"Are you in, or am I going **tomorrow?"**

Gina made a split-second decision. She needed this job. "I'm in. Under one condition."

Wade narrowed his eyes. "I don't usually – "

"We keep it strictly business. Agreed?"

Wade's lips thinned, but Gina stood her ground and kept her focus on his unflinching face.

Finally Wade nodded. "I won't do anything you don't want me to do."

Great, she thought ruefully. Wade hadn't agreed to her terms at all.

House Calls
by Michelle Celmer

ᗝᏯᏀᏋ

What man in his right mind would pass up a few months alone with a woman like Maggie?

The kind of man who knew that she deserved better – that she would expect it. To her, he was just another damaged human being she could fix.

But this wasn't about her. It was about him, and as much as he would have liked to deny it, he wanted his life back. If he did go, and failed, he'd be no worse off than he'd been before. With her help, he'd at least have a chance.

"If you say no, I'll have to reduce myself to kidnapping. You don't want me to commit a felony, do you?"

An honest-to-goodness chuckle rose in his chest and it felt…good. It had been a long time since anyone had made him feel this way. "You win. When do we leave?"

Available in December 2008 from Mills & Boon® Desire™

Married or Not?
by Annette Broadrick
&
Ian's Ultimate Gamble
by Brenda Jackson

ဆၰၦၟ

Christmas in His Royal Bed
by Heidi Betts
&
Rossellini's Revenge Affair
by Yvonne Lindsay

ဆၰၦၟ

Between the CEO's Sheets
by Charlene Sands
&
House Calls
by Michelle Celmer

Between the CEO's Sheets
CHARLENE SANDS

House Calls
MICHELLE CELMER

MILLS & BOON

Pure reading pleasure™

*First published in Great Britain 2008
by Harlequin Mills & Boon Limited,
Eton House, 18-24 Paradise Road, Richmond, Surrey TW9 1SR*

The publisher acknowledges the copyright holders of the
individual works as follows:

Between the CEO's Sheets © Charlene Swink 2007
House Calls © Michelle Celmer 2006

ISBN: 978 0 263 85923 2

51-1208

*Printed and bound in Spain
by Litografia Rosés S.A., Barcelona*

BETWEEN THE
CEO'S SHEETS
by
Charlene Sands

Dear Reader,

I've always wanted to write a story set on an island. What better place to put Wade and Gina than in a resort I've visited dozens of times during my life, Santa Catalina Island! I'd ride the express boat to make the twenty-two-mile journey from Los Angeles to dock at Avalon Bay, the crescent-shaped harbour that was once a pirate's hideaway.

And to make the story complete, I was fortunate to tap into the expertise of my lifelong friends Allyson and Ross Pearlman, owners of the real catamaran yacht, *Between The Sheets*. I thank them for their sailing tips, the inspiration for the title (I stole it!) and those wonderful times on the water. Thanks to them I had an easy time sending Wade and Gina off on their romantic and rocky adventure!

Sincerely,

Charlene Sands

CHARLENE SANDS

resides in Southern California with her husband and best friend, Don. Proudly, they boast that their children, Jason and Nikki, have earned their college degrees. The empty nesters now have two cats that have taken over the house. Charlene's love of the American West, both present and past, stems from storytelling days with her imaginative father, which sparked a passion for a good story and her desire to write romance. When not writing, she enjoys sunny California days, Pacific beaches, and sitting down with a good book.

Charlene invites you to visit her website at www.charlenesands.com to enter her contests, stop by for a chat, read her blog and see what's new! E-mail her at charlenesands@hotmail.com.

To my husband, Don, sole owner of my heart.
And to Jason and Nikki, our wonderful children
who always make us proud.

One

It was the last place Gina Grady wanted to be.

But desperation was an unwelcome persuasion. And Gina was just that: desperate. Her pride and determination also played in the mix.

She needed this job.

She needed to stay in L.A.

Gina was ushered into an empty office. "Mr. Beaumont will be right with you," Mrs. Danner from Human Resources announced before exiting the office, leaving Gina alone with her thoughts.

She walked over to the massive floor-to-ceiling window and took in the view from the twelfth floor of the trendy Santa Monica high-rise, praying the interview would go well. She shouldn't be so worried.

Sam Beaumont had been her friend once. He'd always been kind. Yet, having to take him up on his offer of a job at the Triple B ranked with her top-ten most desperate acts of survival. The Beaumont name alone caused her insides to quake and she wondered at her own sanity in coming. However, it wasn't Sam but his younger brother, Wade, she hoped never to cross paths with again.

The Pacific Ocean loomed on the horizon, the pounding blue surf and white caps filling the view. She shuddered at the sight, and shook off her thoughts of Wade. She had enough to worry about without letting old fears get the better of her today.

She owed money to a whole lot of people and they didn't give a damn that she'd been swindled by a con man she had once trusted as her partner. GiGi Designs, the company she'd struggled to conceive hadn't been given a chance. Her lifelong dream had been destroyed in the blink of an eye. All that she'd worked so hard for had come crumbling down around her.

Now Gina was even more determined to rebuild her clothing design business—from the ground up, if need be.

But first, she needed to pay off her debts.

Gina tidied her long dark hair, making sure it hadn't fallen from the tight knot at the back of her head, straightened her black pinstriped suit and took a seat in front of the massive oak desk, setting her black knockoff Gucci handbag on her lap. She waited for Sam to enter his office.

She closed her eyes to steady her wayward nerves. Calmer, she took a deep breath before opening them again. But when she glanced down, she simply stared in disbelief at the nameplate outlined in solid brass on the desk:

Wade Beaumont, CEO.

"No!" Her heart thudding against her chest, she rose abruptly. She couldn't bear to see Wade again, much less work for him. She couldn't possibly swallow that much pride. She set her purse strap on her shoulder and turned to leave.

"Running away again, Gina?"

Stunned, Gina stopped abruptly and stared into the dark-green eyes of Wade Beaumont. His head cocked to one side, he was leaning against the door where she'd hoped to make her escape. He stared back at her, his lips curled into a mocking smile. "You do that so well."

Gina kept her head held high and tried to appear calm while her insides quivered uncontrollably. She'd foolishly hoped that Wade had nothing to do with Triple B, but now she'd seen the folly in that.

But she couldn't deny how handsome Wade was, standing there in a pair of black trousers and a crisp white shirt, the sleeves rolled up to his elbows. He looked older, more mature and those bold green eyes—she'd never forget the way they use to soften when he looked at her. Or the way his strong body felt crushed up against hers.

Or the day, nine years ago, when she'd run away from him.

"I…this is a mistake. I shouldn't have come," she said on a breath.

Wade ignored her comment. "You applied for a job."

"Yes, I, um assumed Sam would be running your father's company."

"Ah, so you didn't think you'd find me here?"

Gina bolstered her courage as she recalled Wade's onetime contempt for the company his father seemed to love more than his own two sons. Triple B was all Blake Beaumont had ever cared about. When she'd known him back in El Paso, she'd understood Wade's retreat from both the company and his father. She'd never have guessed that he would be at the helm now. Never. "No, I didn't actually. As I said, this is a mistake."

Gina watched his mouth twitch. He walked around his desk and picked up her resume, reading it over carefully.

"I run Triple B now from the West Coast. My father's dead and my brother's remarried and living in Texas. The company fell into my hands some time ago." He stared directly into her eyes. "I suppose you thought I'd work all my life on Uncle Lee's ranch or wind up with a small place of my own back in El Paso?"

"Actually, I hadn't given it much thought," Gina said truthfully. She had thought of Wade countless times in the past—dreamed of him and wondered how his life had turned out—but she never cared what he did for a living. It had never mattered to her.

She'd met Wade while living with the Buckleys in El Paso for the summer. Sarah, her college roommate, had been there for her after her parents had died in a boating accident. Gina had been on the boat, narrowly escaping death that day. Sarah had seen to the funeral, making all the arrangements. She'd held Gina tight, when the caskets were lowered into the ground. And after, when Gina had been uncertain of her future, Sarah had taken her home to El Paso.

The Buckleys' place neighbored Wade's uncle's ranch and the four of them—Sam, Wade, Sarah and Gina—had been inseparable. She came to depend on their friendship and slowly began to heal from her terrible loss, until the day when her world had come crashing down upon her once again.

And now, Wade sat down at his desk and leaned back studying her, his eyes raking her over. She felt exposed and vulnerable, yet unable to draw herself away from his intense scrutiny.

"You hadn't thought about me? Of course, why would you? My father took care of that, didn't he?" He gestured for her to sit down, not expecting an answer. "Take a seat. We'll do this interview."

"No, I—I don't think that would be a good idea, Wade."

"I thought you needed a job?" he said, narrowing his eyes on her.

"I do need a job." She directed her gaze to his without apology. "Just not this one."

He looked down at her resume. "You're more than qualified."

Gina's legs wobbled, so she decided to take a seat, at least for the moment.

"You've got a degree in business. And then you went on to the Fashion Institute. Did my father's money finance that?"

He asked that question so casually that Gina had to rewind his words in her mind to make sure she'd heard him correctly. Wade believed that she'd taken his father's bribe—dirty money that she'd never wanted—to stay away from him.

He believed it because she'd never denied it. She'd let him think that she'd been enticed by a large sum of money to leave El Paso.

But that hadn't been the case at all.

She'd run out on Wade for an entirely different reason. And to have Wade believe she'd accepted his father's bribery had guaranteed that he wouldn't come after her.

She'd hated what he'd done to her.

Hated the high and mighty Blake Beaumont even more.

But if given the choice all over again, Gina wouldn't have changed anything about that summer. Except the night that they made love. Though the sweet memories of the intense passion they shared were always with her, she wished she could take that night back.

Slinging her purse on her shoulder and holding her anger in check, she stood to leave. "I'm sorry," she said, and his dark brows lifted, lining his forehead. "For wasting your time."

Wade stood and glared at her. "You didn't. You're hired."

* * *

Wade watched Gina blink her gorgeous espresso eyes. Nine years had only added to her sultry beauty and it angered him that she could still make his heart race. All Wade had to do was look into those dark, deceitful eyes and admire that voluptuous body and he had trouble remembering the pain she'd caused him. He'd taken her virginity and it had been the highest of highs, claiming her as his own.

She'd run out on him then, leaving town, without so much as a goodbye. She'd gotten what she'd wanted—a load of money from his manipulative father. But if money had been her goal she should have waited. No longer the poor young man working on his uncle's ranch, Wade was floating in cash. But she'd been bought off long ago and had caused Wade enough steaming heartache to fill a Mississippi riverboat.

Gina straightened her pinstriped suit, her chest heaving, the structured material unable to hide the fullness of her breasts. Wade looked his fill, watching the rise and fall as she tried to hide her hot Irish-Italian temper.

Rosy-lipped, with a full flush of color on her light-olive skin, Gina was still the most beautiful woman he had ever seen. From the moment she'd shown up in Aunt Dottie's kitchen with an offering of fresh Italian bread and homemade pasta sauce, Wade had been a goner. She'd knocked him to his knees.

"No. But thank you."

She spoke the words carefully and instincts told Wade that she'd been tempted to take the job. Hell, one look at her and he knew he couldn't let her walk out of his office. Not until they finished what they'd started nine years ago.

"There's a big bonus involved," he said, catching her attention. Her brows lifted provocatively. He shrugged. "I'm in a bind. My personal assistant chose last month to get pregnant. She's down with acute morning sickness and took disability leave. The other qualified assistants are busy with their own projects."

"How big a bonus?" she asked. Wade knew he'd gotten her attention once again. Money, it seemed, spoke volumes with her. Why was he disappointed? He'd known the sort of woman she was, but he had to admit that back in his youth, she sure had him fooled. "It's a thousand dollars a week to start and once the project is settled, win or lose, you get a ten-thousand-dollar bonus. But I'll warn you, you'll be working long hours. Take it or leave it, Gina."

He could almost see her mind working, calculating, *figuring*. She must need a job badly. Wade had the upper hand and he knew it. She was tempted.

He sat down at his desk and rifled through papers, coming up with information on the Catalina project. He had figures to check and hours of work to do before making a bid on the biggest contract Triple B might hope to gain.

He felt her presence, breathed in the heady scent

of her exotic perfume. His better judgment told him to let her go. He'd be better off not complicating his life by choosing to work alongside the only woman he knew who could turn him on with just one look. He'd had to sit down to conceal an unwelcome yet healthy erection that pulsed from underneath the desk.

He must be crazy.

"I must be crazy, but I accept," she said softly.

Wade lifted his head and nodded, more satisfied than he wanted to be. "I expect a decent hard day's work from my employees. If you can manage that, you've got the job."

Her chin jutted up. "I can manage that. I always give one hundred percent."

Wade's mind drifted back to his uncle's barn that night so many years ago. She'd given one hundred percent of herself to him, generously offering up her body with passion and pleasure, but it had all been a trap.

This time, he'd have to be more careful.

"I'll pick you up later this afternoon. Oh, and dress comfortably. We'll be working at my home through the evening."

Gina recalled Wade's instructions and wondered at her sanity. She would never have taken this job if the compensation hadn't been so tempting. She had debtors knocking on her door and that big bonus Wade had offered would surely keep them happy for a while.

She'd changed her clothes three times before settling on a pair of white slacks and a soft-pink knit top. She brought the whole outfit together with a matching short sweater. Comfortable, but still a professional enough look for a woman about to embark on a new job with an old lover.

Gina shook her head. She still had trouble believing she would be working with Wade Beaumont after all these years. He resented her. She'd seen it in his eyes each time he glanced at her. No amount of Beaumont charm could conceal that look.

Gina lifted her briefcase filled with documents that Wade had asked her to review this afternoon. She glanced around the tiny guest apartment she lived in behind the large Spanish-style house in the Hollywood Hills. Once Wade saw where and how she lived, he would realize how desperate she'd been for this job. It was a tidy place with three rooms: a small cozy living space with one sofa, a kitchen that amounted to one wall of the living room with a range, a refrigerator and a café table for two, and a bedroom beyond that.

Her apartment suited her needs. She'd had to downsize everything in her life since Mike Bailey had betrayed her. They'd dreamed the same dreams, or so she had thought, and had gone into partnership together. The day GiGi Designs was born was the happiest day in Gina's life. The day she found out he'd absconded with all of her money and designs only compared with the day she'd had to leave El Paso and Wade Beaumont forever. She'd been heartbroken on both accounts.

Gina sighed and walked out the door, deciding to meet Wade out front. Not a minute later, he drove up in a shining black Lexus convertible. She watched him get out and approach her, his eyes focused on her clothes and she wondered if he approved of her choice of attire. Though not one of her original designs, she always chose her outfits carefully. When the door of the main house slammed, Gina turned her head to find the owner locking up.

"Hey there, Gina. Are you going out?" Marcus's eyes narrowed on Wade and she couldn't help but laugh. Her handsome fifty-something landlord was always watching out for her.

"Yes, but it's business. I have a new job."

"Ah. Well then, good luck." He headed for his car in the driveway.

"Ciao, Marcus. See you tomorrow."

When Gina turned back around, Wade's intense-green eyes burned into hers. "Do you live with him?"

Gina blinked away her anger. Wade had no right to ask her personal questions. She wondered why it mattered, anyway. He had nothing but contempt for her. "No. I don't live with him. I live in the guest-house in the back."

Wade's mouth twitched. "How convenient." He put his hand to her lower back and ushered her inside his car. She took her seat and adjusted the seatbelt as Wade started the ignition. He took one last look at the house and gunned the engine. They drove in silence for a while, until he asked, "Is that guy married?"

Gina leaned her head back against the seat and smiled inwardly. Marcus and Delia had the kind of marriage her parent's had had. That kind of love and commitment was rare and it saddened Gina to think that her parents' love had been cut short by a freakish accident. "Yes, happily."

"He's your landlord?"

"My landlord and a very dear friend."

Wade shot her another glance, this time with a dubious look in his eyes. Gina let the subject drop and stared out the window, her eyes focused on the mountain on one side of the road rather than the blue ocean waters on the other. As Wade drove down Pacific Coast Highway, the wind blew her long hair out of its tight knot.

Ten minutes later and completely wind-blown, Gina was pinning her hair back up, noting Wade's eyes on her as he killed the engine. She marveled at the impressive two-story house that sat on a strip of beach in the Malibu Colony. Wade hopped out of the car and came around to open her door. She stood and looked around for a moment, her gaze traveling past the house to the surging surf and then beyond to the stunning western horizon. "All of this is yours?"

Wade grabbed her briefcase from the car then nodded, staring directly into her eyes. "It's mine." She shivered from the cold assessing look he cast her; a look that said, "It could have been yours, too."

Or maybe Gina had imagined that. It had been nine long years and surely Wade hadn't brooded over her too long. Handsome and successful, Wade wouldn't have to look far for female companion-ship. He had all the markings of a man used to getting his way with women and with life in general.

Gina followed Wade through the front door and into a large vestibule. From there it seemed that she could almost touch the pounding surf as the shore came into view with brilliant clarity through enormous windows. "Take a look around," he said without ceremony. "I'm going up to take a quick shower."

Gina watched him toss both of their briefcases down onto a soft moss-green L-shaped sofa before disappearing up a winding staircase. She felt safest standing there waiting in the safety of the living room, but curiosity forced her to walk through the French doors that led onto a sweeping veranda over-looking the ocean. Wade seemed to have all things necessary for the life of a single man; a hot tub sur-rounded by a cocktail bar sat in one corner of the deck while a fire pit took up the other corner. In the middle of the deck, patio tables and chairs were arranged to enjoy the view of waves crashing into the sand.

Gina walked to the wooden railing and closed her eyes. Taking a deep breath she tried to calm her jittery nerves, but the combination of deep waters and Wade was too much for her.

Wade approached with two glasses of white wine. He handed her one. "To unwind."

Gina accepted the glass, grateful for the forti-tude, and both of them stood leaning on the railing, gazing out. "It looks peaceful here."

Wade sipped his wine. "Looks can be deceiving."

That's exactly what Gina thought, but she was thinking of the deceptive calm of the uncompromising sea. She was certain Wade meant something altogether different.

Rather than stare at the ocean, she shifted slightly so that she could consider Wade Beaumont. His dark hair, still damp from the shower, was slicked back and tiny drops of water glistened on his neck. Late afternoon sunlight revealed a gleam in his eyes and highlighted high cheekbones leading to a beautiful mouth and the masculine line of his jaw. He had changed into a pair of tight-fitting jeans and a black polo shirt. Tan and trim with broad shoulders, his shirt couldn't hide the strength of his powerfully built chest.

Now, as in the past, Gina had trouble keeping her eyes off of Wade. He affected her like no other man ever had. Her heart pumped twice as hard when he looked at her and an unwelcome tremble stirred her body when he came near. In those clothes, he reminded her of the man she'd once known during a time in her life when she could enjoy carefree days and hot summer nights.

Gina took small sips of her wine. She wasn't much of a drinker and needed to remain in control. She couldn't afford any more slipups.

"Only one more sip," she said, "or my head won't be clear for business." Gina set the glass down on the table. Turning to Wade, she hoped that he would take the hint and lead her back inside so that they could begin their work together. She needed to prove herself on this job and, more importantly, she needed to keep her mind on business and not the glowing attributes of her new boss.

Wade didn't move from his stance by the railing. He shook his head, his eyes fixed on hers. "Sorry, Gina," he said, looking anything but sorry. "I can't work with you."

I can't work with you.

Gina blinked as Wade's words sunk in. A rapid shot of dread coursed through her system. She'd begun to think of this job as a means to an end. And she'd resigned herself to working with Wade, whether she liked it or not. Now, just like that, he dropped a bomb on her plans. What kind of game was he playing? She couldn't control the anger in her voice, "I thought you hired me today?"

Wade slammed his glass down on the top rail and turned the full force of his words on her. "Yes, I hired you. Did you think I'd let you walk out of my office without an explanation? Did you think I'd let you go again? You ran away from me nine years ago and I need to know why."

Two

Shocked, Gina stared into Wade's stormy eyes. When she finally spoke, it was softly and devoid of emotion. "We were young."

She had died that night. Leaving Wade had destroyed her and it had been a long hard road getting her life back. She didn't want to dwell on the past or how her friend Sarah had duped her into leaving Wade. The truth had come out a few years later, and she'd long since forgiven Sarah. But the fact remained: Gina had left Wade in El Paso after one secret, glorious night with him.

"Not that young, Gina. You'd graduated from college. We weren't exactly kids."

"My parents died that year. I didn't know what to do or how…or how I would survive."

"My father solved that problem for you, didn't he? He paid you off. And you took the money and ran, for all you were worth."

Yes, Gina had taken Blake Beaumont's money. It had given her a way out of a very serious dilemma. She'd fallen in love with Wade and the night she'd given him her virginity had been wonderful. She'd hoped for a future with Wade, but thinking back on it now, she wondered if she'd been too clouded by grief to see the truth. Later that night all of her hopes had come crashing down around her.

Sarah was pregnant and she'd named Wade as the father.

Gina went to bed that night, tears falling uncontrollably and her heart aching at how she'd been betrayed by the one man who had given her a measure of comfort and happiness after the death of her parents.

Blake Beaumont's offer had come at exactly the right moment. She'd wanted to hurt Wade for his calculated cruelty. She'd wanted to make him pay for his betrayal. She'd hated him.

She remembered so vividly standing there, face to face with the older man who had abandoned his two sons in favor of building his company. Triple B had been Blake's passion, not the two sweet young boys he'd pawned off on his sister and her husband to raise.

Blake Beaumont slid an envelope her way. "Take the money and this airline ticket and leave El Paso. You're a distraction Wade can't afford right now. I sacrificed his childhood so that he would one day stand beside me and run the company and that time has almost come. Sam, Wade and I, we'll build an enormous empire together. There's no room in it for you, dear."

Gina's first instinct was to rip the check up and toss it into Blake Beaumont's smug face. The selfish man wanted his son's full attention. He wanted to dictate his life—a life that didn't include love. Blake Beaumont had made it clear that he fully intended for Wade to immerse himself in Triple B. The only relationship he wanted for Wade was one of dedicated service to the company.

If her heart hadn't been broken, Gina would have laughed at the irony. Blake wanted her out of the picture but how would he feel knowing that it was really Sarah and her unborn child that would disrupt his plans? Gina had wished she could have stayed around long enough to see the look on Blake Beaumont's face when he realized his troubles were just beginning.

Gina accepted the check and ticket out of town. She knew Blake was too ruthless not to tell Wade about the bribe. And that's what she'd counted on.

Wade had a baby on the way with Sarah and that had been all that mattered. Sarah hadn't known about Gina's feelings for Wade and she'd kept it that way. By accepting his father's bribe, Gina guaranteed that Wade would stay in El Paso with his family. She'd hoped that he would realize his responsibilities to Sarah, too.

Gina lost contact with Sarah then, deciding to deal with her pain in her own way. She moved to Los Angeles and dug her heels in, determined to make a good life for herself. It wasn't until a few years later that Sarah had come looking for Gina with the whole truth.

"Answer me, Gina. Why did you run away?"

"I had good reason, Wade. It's not important now. But you have to believe that leaving El Paso when I did broke my heart."

"It broke your heart?" he said, coming to stand right in front of her, his anger almost tangible. "Funny, but I remember it differently. I remember you letting me strip you naked and take you in my uncle's barn. I remember every little moan, every whimper, every time you cried out my name. I never once heard you say your heart was broken and that you were leaving town the next day."

Tears welled in Gina's eyes and her body trembled with unspoken grief. She had loved Wade then and had felt the cold slap of his betrayal. She shed tears all the way to Los Angeles, but had made up her mind not to look back.

"Wade, when I came to see you that night I didn't know I would be leaving so soon. I…wanted you."

Wade let out a derisive laugh. "And Gina always gets what she wants, right?"

Gina hadn't gotten what she wanted. She'd lost her best friend that summer and the man she'd loved.

Wade had been so sweet, so caring. Once he kissed her and touched her skin, she'd reacted with primal, desperate need. She'd wanted Wade, thought maybe they could have a future together. His every touch and caress excited her, warmed her, told her that she'd been smart to wait to give up her virginity to the right man. They'd spoken of love and the future in vague terms, the relationship too new to know for sure. But Gina fully believed that Wade Beaumont had been the right man for her.

"It wasn't like that," she said in a calm voice, one that she almost didn't recognize.

But Wade didn't really want her explanation. He wanted to lash out. "You were a virgin, Gina. Don't think that didn't weigh on me. I wasn't a boy. I was a twenty-one-year-old man. I didn't know if I'd hurt you physically or emotionally. I didn't know what to think. I was half out of my mind when I learned that you had left El Paso the next day, catching the soonest flight out of town.

"I made the mistake of telling dear old Dad that I'd found the right girl for me during a phone conversation days earlier. Even before we made love, I knew I wanted you in my life. Next thing I know my father makes a rare visit to El Paso. He couldn't wait to tell me that you'd taken a hefty bribe from him. The man was so damn cocky. He didn't realize that I'd hate him for his part in it. He thought I'd appreciate knowing that I'd been wrong about you. But it didn't matter anymore. I pretty much wrote you off as the biggest mistake of my life."

His harsh words cut like a knife. He didn't know the agony she had gone through that night, her emotions running hot and cold, thrilled to have finally given herself to him only to find out later that he had been deceitful. She managed to bolster her courage and hoist her chin. "If that's the case, why did you bother seeing me today? Why did you *hire* me?"

"Because Sam asked me to. I did it as a favor to him, Gina. And now we're stuck with each other."

She gasped silently from the immediate shock to her system. She'd seen Sam a few months ago, crossing paths with him at the airport, his new family in tow. They'd exchanged pleasantries and when he'd found out that she was living in Los Angeles he'd offered her a job if she ever needed one.

With her pride deeply injured, Gina shot back. "Consider yourself, unstuck. I won't ask you to work with the *biggest mistake of your life.*"

Gina turned her back on Wade and walked toward the French doors. She wanted out, away from Wade for good. But just as she stepped inside the house, Wade grabbed her from behind, his hands holding her gently just under her breasts, the zipper of his jeans grinding into her derriere. She felt the pins being pulled from her hair, freeing the tresses from their knotted prison. Wade wove his hand in her hair and brought his lips to her throat, his voice a gruff whisper. "Don't run away again."

Gina's traitorous body reacted to Wade and, angry as she was, she couldn't deny the overwhelming heat pulsing through her. "You don't want me here."

"That may be true." And then he added softly, "But I need you."

Gina slammed her eyes shut. She felt herself softening to Wade and when she turned in his arms to face him, she witnessed the depth of his sincerity. "You need me?"

She glanced at his mouth just as his lips came down onto hers. He cupped her face and deepened the kiss, slanting his mouth over hers again and again. Gina reacted with a little whimper, urging her body closer. His heat was a fire that burned her. And when she sighed, he took the opportunity to drive his tongue into her mouth, mating them together. Soon, Gina's body swayed in rhythm and Wade wrapped his hands around her waist, his fingers pressing into the curve of her buttocks, drawing her closer.

She felt his erection, the hot pulsing need rubbing into her. Heart pounding out of control, she felt dizzy and wanted Wade with undeniable urgency.

"Yoo-hoo, Wa-ade? Are you home? I brought you chili, honey. Just the way you like it, hot and spicy," the low throaty rasp of a woman's voice startled Gina. She pulled away from Wade in time to see a young redhead coming up the deck steps from the beach. In a flowery bikini covered only by a hip-riding sarong, the woman held a hot bowl in her pot-holder-clad hands. She stopped up short when she reached the deck, finding Wade and Gina together. "Oh, sorry, Wade. I guess I had the wrong night. I thought we were on for the hot tub. My mistake," she said casually. "I'll just leave this here for you." She set the chili on the deck table.

"Shoot, Veronica. Sorry. I forgot." He winked at her and smiled. "I'm working tonight."

"I can see that," she said, taking a quick glance at Gina, before backing down the stairs. "Don't work too hard, honey." Gina heard her chuckle as she disappeared onto the beach.

Gina stared at Wade and abruptly everything became clear. For a moment she thought that she was back in El Paso with the young, sweet man she had given herself to unconditionally. Suddenly, she felt foolish. And stupid for thinking that nothing had changed, when, actually, everything had.

She tried to brush past him to get away, but he was like a block of granite, too strong to move without his willing surrender. He reached for her arms and held her without budging. When she glared into his eyes, he shrugged and said calmly, "She's a friend."

Gina wasn't a fool. She doubted Wade had female "friends" who came over just for a quick meal and a splash in the hot tub. She shook her head adamantly. "I think not. I'd better go. Will you drive me home or shall I take a taxi?"

"Neither. We have work to do. When I said I needed you, I meant it. I need a personal assistant for this project and we have to catch you up on the details."

"You mean you'd give up your hot-tub date?" Her voice was deliberately rich with sarcasm.

"I just did, didn't I?" Wade shot back.

Gina bristled. "Yes, you did. You dismissed her quite easily. But what about what just happened between us? Can you dismiss *that* just as easily?" His kiss had stole Gina's breath, but she had regained normal breathing.

Wade pursed his lips. He stared at hers, well-ripened and swollen from his powerful assault. "I never could dismiss you, Gina. You're hardly the kind of woman a man can forget."

"That does not answer my question."

"Listen, maybe I was out of line a minute ago. But I'm not kidding when I say I need you. As my assistant. We're setting sail first thing tomorrow so—"

Gina snapped her head up. "Setting sail? For where?"

"For Catalina island. You should have been briefed during the first interview with Helen in Personnel. It was a stipulation of the job."

Wade seemed full of surprises. First he stunned her with that incredible kiss and now this unexpected announcement of an island trip. "I wasn't informed about a trip."

"You knew about the latest project the company plans to bid on. It could be the biggest contract in Triple B's history and I intend to get it. It's right there in the file I gave you to review."

"Yes, but I didn't think—"

"It's the reason for the big bonus, Gina," he interrupted to clarify.

"But that's what I don't understand. That's a great

deal of money for a trip to Catalina. It's only a few hours away. Surely, one day isn't worth such a large sum of money."

"One day? Gina, we'll be on that island for a minimum of one week and I guarantee you'll be working long hours."

Gina slumped her shoulders. "One week?"

He nodded. "Seven days, including the weekend. So are you in or am I going it alone tomorrow?"

Gina slammed her eyes shut. She hated her own cowardice. She hadn't been on the water in any capacity since the boat accident that claimed her parents' lives. She'd dealt with the guilt at being the sole survivor, but she hadn't been forced to face her fear—until now. And she was ready. She'd been praying to find a way to conquer her anxiety and now she had the opportunity. If she didn't face her fears, she'd not only lose the revenue to rebuild her future, she'd lose part of herself all over again.

Gina made a split-second decision. She needed this job for more than one reason. But she would accept the position under one condition, and one condition only. "I'm in. Under one condition."

Wade narrowed his eyes. "I don't usually—"

"We keep it strictly business." Gina had allowed personal feelings to get the better of her in business once before and that had landed her with a pile of bills, slimy pawnshop receipts and creditors pounding on her door. She couldn't let that happen again to her pocketbook or her heart. "Agreed?"

Wade's lips thinned.

She stood her ground and kept her focus on his unflinching face.

Finally Wade nodded. "I won't do anything you don't want me to do. Now, let's go over those files. I don't want to get you home late. We'll be setting sail at eight sharp."

Gina drew in a deep breath wondering how she would fare spending her days and *nights* with the only man who could anger her, confuse her and make her ache desperately for his touch.

I won't do anything you don't want me to do.

Great, she thought ruefully. She'd just realized that Wade hadn't agreed to her terms at all, but instead, issued her a challenge.

She felt herself slowly sinking and she had to paddle fast to keep from going under. Which was saying something for a woman who had a dire fear of water.

Three

The next morning, Wade watched Gina make her way down the ramp that led to his docking slip at Marina del Rey. He'd told her to dress comfortably for the trip over to the island but as he watched her descend the steps he was almost sorry he'd given her that instruction. Her flowery sundress hugged her body perfectly and the tight white jacket she wore only accentuated her full breasts and slender waistline. July breezes lifted the hem enough to show her shapely legs as she strolled toward him. She'd pinned her hair in that knot again, but the breezy weather wouldn't allow it and those chestnut tresses fanned out in tempting disarray. The vision she created of simple elegance and unquestionable beauty turned heads at the marina. Wade winced as he caught men stop what they were doing on their boats to watch her walk by.

Wade muttered a curse and told himself this was a business trip where he needed to keep his focus. He'd never let a woman get in the way of what was important to the company. Yet, when Gina approached his yacht he had a hard time remembering that. He peered up from the stern of the boat to greet her. "Morning," he said, none too pleasantly.

"Good morning," she said, but her eyes weren't on him, or his yacht. They focused off in the distance, to the ocean that lay beyond the calm marina.

"You're right on time."

She took her eyes off the ocean long enough to answer, "Thanks to the driver you sent to pick me up." She bit down on her lip and stood there looking quite businesslike, her chin at an unapproachable tilt and her stance slightly rigid. But that dress…that dress could make a man forget his own name.

"Come aboard," he said, putting a hand out to help her.

She scanned the length of the boat and drew a deep breath as if steadying her nerves.

"You haven't changed your mind, have you?" he asked.

She gazed once more at the ocean beyond the marina and shook her head, but her soft tentative answer left room for doubt. "No."

Wade gestured with his outstretched hand. "Come on, Gina. We have to set sail soon."

From the minute he'd seen it, Wade had known he had to own this fifty-two-foot Jeanneau sloop. It hadn't mattered that he didn't know how to sail. He'd made it a hobby and a far-reaching goal to master the craft when he'd first arrived in California. And he'd never been sorry.

Gina's gaze scanned the deck and the steps leading to the quarters below. "I don't see the crew? Are they late?"

"You're looking at the crew."

Gina's dark almond-shaped eyes opened wide. "You?"

"Sam's the pilot in the family and I'm the sailor." He stepped from the boat onto the ramp and grabbed the suitcase from her hand. "Come aboard and I'll show you around."

After a moment's hesitation, Gina accepted his help and he guided her down onto his boat, releasing her the moment her feet hit the deck.

"I had no idea this was how we would arrive in Catalina."

Wade had purposely left that detail out. He didn't know how she would've reacted to his sailing them across to the island. Some people got jittery when they realized only one man had full charge of the boat. But that was what appealed to him most about sailing—the solitude and the challenge of being at the helm. And since he'd had a hard enough time convincing Gina to take the job last night, he'd thought it best to leave their travel arrangements out of the conversation.

His old man once told him that timing was everything. Wade believed him. He knew that after that kiss last night and then the untimely appearance from Veronica, he was on shaky enough ground with Gina. She'd been ready to walk out of his life again.

But that kiss had him tied up in knots all night long. Gina had melted in his arms. That much hadn't changed. She'd tasted like wine, her lips soft and full and ripe. Her body molded to his, they fit each other like two puzzle pieces. He couldn't hide his reaction to her any more than she could to him. Wade had lost himself in that kiss and he realized that he couldn't let her go until they'd cleared up all of their unfinished business. Then and only then, would he say farewell to Gina for good.

"Can't say that I ever imagined I'd get you on Total Command."

Gina arched her brow. "Excuse me?"

"*Total Command.* The name of the boat. And the only way I operate these days.

Gina cast him a disapproving look.

"Listen, I'll get us both to the island safe and sound. There's no need to worry." Wade picked up her travel bag and stepped down into the living quarters of the boat first and reached for her hand. She advanced carefully down the steps. But when the boat rocked slightly, she lurched forward. Wade grabbed her and their eyes met as their bodies collided. Intense heat sizzled between them. She was soft where she needed to be soft, and firm in all the right places. Wade held her for only a second before stepping aside.

He showed her the open space that would serve as a living room and then they walked through the galley where he had fixed them a mid-morning snack of fresh fruit, cheese and coffee.

Next he explained about the VHF radio and the SSB, the Single Sideband system used for a wider perimeter of communication. He'd even explained to her how she should call for help in case of an emergency. "But don't worry about that. The weather is clear, the wind perfect, I'm in good health and we'll be in Catalina before lunchtime."

Gina nodded, but he didn't miss her wide-eyed expression when he described to her how she could reach the coast guard if necessary.

"And what's in there?" she asked gesturing toward a doorway.

"The master bedroom and bath. There's two more bedrooms on the opposite end of the boat."

"You don't expect, uh, you don't expect me to sleep down here."

Wade wouldn't get a lick of work done if she did. "That's not in your job description. You'll have a room in the finest inn on the island."

"And you?" she asked. "Where will you be?"

"Right here. I stay on the boat when we moor. I don't get as much time as I'd like on the boat. So I've set up an office in one of the spare bedrooms."

He guided her back to the stairs, catching a whiff of her perfume, some exotic fragrance that reminded him of sultry tropical nights. As she climbed up the steps to the top deck he admired the wiggle of her bottom and those long tanned legs as he followed her up.

"Ready?" he asked.

She drew another deep breath into her lungs then put on dark sunglasses. She looked mysterious in them, a superstar trying to conceal her identity. And in a way Gina was a mystery to him. He didn't know her mind, how it worked, what made her tick. He'd known her body and, hopefully, would try his best to know it again, but he would never believe he knew what she was thinking. He refused to make that mistake again.

Wade prepared the yacht for their departure, untying the ropes and setting the sails. Soon they were moving through the marina, past the rocks that harbored the bay, picking up wind that would take them into the Pacific Ocean.

Gina shook with fear the moment the boat began its journey out of the calm marina waters. She took a seat in the cockpit area as salty sea spray lightly drizzled her. With slight desperation she tried to block out images of the last time she'd been on the water, the last time she'd seen her parents alive.

She prayed for enough courage to sustain her through this trip and placed her faith in Wade and his sailing abilities. She watched him move along the sheets and sails, making adjustments and setting the course.

In faded blue jeans and a white tank, Wade might have looked like a typical sailor except his muscles strained harder, his body held more steadfastly, the concentration on his face appeared deeper than on any man she had ever known. Studying his fluid movements along the rigging, Gina could only admire him.

His kiss last night had been *something*.

But it had meant nothing to him.

I need you.

Yes, she understood that he needed her as his personal assistant, a right-hand man and a secretary all rolled up in one. He didn't need her in any other capacity. Not in the way she had needed him nine years ago.

Wade took his place behind the wheel and they sailed in silence for a short time. The boat rocked and waves smashed up against the hull as they sailed along. Gina shuddered, unable to suppress the trembling of her body.

Wade turned at that very instant, catching her in a moment of fear. Their eyes held for a moment before he angled around again and Gina hugged her middle, tamping down the tremors that passed through her.

A few minutes later, Wade left the wheel and handed her a life jacket. "Put this on. You'll feel better."

Gina didn't bother to protest. He was right. But though wearing a life vest might help with her fear, it wouldn't erase the memories she had locked away that were surfacing. She put her arms through the armholes and closed the jacket taut.

Wade helped her fasten the snaps and tied it for her. And when she thought he would return to the wheel, he surprised her by taking a seat by her side. "Feeling seasick?"

She shook her head. Her queasiness had nothing to do with the motion of the sea. "No."

"You're trembling and pale, Gina."

"I'm not—"

"You are."

"No, I meant to say, I'm not seasick, but this is the first time I've been on the water since…the accident."

Wade's dark brows rose. He appeared genuinely surprised.

"I realize that this is the ocean and the accident happened on a lake, but—"

"You haven't been on the water since?" he asked.

Gina closed her eyes. Memories flooded in of the ski boat, the laughter, her mother's smiling face and then…the collision. Gina went flying into the water, out of danger. Her parents hadn't been so lucky.

She shook her head and stared at the hands she'd placed in her lap. "No. I haven't had the courage. It's been almost ten years."

"So, why now?" Wade asked softly.

But she sensed he was really asking her, "Why me?" Why would she take her first boat trip with him? She'd been desperate for work she'd wanted to tell him. She needed the money and was determined to start her business again, without anyone's help this time. She'd been betrayed, but not destroyed. She wouldn't give up, and if that meant facing her fears, then so be it. She peered into a face filled with concern, an expression reminiscent of the sweet, caring Wade Beaumont she'd once known. "It's time, Wade. That's all."

Wade leaned back in the seat and put his arm around her. "That's not all. Tell me about the accident."

"I—I don't talk about it." She'd never really spoken about that day except with a support group that had really helped and understood what she'd been through. Losing both parents had been devastating enough, but to be the sole survivor of the crash that had taken four lives had been equally difficult. The result was major survivor guilt.

"Maybe you should. Maybe it'll help you overcome your fear of water."

She shook her head and gazed out upon the open sea. "I doubt that."

Wade took her hands in his and the look on his face, serious but earnest, urged her on. "Try, Gina. We're going to spend a week on an island surrounded by water. There'll be times we'll have to come back to the boat." He cast her a slight hint of a smile. "I can't have you fainting on me."

Gina peered into his eyes. They were warm with concern. But she wondered if that look was about keeping his personal assistant calm or if it was truly for her benefit.

He squeezed her hands gently, coaxing the words that she hadn't spoken to anyone but her support group. "It was Memorial Day weekend," she began, "and we never once thought to worry about drunk drivers on the water…"

Emotions rolled in the pit of Gina's stomach. She'd purged herself of her burden, sharing the events of that horrible day with Wade. He'd listened to her as she tried to communicate without tears, but at times her voice broke and she choked up. Wade sat there with a soothing arm around her shoulders, listening. And when the last words were out of her mouth, he thanked her for telling him.

"Are you feeling better?" he asked.

Gina nodded feeling a small sense of relief. "A little."

He stood and peered down at her. "You need to eat something."

"No," she said, placing a hand to her stomach. "No, I couldn't."

"If you don't want to eat, there's coffee down below." He glanced at the blue skies overhead then looked into her eyes as if deciding what was best for her. Then he took hold of her hand, guiding her up. "You look tired, Gina. Take a little rest. Get away from the water for a little while."

He spoke softly and his tone comforted. She thought she could fall for him again—if she hadn't sworn off men completely and if he would always look at her like he was now, without contempt and regret in his eyes. "Maybe I will go down below."

He walked her to the steps and turned, tugging

her close. She nearly bumped into his chest when the boat swayed. He steadied her with both hands on her shoulders then, with a slant of his head, brought his lips to hers. The kiss was brief and chaste and when it was over she gazed deeply into his eyes and smiled.

Wade looked off toward the horizon a moment then returned his focus to her face with narrowed eyes. His soft expression turned hard once again.

"Don't think I gained any satisfaction seeing fear in your eyes or hearing pain in your voice, Gina. I'm not that big a bast—"

Gina pressed her fingers to his mouth. "I know, Wade. You're not—"

He pulled her fingers from his lips. "I am. Make no mistake. But I draw the line at preying on another's weakness. Take that as fair warning."

Gina shuddered at Wade's harsh tone. He'd let her glimpse the man he'd once been, but only for a moment. The young man she'd fallen in love with was gone, she feared, forever. And she'd had everything to do with his demise. "Consider me fairly warned." She turned to walk down the stairs, feeling Wade's penetrating gaze following her every step of the way.

Wade guided the boat toward the mooring can in Avalon harbor on Catalina island and set about tying the lines to secure the boat from bow to stern. The trip had been uneventful, the weather calm, the sailing smooth. But his passenger had yet to return to the deck.

With the dinghy ready to take them ashore, Wade made his way to the cabin below. The galley was empty, the food he'd set out was untouched and there was no sign that Gina had even been there.

With a curious brow raised he walked to his master bedroom and bath, finding that room empty as well. He'd have guessed as much and smiled to himself, but his smile faded quickly when he finally found Gina, sprawled out on the bed in the guest-room.

"Gina," he said quietly.

When she didn't rouse, he entered the room and gazed down at her, lying across the bed, her hair in a tangle, the dark tresses half covering her beautiful face. The dress she wore rode up her thigh, the material exposing thoroughly tanned, shapely legs. She'd kicked off her shoes and made herself comfortable on the dark-russet bedspread. She looked peaceful and more tempting than a woman had a right to look. Hell, even her polished scarlet-red toenails turned him on.

Her eyes opened slowly, as though she'd sensed him watching her. With a sleep-hazy sigh, she stretched her limbs, reminding him of a cat uncurling after a long sleep.

"Mmmm…Wade," she purred and continued that long slow sensual stretch while keeping those lazy half-lidded eyes on him.

God, she was sexy.

But deceitful, too, he reminded himself. He could scarcely believe he'd hired her. She was his employee now and one he wasn't sure he could trust. But his brother Sam had vouched unconditionally for her. "Give her a chance, Wade," he'd said. And Wade had because of Sam's request. But the truth was that if she'd walked into his office without the benefit of his brother's recommendation, he would have hired her anyway. They had unfinished business. Period.

"I'd love to join you, Gina," he said softly, meaning every word, "but we've got a full day ahead of us."

"Oh!"

Gina bounced up from the bed, realizing where she was and with whom. Wade enjoyed every second of that bounce and struggled to keep his lust from becoming visible. Wouldn't take much to throw all rational thought out the porthole and spread his body over hers.

"Sorry, Wade." She untangled the hair that had fallen into her face. "I guess I fell asleep. The rocking of the boat…"

She bent to put her shoes on and treated him to a luscious view. From his position, the dress barely contained her full breasts when she leaned over.

"This is embarrassing," she said. "I've never fallen asleep on the job."

"I won't hold it against you. Anytime you want to slip into one of my beds, feel free."

Gina rose then and looked into his eyes. "Too bad we have a full day ahead of us," she bantered back, repeating his words.

Wade hid his amusement.

"Are we on the island?" she asked.

Wade shook his head. "Not yet. There's a little matter of a dinghy ride to the dock."

The sleep-induced rosy color drained from Gina's cheeks. "How far?"

"Not far," he said. "We'll be ashore in less than five minutes."

Gina groaned and Wade almost felt sorry for her.

"That's five minutes too long."

"Gina, you're gonna have to trust me. I'll keep you safe."

She angled her chin and probed him with those dark sensual eyes. "Trust goes both ways, Wade. Do you trust me?"

Wade held her gaze for a moment then refused her an answer and walked out the door.

Trusting Gina had never been an option.

Four

Gina held her breath through most of the dinghy ride to the mainland. Wade glanced at her from time to time, but his primary focus was on getting the small boat to shore and mooring at the dock. Once there, he secured the dinghy and stepped off the boat with her suitcase, then reached for her hand. "You okay?"

Gina nodded. "I will be as soon as my legs stop trembling."

Wade glanced down and raised a brow. "They look fine to me," he said, with a gleam in his eyes. "Come on, let's get you settled into your room."

Gina got control of her legs once she'd reached solid ground. The sun shined in the clear-blue sky and children's laughter rang out from the nearby beach. Catalina island was a nest for summer travelers wishing to get away from the daily grind of the big city. The mainland, visible on a clear day, was just twenty-two miles away. As they walked along the sidewalk, Spanish influences surrounded them, marking some of the history of the island. She noted a lovely tiled fountain bubbling up with a cool spray in the middle of a circular paved drive. Wade stopped for a minute in front of the fountain.

"Santa Catalina was originally named after Saint Catherine, the patron saint of spinsters," he said. "Lucky for my company, the island is now a resort for lovers."

"So the developer wants the resort to be known as an elite honeymoon destination?" she asked.

Wade nodded. "Can't think of a better place locally. Most of the hotels have no phones and televisions in the rooms. People get real creative to entertain themselves. This whole island spells romance."

Gina nodded as they walked past a row of swaying palms, the gentle sea breeze blowing by, the scent of sand and surf filling her nostrils. She supposed for most people that potent scent meant fun and sun and time away from the hassles of everyday life, but a resort surrounded by water only reminded her of things she'd rather forget.

Within a minute they were at the quaint town of Avalon and Gina looked down a long avenue, which she deemed to be the main street of town. The shops and cafés faced the water and swimsuit-clad vacationers swarmed them as others biked their way down the street. The only other vehicles on the busy thoroughfare were canopied golf carts. Wade continued to lead the way but soon stopped again, this time at a hotel. Villa Portofino. "Here we are," he said. She looked up to see a hotel with all the trademarks of Italy.

Gina nodded. "Nice."

"None better, unless you take a trip to Tuscany."

Gina eyed him carefully, wondering why he'd picked such an expensive place for her to stay. This was just business and she would remind him of that again, if she had to. "So your hotel will have competition."

"Not at all. We plan to build a lavish honeymoon resort with pools, tennis courts and a golf course. The Portofino is a great little beachfront hotel. It won't give us any competition at all. This is where our employees stay when in town working on the project. You won't be disappointed."

Disappointment was the furthest thing from her mind when she entered the Bella Vista suite. True to its name, the suite's wraparound balcony had a grand view of the lush hillside as well as the Catalina harbor. A king-size bed in the center of the room faced a large built-in fireplace and a table for two adorned by a vase filled with tropical flowers. The bath was full-size and encased with fine Italian marble. The whole suite was larger than her tiny guesthouse in Hollywood.

Wade set her bag down and walked to the window

to stare out at the harbor. He'd waved off the bellboy, insisting on bringing her up here himself. "It's a far cry from El Paso."

Gina sucked in her breath. What could she say to that? Wade had made something of himself, despite his father's meddling. He was his own man and he'd made the West Coast Triple B a success. Gina couldn't argue with that. "I liked El Paso, Wade. It was the best summer of my life."

He whipped around to stare into her eyes. "I thought so, too…once." His eyes hardened on that last word.

Gina remembered her final week in El Paso. Sarah had been gone during that time, traveling from Dallas to Austin with her mother to interview for teaching positions. Mr. Buckley had been busy at work and Gina had been left pretty much on her own.

After their work was done on their uncle's ranch, Gina would meet Wade and Sam for ice cream or a movie or just to talk. But before long, it was only Wade coming around. They'd gotten close that last week, closer than she might have imagined, spending all of their time together. And they'd fallen in love over hot-fudge sundaes, hot summer walks and hot sizzling kisses.

No one had really known that their friendship had escalated. It hadn't been a secret, but they hadn't made any announcements either. Certainly Sarah hadn't known. Gina hadn't the time to confide in her and when she'd returned from those interviews,

Sarah had been edgy, anxious and unhappy, until she finally revealed her pregnancy to Gina and her parents.

Gina bit back her need to tell Wade the entire truth about Sarah. But destroying his friendship with Sarah wouldn't make up for what Gina had done. She hadn't trusted Wade and she *had* taken his father's money and left El Paso. Her reasons wouldn't matter to him, because Wade was a man who expected total loyalty. She had loved him back then, very much. But he wasn't the same man she'd fallen in love with. And she wasn't the same woman. The years had taught her hard lessons.

"What now?" she asked.

Wade became all business again. "Now? We have a late lunch meeting with James Robinique from the Santa Catalina Island Company. It'll take a few hours." He glanced around the room. "Enjoy yourself. Because after that, we'll be working our tails off."

Gina nodded. At least now they would get down to business. She never minded hard work. "How should I dress?"

Wade toured her body with a possessive eye. "Robinique is a lusty Frenchman with an eye for beauty. It won't matter if you wear a burlap sack, he'll still want to get you into bed."

Gina's mouth gapped open as Wade strolled out the door. Had that been a warning? Or had Wade coaxed her into coming here for an entirely different reason? She knew how important this project was to him, but enticing an island dignitary wasn't in her job description.

Gina couldn't believe it of Wade.

But the thought niggled at her far too much.

She grabbed a down pillow and flung it at the door Wade had just closed. The pillow smacked almost silently before falling to the floor, but it was enough to satisfy Gina's frustration.

"There, now I feel better," she muttered, wishing she had a burlap sack in her wardrobe. Because if she had one, she would surely have worn it just to spite Wade Beaumont.

A little later, Gina unpacked her bag, making sure to hang all of her clothes up carefully. She'd only brought one suitcase, packing enough clothes for the week, but she could make her wardrobe last two, if need be. She knew how to accessorize, how to mix and match and stretch out her clothes for maximum versatility. She prided herself on that. She loved design. She loved to create and one day, she vowed, her creativity would pay off.

A cooling breeze lifted her hair and she strolled to the wide French door Wade had opened, but instead of closing the door, she stepped outside. On a breath, she leaned against the balcony railing and gazed out at the ocean, tamping down shivers of fear, realizing that she'd crossed this ocean today with Wade by her side. She'd spent the better part of the trip below deck, but regardless of that, it was a first step to overcoming her fear.

Here she was on a small stretch of land, completely surrounded by water, working for Wade Beaumont. "Who would have guessed," she whispered into the breeze. She was living through the two scenarios she dreaded most. And the one man she hoped to never see again had orchestrated both.

Gina decided on taking a leisurely shower, luxuriating in the scented soaps, oils and body washes provided. Feeling rejuvenated, she sat down at the dressing table and brushed her long hair, deciding on another upswept do, this time leaving strands of hair down to frame her face. She used a little mascara on her eyes, highlighted the lids and put on a light shade of lipstick.

She decided on a conservative black pencil skirt and white-linen cuffed blouse to wear for the lunch meeting. Gazing in the mirror, she nodded in approval. This was business and, despite Wade's cutting remark, she wanted to appear every bit the professional.

An hour later when Wade knocked on her door, she was more than ready. "I'm all set," she said, opening the door.

Holding a briefcase in one hand and wearing equally professional dark trousers and a white shirt, he had a no-nonsense appearance: tall, dark, imposing. *Handsome.*

He made a quick sweep of her attire and she bit back a comment about burlap as he glanced down at her black-heeled sandals. "We have some walking to do."

Gina lifted one leg and twirled her foot. "These are the most comfortable shoes I own."

Wade arched a brow, taking time to stare at her toes. "Tell me that once we're back and I might believe you. Let's go."

She grabbed her purse, locked up her suite and Wade guided her downstairs with a hand to her back. "We'll go over the details once again about the Santa Catalina Island Company," he said as they walked along the streets.

Gina had read much about it in the reports, but Wade insisted on going over all pertinent information, more to reaffirm his knowledge, she believed, than to clue her in. He would do all the talking. Gina was there to take notes and provide any assistance Wade needed.

Wade explained once again how important this lunch was. The island company had been granted more than forty-thousand acres dedicated to conservation. Rarely did they agree to any building on the island. Anything proposed had to be in tune with the land and provide sanctuary for the wildlife and flora. The developer had sealed the deal, but Mr. Robinique needed to hear the plans directly from each contractor—whoever convinced him that the land would be best protected would gain the upper hand and have the best chance at winning the contract. Robinique's influence over the final proposal couldn't be discounted. Wade had three competitors, he reminded her, but only John Wheatley of Creekside Construction could truly compete with Triple B.

They climbed a hilly street to reach the snug

Harbor Inn and, once inside, Mr. James Robinique rose from his table to greet them. He shook hands with Wade and then smiled at Gina.

"This is my assistant, Miss Grady," Wade said.

Gina offered her hand and Robinique took it, clasping both of his over hers. "It's a pleasure," he said, his blue eyes never wavering.

Gina smiled at the good-looking Frenchman, taken aback by how young he appeared. From Wade's accounting, she'd expected a more mature man. But James Robinique appeared no older than her. He clasped her hand a little longer than she deemed necessary and slowly removed it from his. When she took her seat, the two men also sat down.

Once the meals had been ordered and served, the two men enjoyed healthy portions of halibut sautéed in wine sauce and conversed while Gina nibbled on her chicken salad. Wade drank beer on tap and Mr. Robinique sipped on pinot grigio. Gina opted for iced tea. She was on the clock and taking copious notes.

"Let me assure you that we have every intention of preserving the environment on the island. As you can see from the architectural layouts, there's a bird sanctuary on the grounds, not one tree will be downed and we have enhanced the outer perimeters with ponds and streams that will add to the island's beauty and invite the natural inhabitants."

With the layouts spread across the table, Robinique looked over the designs, making mental notes, nodding his head as Wade continued to make his case.

Gina jotted down his comments and questions, something Wade had asked her to do. Wade was nothing if not thorough and he wanted no stone left unturned.

Gina had to admire Wade's tenacity. He went after what he wanted without compromise. To hear him talk, you'd never guess that the resort—which would house seventy-five rooms, forty deluxe suites, six eloquent cottages, a horse-filled stable, three pools, tennis courts and a golf course—would disrupt the land in any way.

Yet, Mr. Robinique wasn't a pushover. He didn't appear completely convinced. He had specific, detailed concerns pertaining to the ninety acres in question. Wade admitted that he must do one more survey of the land before he could satisfy those questions.

Robinique agreed to meet with him later in the week, suggesting that Wade make use of the nearby stables to go over the entire acreage.

When Wade nodded in agreement, Robinique glanced at Gina. She had stopped writing and he spoke directly to her with just a hint of a French accent. "What do you think of all this, Miss Grady?" With a wave of his hands, he gestured to the plans.

"I think Mr. Beaumont and the staff at Triple B have worked diligently to try to satisfy both the developer and your company."

He kept his focus on her and smiled. "And I think Mr. Beaumont has a loyal employee."

Gina lifted her lips.

Wade kept his gaze tightly fastened to Robinique.

"Tell me, Miss Grady, are you through now, taking all those notes?"

Gina glanced at Wade. He nodded and she slipped the notepad into the briefcase. "Yes, I think so."

"Then your work is done for the day?"

"I'm not sure." She looked at Wade.

"If you are satisfied with the presentation, then I would say that our work is done for now," Wade offered. "But we will meet again later in the week."

"Then, we are finished," Robinique said, "unless you would care for coffee and dessert?"

Wade shook his head and looked at Gina. She too, shook her head. "No, thank you."

When Robinique stood, Wade took his cue and the two men shook hands. "I'll call you soon," Wade said, lifting his briefcase.

"I will expect your call," James Robinique replied, then turned to Gina. "Excuse me, Miss Grady" he began, his eyes a striking blue when focused solely on her, "but I cannot let you go without offering you our island hospitality. Would you care to join me for a drink later this evening?"

Gina felt Wade's eyes on her. He had a way of doing that, blatantly watching her with those intense-green eyes. But it was the charming blue eyes on a man with impeccable manners that had caught her off guard. Wade's words from earlier today flitted through her mind.

Lusty Frenchman.
Burlap sack.

Get you into bed.

James Robinique was certainly charming, but Gina wasn't interested in him. At one time in her life, she might have agreed to spend some time with the handsome man. Now all she wanted was to do a good job. She was here on business and she needed to keep her head in the game. She opened her mouth to answer, but Wade beat her to it.

"I plan to keep Gi-Miss Grady busy most of the night...*working.*" One side of Wade's mouth quirked up.

James Robinique blinked his eyes, then darted a glance her way before looking at Wade with a hint of envy. "I see. You are very dedicated then."

Wade nodded. "This project is important to my company."

Robinique gazed at Gina again, this time with more discerning eyes. "Yes, I can see that."

Gina's face flamed but, lucky for her, she'd always been able to hide her embarrassment under her olive complexion. Inside, she fumed. Wade had practically announced that they were lovers and all three of them knew it.

Nothing was further from the truth. Despite her need for job security, she couldn't let Wade get away with this. "I'm sorry, Mr. Beaumont, but I must take some personal time today. I've suddenly developed a terrible headache."

Blinding anger offered up the courage she needed to march out the front door of the restaurant and never look back.

* * *

Gina walked along the main streets of town until her feet ached, her anger ebbed and her heart had stopped racing like she'd just run a marathon. She peeked into shops but had no urge to stop. When tourists smiled at her she didn't smile back. She felt trapped on this island. Trapped in a job she shouldn't have taken—one she couldn't afford to lose.

She'd been out for two hours, enough time to simmer her hot Irish-Italian temper. She headed back to the hotel, contemplating a quiet night with a good book. As soon as she entered her suite, she kicked off her shoes. One flipped up and back hitting the wall behind her, the other slid across the floor to meet with another pair of shoes—a pair of *man's* shoes.

She looked up.

"Where the hell have you been?" Wade's angry voice startled her. He glared at her, arms folded, his face as firm and set as his tone.

"What are you doing in here?" she asked, none too pleased to find her boss invading her private space. "How dare you show up in my room like this!"

"You're on company time, Miss Grady. And this is a company suite."

"Oh, no. No way, Wade. This is my room and while I'm on this island, you have no right entering it without my permission. You're not paying me enough to…to—"

Wade stepped closer, until he was nearly in her

face, his green eyes, holding hers, his voice menacing. "Sue me."

Gina blinked. Anger she'd ebbed earlier rose up again with striking force. She turned her back on him, opened the front door and spoke with a quiet calm she didn't know she possessed. "Get out."

Wade strode to the door and, staring into her eyes, shoved it shut. "No one walks out on me, Gina. And no one dismisses me."

"You're so wrong. Maybe I can't throw you out of here, but I've already dismissed you." On shaky legs, she moved away from the door, away from him.

"What's got you so riled up anyway?"

Gina twirled around. Was he serious? Didn't he know how he had portrayed their relationship? "You deliberately let Robinique believe we were lovers, Wade. You staked your claim, though nothing's further from the truth. But more than that, you had no right to make that decision for me."

"Sleeping with Robinique would compromise the company."

He *was* serious. He'd actually thought she would— Furious, Gina calmed herself and took a different approach. "Quite the contrary, Wade," she began with a slow easy smile, "if I slept with him, the company would only benefit."

Wade couldn't really argue with that, though it galled him just thinking about Gina with James Robinique. Visions of making love to Gina, her soft pliant body meshed with his as they laid down on a soft cushion of hay, were never far from his mind. He remembered her, every inch of her, all too well. That night in El Paso had been magical. Though not experienced, Gina had pleased and pleasured him like no other woman had. "So, you're willing to take one for the team, so to speak?"

Her dark espresso eyes turned black as ink. She stood barefooted, hands on hips, looking at him with defiance. Only the king bed separated them and Wade's thoughts turned to it and how making love to her here would be on a soft mattress and silky sheets.

Gina's voice was deceptively calm, but the fury in her eyes gave her away. "I came here to work with you. Whether you believe me or not, I can be trusted. And if you'd given me the chance, you'd have seen me refuse Mr. Robinique's offer. I have no intention of sleeping with him or any other man. So no, I wouldn't have taken one for the team, Wade. Not like that. Now, please, it's been a long day. If there's nothing else you need from me, I'd like you to leave."

Wade stood his ground. He'd never trust Gina again, but he felt great satisfaction knowing that she would have refused Robinique. Though she'd been wrong on one account. She would sleep with one man while on this island. "Sorry, sweetheart, but you're forgetting who's the boss. And there is something else I need from you. I wasn't lying to Robinique when I said we'd be working into the night."

Gina's ire seemed to vanish. "Oh?"

Wade headed for the door. "We have a dinner meeting in exactly two hours. Be ready when I pick you up."

Gina stood there with a confused look on her face, her eyes softening, her rigid body relaxing. He glanced down at her red toenails and had never wanted a woman more.

Wade whipped the door open and exited.

Before he told her what he really needed from her.

The dinner meeting, held at a small eatery on Avalon's main street boasting buffalo milk, ended after ten o'clock. Gina had eaten quickly and immediately returned to taking notes. Wade had set up this dinner with local shop owners and proprietors to gain their support and trust, to get to know them, to assure them that if Triple B won the bid, their workers would add to the economy and not cause any trouble. Gina learned from day one that Catalina island thrived on the tourist trade. It was essential that there be no unsavory incidents and no bad press on the island. Wade was smart enough to know that, to understand their concerns.

When all was said and done, Wade escorted her outside and, as they headed toward her hotel suite, he asked. "How do you think that went?"

"By their own admission, not one of the other builders had approached them. Your assurances went a long way. I'd say you scored points."

Wade nodded. "I want to be on friendly terms when we win the bid. Our crews are the best, but get a bunch of men working in a confined area for too long and that might spell trouble. They needed to know I'd do everything in my power to keep things running smoothly."

"I think you convinced them." Wade wasn't just blowing smoke. Gina really believed he meant what he said. Nine years ago, she would never have believed that the roughriding rancher with the sweet nature would become such an astute businessman. She never pictured him in that role. Yet here he was, talking the talk, making the deals. Gina shook her head.

Wade caught the slight movement. "What?"

"Nothing, really. It's nothing."

Wade was silent for a while, then before they reached her hotel, he stopped. "I could use a drink. There's a nightclub up the street known for their tropical drinks. Care to join me?"

Gina hesitated. A nightcap sounded wonderful. She'd had a tumultuous day. She was physically exhausted but the idea of relaxing with a piña colada and some good music sounded great. "I bet the music's real loud."

"Probably," Wade replied honestly.

Gina nibbled on her lower lip. "It's probably crowded."

"Without a doubt."

"Am I on the clock?" she asked. Looking into Wade's beautiful green eyes what she really wanted to know was if his request had been a demand of the job or a simple invitation.

Wade shook his head. "Not at all. I don't like to drink alone, but if it's not what you—"

"I could use a drink, too."

"Great. Let's go," he said, with a pleased look on his face. They strolled up a slightly inclined street and, somewhere along the way, Wade twined his fingers with hers and they entered the nightclub hand in hand.

For Gina, it felt as natural as breathing.

Five

"I want to make love to you," Wade whispered in her ear, his warm breath combined with those softly spoken words caused havoc to her nerves and brought tingles to her toes.

With her arms wrapped around his neck, their bodies brushing, swaying to the jazz band's bluesy sensual ballad, Gina rested her head on his shoulder. After two piña coladas, her brain was fuzzy, but not fuzzy enough to disregard what was happening between them. She was fully aware of what Wade wanted. "It's not in my job description," she whispered back softly.

She felt Wade's smile. It was difficult not to feel the same arousing sensations, not to succumb to his body heat or the pressing evidence of that desire. Gina wanted him, too.

"I told you before, you're not on the clock, Gina."

Wade dropped his hands down lower on her back, his fingers splaying across her derriere. He made soft caressing circles as he drew her closer. "Remember how it was between us, Gina? It can be that way again."

She shouldn't allow him such liberties. The fact remained that he was still her boss. They had a job to do here on the island. But the sensations swept through her with blinding force. His touch heated her, his words enticed her and his hard body stirred her softer one. She raised her head from his shoulder to look into his eyes.

It was a mistake.

Wade's intense gaze blazed into hers, before his lips came down in a soul-searing kiss, right there on the crowded, smoky dance floor. They kissed. And kissed.

Gina's body ignited, but dire warnings fanned the flames quickly. She couldn't allow Wade in. Not again.

She shoved at his chest and pulled away from him, her body swamped with heat, defying her reasoning. "I didn't come here for this," she breathed out. "It's not a good idea."

Wade reacted immediately. "I can't think of a better one."

Rather than make a scene right there in the nightclub, Gina moved off the dance floor. She walked outside, letting the cool sea breezes clear her head. Wade was beside her instantly. "You're still a liar, Gina."

Gina scoffed and began walking down the street. "Your bedside manner needs improving, Wade."

Wade kept pace, his hand placed possessively on her back. "There's not a damn thing wrong with my bedside manner. And you'll find that out as soon as you stop lying to yourself and admit what you really want."

Gina heaved a big sigh, her head in as much turmoil as her quaking body. "What I *want* is to go to bed. Alone."

Wade curled a hand around her neck, bringing her face close, as he came around to block her from walking past him. She was forced to look into those smoldering green eyes.

They stood under the moonlit night sky with twinkling stars overhead, right outside the entrance of her hotel. "Sorry, sweetheart, but what you want is for me to crawl up inside your sheets, strip you naked and rock your world."

Gina's mouth opened. Then closed.

"It's going to happen, Gina. Bank on it."

He left her standing on the front steps of the hotel, captivated by the steamy image swirling around in her head, more angry than she ever remembered being and wishing that, more than anything, Wade Beaumont had been wrong.

Wade dressed in a pair of Wranglers, faded not by the manufacturer, but by hard work and long wear, a plaid shirt and his Stetson. He put on his boots and left *Total Command* to pick up Gina this morning.

Although clothes didn't make the man, Wade was comfortable in these, the old standbys, the worn leather of his boots and the soft cotton of his shirt reminding him of his time at Uncle Lee's ranch in El Paso. He wasn't that young man anymore. Time, with all the hardships, heartaches and headaches, had a way of changing a man.

His heart had hardened. And he knew it. He was relentless when he wanted something. Maybe that much of his old man had rubbed off on him. Wade wanted two things. He wanted to win the bid on the Catalina project and he wanted Gina.

Neither one would escape him. He would see to that.

He knocked on her door at precisely 8:00 a.m.

When she didn't answer, he knocked again, harder.

"Are you looking for me?"

Wade whipped around in the hallway and caught Gina's unfettered expression. She hadn't recognized him, that much was obvious. And once she had that genuine look vanished.

"Oh," she said, standing there, her breaths coming quickly, with sweat on her forehead, dressed in killer shorts and a white spandex top. "Wade, I didn't—"

"Do you run?"

A quick smile curled her lips. "I try."

They stood silent for a moment, gazing at each other, but Wade couldn't miss Gina's probing eyes and those few rapid blinks as she took in his appearance, as if trying to figure out which man he really was: the fast, hard businessman or the easy, kind cowboy she'd once known.

The confusion in her eyes bothered him, so he ignored her expression and swept his gaze instead to her long legs, and tanned smooth skin. More leg than she'd allowed him lately. And as his gaze traveled upward, he noted her breaths coming fast and the spandex top unable to confine the swell of her breasts and the damned enticing tips of her erect nipples.

Her hair was pulled back in a ponytail. She looked sweaty and hot and sexy enough to have for breakfast.

"I thought I had an hour before going to the stables," she said, opening the door to her suite and entering.

Wade followed her inside. "You do, but we need to eat something first. I ordered room service. Breakfast will be here soon."

In a single fluid move, Gina pulled the elastic band from her hair and chestnut strands flowed onto her shoulders, framing her face. "Let me guess, last night you didn't want to drink alone and today you don't want to eat alone."

Wade shrugged off her comment as he tossed his hat onto her bed. "Doesn't figure for me to eat alone when I have a beautiful assistant at my disposal."

"I may be at your disposal in business, Wade, but that's the extent of it."

Again, he ignored her. "You look *hot.*"

Gina frowned. "I know. I'm hot and sweaty. I must look a mess." She ran her hand through her hair in an unconscious move that had Wade approaching her.

"Not a mess." He strode the rest of the distance separating them, facing her toe to toe. *"Sexy as hell."*

Gina blinked then captured his gaze as well as his meaning. She backed up a step, her tone filled with warning as she shook her head slightly. "Wade."

Wade reached for her waist, encircling his arms around her and pulled her close. A combination of female and salty scents drifted up as she looked at him with hesitation in her eyes.

"Don't fight it, honey." Wade swooped his mouth down and took her in a long, slow, deliberate kiss that had her molding her body to his. A little moan escaped her throat when Wade cupped her buttocks, pressing her to the juncture of his thighs.

She fit him perfectly. She always had. Immediate heat swamped him and his groin tightened envisioning her on the bed with him, just a few feet away. He'd wanted her, wanted *that* ever since she'd walked into his office a few days ago.

A knock at the door broke the moment.

Wade winced at the bad timing. And, as he tugged his mouth from hers, he whispered, "Room service." Wade had a notion to send the waiter packing and finish this. Just as he began to utter those commands, Gina backed away.

"I—I need a shower."

Wade glanced at her chest, the tempting swell of her breasts straining against her spandex top with her breathes coming hard again, only this time, he knew her fast breathing had nothing to do with the run she'd just taken. "So do I—a cold one."

Gina's gaze slipped down to his jeans, her eyes riveted below his waist.

Wade ground out a warning. "Don't tempt me, Gina."

"I never mean to."

That was the problem. Gina, just being Gina, was enough of a temptation. Didn't matter what she wore, how she looked, Wade found himself wanting her, no matter what. She was beautiful to him. That much hadn't changed. From the moment he'd set eyes on her almost ten years ago, he'd wanted her. Had to have her.

The only difference between now and then was that now he knew he'd have her but he'd never keep her.

The knock came louder this time, announcing, "Room service!"

Wade let out a deep sigh, restraining his desire. "I'll get the door. You get your shower."

Gina nodded and, without a word, entered the bathroom. After a second, he heard the decided click of the bathroom door's lock.

Gina mounted a bay mare, fitting herself as comfortably as she could on the saddle. It had been almost ten years since she'd ridden a horse. She'd been taught by the best; Mr. Buckley, Sarah and

Wade all had a hand in teaching her how to ride. But she was rusty and uncertain.

"Don't let her know you're nervous," Wade said, gripping the reins, holding the mare steady from the ground. Gina took a deep breath and nodded.

"You'd think a girl born and bred in Texas would know more about horses than how to hang onto the saddle horn."

Wade grinned. "You were from Austin. That doesn't count."

"Austin was full of horses." Gina tipped her chin up in defiance.

"Right. And you rode how many?"

Wade didn't wait for an answer. He handed her the reins, then swung his long legs up and over his saddle, mounting a tall dappled-gray mare. "Follow my lead. Loosen up on the reins and use only slight motions to guide the mare. You'll do fine."

"I can't take notes and ride. Why do you need me?"

"I need another pair of eyes."

Gina doubted that. She knew for certain that scores of Triple B's finest—from architects to financial accountants—had surveyed the property already.

"Ready?"

Gina squirmed once more in her saddle and adjusted the straw hat Wade had purchased in town for her. "Ready."

Wade made a soft sound to his mare and with just the slightest click of his boot heels, the horse took off. Gina's mare followed and they rode off the stable grounds and away from the road, heading further into the interior of the canyon.

Ten minutes later, Wade reined his horse to a stop. Saddle leather creaked when he turned around in his seat. "Take a look," he said.

Gina's gaze flowed in the direction he was pointing. They had steadily climbed and had come to a low rise that overlooked the entire town of Avalon and the crescent-shaped bay below. From this distance and under clear-blue skies, the ocean seemed less threatening with a throng of boats harbored in the stunning turquoise bay. "It's remarkable."

Wade agreed with a low grumble. "It's hard to believe this place once was home to pirates and trappers."

"Yes, but I can picture it, can't you? The wildness here, the untouched land and those men coming here, some for honest work, others to do harm or hide out."

Wade cast her a long thoughtful look, his eyes narrowing as if picturing it. "Yeah, I can see that," he said, his lips quirking in a distant smile, before turning back around.

Once again he *looked* like the Wade she'd known in El Paso, only more mature, stronger, more capable, if that were even possible.

"Not much longer now," Wade said, as they passed oaks and sage and tall limber stalks of sun-yellow and white poppies.

They met up with a road again and Gina saw the gates that led to a clearing. No Trespassing signs cordoned off the area.

Wade dismounted and used a key to unlock the chains on the gate before mounting his mare again. Gina followed him inside.

The clearing where the resort was to be built was anything but clear. Tall cottonwoods blocked the sun, natural formations jutted up from the earth and canyon walls provided the backdrop.

"The architects have done a great job in preserving most of what you see. We won't down these trees. They'll be a natural part of the landscape. Out there in the distance, a wildflower meadow allows just enough land to build the main hotel and facilities. About half a mile down the road there's a secluded cove that we'll utilize for special occasions and weddings. You name it. This is the first project I've been involved with where the land dictates the building, instead of the other way around. I think Robinique understands that."

Wade spurred his mare on. "Come on. I need to see it all one more time and get your opinion."

"I've seen the plans on paper, Wade. But it's hard for me to picture it. Seems like this place needs to stay untouched."

"*Nothing* stays untouched, Gina." He cast her a narrow-eyed look from under the brim of his Stetson. "I learned that lesson a long time ago."

"So as long as it's going to be *touched,* you might as well be the one doing the touching?"

Wade stared deeply into her eyes, capturing her and making her flinch from his intensity. "That's right."

Heat crept up Gina's neck. She wanted out of this conversation, knew she should let the comment go, but she couldn't. Wade had twisted her words and suddenly they weren't speaking about the land any longer. She fought her rising anger. "When did you become so ruthless?"

Wade's voice held contempt. "You know the answer to that."

Gina slumped in the saddle. Telling him the truth now wouldn't do any good. Wade had changed. He was a man walking in the shadow of his father. He was just as driven, just as bitter. Getting involved with him again would be a big mistake. She'd already had a bad relationship with one unscrupulous man and she feared Wade Beaumont, too, would only use her then toss her aside.

Gina kept Sarah's secret close to her heart. It wasn't her secret to divulge anyway. If Sarah wanted Wade to know the truth, then she would tell him in her own time. Long-standing friendships were at stake here and Gina wanted no part in destroying Sarah's relationship with Wade. Gina was the outsider and she would always remain so. "We'd be better off just sticking to business, Wade."

Wade cocked his head and sent her a crooked smile. "That's all I was talking about. Business."

Gina's temper rose with lightning speed. There was no stopping the rage within her. She silently cursed Wade and his infuriating hold on her. She needed to get away from him. She kicked her mare's flanks just as a wild hawk swooped down from a cottonwood. The horse reared up in fright—nearly tossing Gina from the saddle—then her front hooves landed hard onto the ground and the mare took off running.

Startled, the reins dropped from Gina's hands. She grabbed for the saddlehorn, bouncing on the seat as the mare raced across the meadowland. Her hat flew from her head as she hung on.

She heard Wade's commands from behind, knew he was racing behind her, trying to catch up. Gina held on for dear life. Her shoes came out of the stirrups from the turbulent ride. She lost her balance in the saddle and her grip on the horn. Within seconds, she was tossed off the horse.

She hit the ground hard.

Dazed from the fall, she heard Wade's footsteps fast approaching. And then he was leaning down beside her with fear in his eyes and a voice filled with gentle condemnation. "Damn it, Gina. You're always running away."

Six

With her head pounding, her body twisted and the air knocked out of her, Gina squinted into the morning sun. Wade moved to obstruct the light, his tone fierce but his hands gentle as he touched and surveyed her body for injuries. "Did you hit your head?"

She gazed into his eyes as his fingers searched for a bump. "I have a hard head."

"Tell me about it," he muttered, yet the softness in his eyes belied his tone. When he didn't find a bump on her head, his hands traveled to her face, gently turning her right to left, searching for injury. "Can you untwist your body?"

Gina did exactly that. She straightened her form

then winced. "I'm sore, but at least everything's moving."

He frowned and spoke quietly, "The fall won't really hit you until tomorrow."

Gina looked up into his eyes. She liked what she saw there. In an unguarded moment, Wade let down his defenses and she witnessed the depth of his compassion. "You mean I have aches and pains to look forward to?"

"Remember when I tried to break Rocket? That horse wouldn't give in. He must have thrown me a dozen times."

Gina nodded, recalling Wade's determination to break the wild stallion his uncle Lee had captured in the mountains. After several bronc-busters had tried, his uncle Lee had just about given up and had been ready to turn the stallion loose. But Wade had been more stubborn than the stallion and had finally tamed the beast. "I remember that you had trouble walking the next day." Then it dawned on her. Slightly panicked, she tried to rise up. "You're not saying I'm going to feel like that?"

Wade placed a calming hand to her shoulder. "Hold still, honey."

In one grand sweeping movement, Gina was lifted up into Wade's arms. She automatically roped her arms around his neck. He carried her to the shade of an ancient oak.

He felt solid and warm and, when he peered down at her, she couldn't miss the concern in his beautiful green eyes.

"You're not as tough as you let on," she whispered near his ear. "Sometimes, I see the man you were in El Paso, Wade."

"I don't think he exists anymore, Gina." Wade pitched his Stetson and Gina watched the hat land near her mare's hooves. It was so telling, so obvious what that toss of the hat meant. Wade didn't want to go back. He'd moved into the role of a high-powered executive and was comfortable there.

She let out a quiet sigh. "A girl can hope, can't she?"

Wade stared into her eyes for a long moment and nodded then lowered down to sit against the base of the oak, keeping Gina firmly in his arms and on his lap. "Are you hurt? Do you feel dizzy?"

She shook her head, "I'm not hurt at all. My head's fine. You can let me up now."

"I can't," he said.

Her brows lifted. "Can't?"

"Don't want to, won't."

He smiled, right before his lips touched hers. The brush of his mouth over hers sent warm comforting shivers throughout her body.

She wound her arms tighter about his neck and he deepened the sweet kiss, coaxing her mouth open. From there, Wade took complete control, mating their tongues in a slow fiery seduction while his hand stroked her face then her throat. Gentle fingers traveled lower, unfastening the top buttons of her blouse.

Wade had her in his arms, at his mercy. Gina

couldn't fight her desire any longer. She was where she wanted to be. The Wade she'd known was still there, inside, somewhere in the soft caress of his eyes, in the caring way he held her and in the coaxing brush of his lips. She wanted Wade Beaumont to return. She wanted the man she'd once loved. She'd do anything to bring him back to her.

He slipped his hand inside her blouse. She moaned when he touched her breasts, remembering those fingers, gentle yet rough against her skin. She strained against him. He took more, easing her bra down, cupping her, flicking her nipple until she moaned louder, feeling the pulse of his erection against her thigh.

When he broke off the kiss, they looked deeply into each other's eyes. "Definitely feeling dizzy now," she whispered softly.

Wade smiled again and spoke in a low, raspy voice. "You want me."

It wasn't a question but a statement of fact. One she couldn't deny. "Yes."

Wade kissed her again and palmed her breast until spiraling heat curled up from her belly.

"This is a long time coming, Gina."

He pressed her down lower on his lap and, leaning over her, he slipped his hand under the waistband of her jeans, his fingers trekking slowly, teasing, tempting, until finally he reached her.

Gina welcomed him. His touch, the stroking of his fingers as they kissed, brought damp moist heat and an ecstasy she'd only known in his arms.

Suddenly, Wade froze, his head shooting up and he muttered a foul curse.

"What is it?" Gina asked, stunned by his quick abandonment.

"Security jeep. Coming from down the road. They must have seen the gate unlocked."

He lifted her off him and together they stood facing each other, Gina's clothes as disheveled as her mind.

"Get dressed," he said. "I'll go meet them. Explain who we are."

No words came. She could only nod.

Wade plucked his hat from the ground, yanked it onto his head and strode over to his horse. Before mounting, he turned to her with deep regret in his eyes, as he watched her button her blouse. "One of these days I'm going to make love to you in a damn bed."

Wade escorted Gina back to town, leaving her in front of the hotel. She'd been quiet on the ride back to the stables and then, as they walked back to the hotel, she hadn't said more than a few sentences. Wade wasn't in the mood for talking either. He'd had a few choice words for the security guards who needed convincing that he wasn't a trespasser. Their interruption had cost him. His desire for Gina had gone unsatisfied and that made him want her all the more.

It irritated the hell out of him how much he wanted her. She couldn't be trusted and he'd never forgive her for her betrayal, so why wasn't he satisfied with all the other women he'd had in his life?

"Take a few hours to rest. We have a late lunch meeting. I'll go to the boat and do some work. I'll be back later to pick you up."

Gina nodded, but kept her eyes from meeting his. "Okay."

Wade cupped her chin and forced her to look at him. "Are you up for it?"

She shot him a look of defiance. "I came here to work, Wade." She backed away, releasing his hold on her. "So yes, I'm up for it. But back there, that was a mistake. We've both changed. We're not the same people we were when we knew each other in El Paso. You're paying me to be your personal assistant. I don't believe sleeping with the boss is in my job description."

Wade tamped down rising anger. "*That* had nothing to do with business or the fact that I'm your boss. As I recall, you said yes and couldn't wait for me to get into your pants."

Gina's dark eyes went wide. She lifted her hand and Wade warned her with a searing glance not to even try it. When she lowered her hand, she spoke with quiet calm, her words more potent than any slap to the face. "I thought I saw an inkling of the man you once were, Wade. The man I wanted above all else, the man who was kind and generous and caring. But I was mistaken, you're *nothing* like him."

Wade jammed his hands in the back pockets of his jeans, watching her spin around and walk into the hotel lobby. Her words stung but he wouldn't be played for a fool ever again.

No matter how much he wanted her.

* * *

Wade poured himself a whiskey on the rocks, something that always soothed his bad temper, and took a seat at his desk. He let the mellow rocking of the boat and the fresh sea breeze calm him for several minutes before opening his e-mail account. He punched in his password and viewed more than a dozen messages forwarded to him from Triple B.

As he went through half of them, all having to do with the Catalina project, Wade came upon one message he hadn't expected, from Sarah Buckley.

He hadn't spoken with Sarah in over six months. They'd always remained friends, but ever since that episode with Gina years ago, their relationship hadn't been quite the same. He'd left El Paso shortly after that tumultuous summer to work at Triple B with his father. Maybe his imagination was in overdrive, but whenever he had visited his uncle and aunt in El Paso, he'd also made a stop in to see the Buckleys and, oddly, they'd been slightly distant, polite but not as friendly as he remembered. And Sarah, too, had seemed more cautious with him.

He punched in and opened the e-mail.

Wade, I know you're out of town, but it's important that you call me when you return. We need to talk.
Always,
Your friend,
Sarah

Wade sipped his drink, staring at the message for a moment, making a mental note to call Sarah once he returned to Los Angeles. Right now, he had enough to deal with, Gina being right up there on his list.

He realized his approach with Gina had been completely wrong. She wasn't an easy female to figure out but he did know that when she was backed into a corner, she came out fighting. Though she was as headstrong and volatile as she was beautiful, Wade wouldn't let her get away this time around. She had become nearly as important as the Catalina Project and both were challenges he fully intended to win. He finished his drink, took a quick shower and changed into different clothes. Before meeting Gina at the hotel, he had one important errand to run.

Gina glanced at the digital clock on the bed stand. It was ten minutes after two and Wade was late. It wasn't like him to be late for a meeting.

She glanced at her reflection in the framed beveled mirror, straightening out her tan skirt and cream knit shell top. She tossed the short tailored jacket she'd donned minutes ago onto the bed and headed to the wraparound balcony for a breath of fresh air.

Her nerves had been wrought ever since she'd come to this island. The trip over here in Wade's yacht had nearly done her in and she hadn't thought things could've gotten any worse. But they had.

She didn't know where she stood with Wade. He was her boss, that was a given. He wanted to be her lover. That's where it all got confusing. She knew enough not to get involved with him romantically, yet when he kissed her and touched her tenderly, memories flooded in, sweet hot wonderful memories of the times they had shared in the past. Gina had succumbed to him earlier today and the heat of his touch still sizzled on her lips and other highly sensitive parts of her anatomy. Wade had left his mark on her body.

A light-hearted tap on the door surprised her. She strode the distance wondering who it could be. Certainly Wade's knock had always been more commanding. When she opened the door to her suite, she stood in awe, looking at a smiling Wade, dressed in khaki shorts and a tan polo shirt, black beach sandals on his feet.

"Our meeting was cancelled," he said, walking in holding a shopping bag. "I figured we both could use some down time."

"Down time?" Gina asked, confused by Wade's uncharacteristic light mood.

"Yeah, you know…relax, soak up some sun, enjoy the beach."

Gina stared at Wade. "That sounds nice," she fibbed. The last place she could relax was staring out at the fathomless ocean. "But I'm afraid I didn't bring 'down time' clothes with me. Sorry, you'll have to go it alone." She sent him a small smile.

Wade lifted up the bag. "That's why I brought this."

Gina watched him set the bag on her king-size bed. "Oh, I was hoping that was lunch."

Wade shot her a sweeping glance, his eyes raking in her body from top to bottom. "Depends on how you look at it."

"What? What did you bring me?" Gina walked over to the white bag and tossed the contents onto the bed. Swimsuits, sarongs and fancy rhinestone flip-flops scattered. Gina lifted up a pure-white dazzling bikini. "A thong?" She turned to face him. "Not on your life."

Wade laughed. "I had to try." He gestured to the others. "What about the black one?"

Gina eyed him cautiously, before picking it up and scanning it over. The bikini had a tad more material than the thong, she noted. She shook her head. "You don't know my size."

Wade stepped closer to her and looked into her eyes. He spoke softly, with confidence. "I know your body, Gina. They'll fit."

Heat rushed up, warming her throat and blistering her face. Once again she thanked the Almighty for her olive complexion. At least she could hide her blush from Wade, if nothing else. She set the suit down. "I'd really rather stay in."

Wade folded his arms across his middle. "Okay, we'll stay in." He glanced at her then the bed. "What do you suppose we can do in here all afternoon?"

Gina flinched. "I wasn't inviting you."

Wade took a seat on the sofa, his arm spread along the top cushion. "Gina, what are you afraid of? We'll go down, have lunch at a café, then relax on the beach for a few hours."

"You know I don't like the water."

"You traveled twenty-two miles over that water to get here."

"I know. I'm dreading the trip back." Just the thought brought shivers.

Wade pointed to the clothes on the bed. "Try the red one, Gina. It's a one-piece."

Gina glanced at it and frowned. "With more cutouts than Swiss cheese."

"You noticed that, too?"

Wade didn't even try to hide his amusement. "Come on, Gina. You must be starving by now."

Gina's stomach rumbled quietly. Thankfully, Wade didn't seem to hear. She was hungry and it seemed the only way to get Wade out of her hotel room was to leave with him. "Okay, fine. I'll wear the red one."

Gina grabbed the swimsuit, a multicolored sarong and sparkling rhinestone flip-flops and stomped into the bathroom, ignoring Wade's satisfied chuckle from the sitting area.

She knew he'd be right. Everything he bought would fit her.

Perfectly.

Gina sipped her piña colada, the coconut-and-rum tropical drink sliding cold and smooth down her throat. Wearing the cherry-red swimsuit underneath the sarong cover-up, she faced Wade from her seat at the beachfront café, surprised at his casual demeanor. He'd dominated the conversation, opening up to her about his time at Triple B working with his father, learning the business, then taking over after his father died and Sam remarried and started a new life at Belle Star Stables. He'd filled her in on his life from the time he left El Paso to the present. Of course, she was certain that he'd left out choice bits about his love life and he'd skirted the issue about their onetime hot and steamy relationship.

If he'd wanted her to relax, he'd succeeded. The two empty piña colada glasses in front of her might have had something do with it as well, but Gina wouldn't look a gift horse in the mouth.

"So what about you? What did you do once you landed in Los Angeles?" he asked, his tone light, his eyes holding nothing but curiosity.

Gina had always wanted Wade to understand what her life had been like before and after she met him. There had been so many things left unsaid. Perhaps now was the time, after all this time, to come clean, at least partly. She'd always wanted Wade's trust and maybe this was the first step in gaining it back.

"I'd always liked Los Angeles. Sarah and I roomed at UCLA for four years together. We were girls from two different worlds. Though I was raised in Austin, my parents were city folks. They owned a small Italian restaurant. My mother was a terrific cook."

"As I recall, so were you."

"Thank you. It was a family-run operation. I worked there until I left for college."

"And after college, when you left El Paso, what did you do?"

Gina peered at Wade. He'd just polished off a sandwich and was working on the fries and his second beer. Because she didn't find any sign of resentment, any hint of a trap, she continued. "I looked for work and did some odd jobs here and there. Nothing too stimulating, but all the while I'd been working on clothing designs. That's when I realized I'd probably wasted four years of my life in college. I should have been following my heart. I entered the Fashion Institute and loved every minute of it. When I got out, I ventured into my own business. Or at least, I tried."

"What do you mean, you tried?" Wade asked. "What happened?" He plucked another fry up and shoved it into his mouth.

Gina took a deep breath and surged on. "I didn't have any money, so I took on a partner. A man. He seemed to have more business sense than me, some really good ideas. We took out loan after loan to fund our venture. I...trusted him."

Wade took a pull from his beer. "Mistake?"

"Big, big—huge—mistake."

Wade set his beer down and leaned in, his elbows braced on the table now. "I'm listening."

"He stole my designs and every bit of money we'd borrowed. I have no idea where he is or what happened to him."

Wade studied her a moment as if sorting something out in his mind. "Were you involved with him?"

Gina paused, hating to admit this to Wade. She'd been such a fool. "Yes. He was charming and so easy to be with…a charming con man."

Wade sat back in his seat, looking at her. "I get it now. Why you took the job working for me."

"I'm in debt, Wade. I owe a lot of people a lot of money."

"You shouldn't have to pay it all back."

Gina bit her lip, and swallowed. "Some of the loans were in my name only—a good many of them."

Wade nodded and had her gratitude for not telling her what a gullible fool she'd been.

"I plan to repay every loan. There isn't anything I won't do to clear my name. I still want my dream. I still have the designs in my head. I know I can do it, but first I need to clean up my debts."

He eyed her now, holding her gaze. He was a wealthy affluent man and her debts might seem trivial to him, but to her, the thousands she owed were monumental. "How much are we talking about here?"

Gina shrugged and smiled. "You don't want to know. It doesn't matter. Like I said, I'll do whatever it takes to get out from under all my debt. Then I plan to start GiGi Designs on my own. I'm determined."

Wade shot her a look of admiration and she wondered where that had come from. Nervous and uncomfortable from his perusal, Gina changed the subject. "Are you through with lunch?"

He smiled. "Do you see anything left on my plate?"

"Then I guess we should get the relaxing on the beach and soaking up the sun over with."

Wade stood, tossed some cash onto the table and took her hand in his. "It's hardly cruel and unusual punishment."

Gina only smiled at the comment, but for her that's exactly how it seemed. She doubted she'd ever be comfortable sitting on the beach just steps from the ocean.

Ten minutes later, they were lying against rented sand chairs, lathered in sunscreen, watching children play in the water. Wade's eyes were closed under his dark sunglasses, his chest bare and his long lean legs stretched out along a beach towel. He looked magnificent.

When one little girl slipped and went under a wave, Gina rose up and gasped. "Oh no."

Wade glanced up, noting Gina's distress. They both watched the child lift up from the water, dripping wet, her face animated and her joyous laughter ringing through the noisy beach.

Relieved, Gina sank back down, trying hard to control her irrational fear. It was enough that she couldn't stand the water, but she should be able to see others enjoying themselves without thinking the very worst. Without those terrifying flashes of memory hitting her.

"Come on, Gina. We're going for a walk."

Gina hadn't noticed Wade rise up from his chair to stand over her. He blocked the sun, peering down at her through those dark shades. "Where?"

"Along the beach."

Gina shook her head fiercely. "No, thank you."

"It'll do you good."

"I...can't, Wade." Didn't he understand her fear? She explained to him that she hadn't stepped foot in a swimming pool—or any body of water—since the accident. Her bathtub days were over as well—she was unable to sit in a tub full of water for any length of time. Sitting just feet from the bay did enough to jangle her nerves.

He reached for her hand. "I think you can. Trust me, on this." He removed his sunglasses to peer deeply into her eyes. "Come on. You'd be doing me a favor."

"A favor?" she asked incredulously. "How so?"

He swept his gaze over her, then zeroed in on her breasts, which were nearly popping out from his most conservative choice of swimsuit. Conservative for a showgirl, that is. "It's torture sitting next to you wearing that thing. Making out on a public beach isn't my style. So do me a favor and take a walk with me. I need the distraction."

Gina laughed, despite her fear. "You're such a liar, Wade. I know what you're trying to do."

"Don't be so sure that I'm lying." Then he leaned down to within a breath of her. Her gaze flowed over his strong, muscled chest, then up to his face, the hot gleam in his green eyes. "And don't tempt me. I'd rather be on a private beach with you, but this just might have to do."

Gina didn't believe him for a second, yet his

powers of persuasion couldn't be denied. "Okay, let's go for a short walk."

Wade nodded, slipped his sunglasses on and took her hand. "Let's go."

The short five-minute walk Gina had hoped for ended up being a thirty-minute stroll along the beach with Wade doing all the talking, *all the distracting*. He held her hand and she knew this time it was to lend moral support rather than any need he had for intimacy. Once they reached a secluded cove, far away from the loud boisterous beach crowd, Wade stopped by the water's edge and turned her by the shoulder to look into his eyes.

"Just stand here." He took both of her hands now and held on. They faced each other, her back to the ocean. "Keep looking at me."

Gina held her breath, her bare feet digging into the hot sand. "If you're trying to torture me, you're doing a fine job."

"I'm trying to help. The surf's coming up."

Gina flinched.

Wade held her firm. "I've got you. Don't move. Just let it wash over your toes. Gina, look at me!"

She did. She looked into his eyes. This was his best revenge. If he meant her harm, wanted to hurt her, this was the way. But for once, Gina gave him the benefit of the doubt. She believed he was sincere, wanting to help. And the only reason she came up with was that Wade couldn't stand to see weakness in others. He couldn't relate. He had no clue how hard it was for her to stand on this beach and give him her full trust.

Water lapped over her feet.

She closed her eyes and fought from running onto dry land. The chill hit her first, then the moisture as her feet dug in again, this time into cool wet sand. It lasted only seconds and once the water ebbed she opened her eyes.

Wade was there, watching her, still holding her hands tight.

"You did it." There was admiration in his voice. "I know it wasn't easy."

"Can I go back to the hotel now?"

Wade smiled. "Once isn't enough. It never is with you."

And then he brought her closer, crushing his lips to hers, lifting her onto the tips of her feet.

She barely felt the next wave as it curled around her toes.

Seven

The next few days flew by and Gina felt she'd earned every dollar Wade was paying her. She attended meeting after meeting and spent a good deal of time on the boat working on the proposal, double- and triple-checking everything. Wade was tenacious in his approach and meticulous with details. He worked with total concentration. It was only once they were done for the night that he would look at her as if he could devour her.

But they were both drained physically and mentally and Gina was grateful he kept his distance. Three days had gone by since that first episode on the beach where Wade had taken her to the water's edge. And every morning since, he'd persuaded her to take a barefoot stroll along the beach for only a minute or two with him. He'd roll his pants up, remove his shoes and urge her to do the same.

Gina had gotten accustomed to the feel of water lapping over her feet. She'd even gotten used to being below on the yacht, working in Wade's small office or at the navigation station. It was the dinghy rides back and forth to the boat that still frightened her. The small tubular boat that Wade made sure to power slowly to the dock and back, brought her close to the surface of the water and even closer to facing her fears.

And now as she sat in the dinghy, ready to head back to the hotel, Wade made the same request he'd made for the past three days. "Put your hand in the water, Gina."

And Gina gave him the same answer she'd given him for the past three days. "Not today, Wade."

But this time, Wade frowned and shot her a determined look, one she'd readily recognized from days of working alongside him. "We're almost through with our work here. It's now or never."

Gina crossed her arms over her middle. "*Never* sounds good to me."

"Then we may *never* get to shore." Wade steered the dinghy away from the shore, slowly heading the boat out of the bay.

Gina froze. Every muscle in her body tensed. Wade couldn't be serious. He wouldn't do that to her. "Wade, don't."

When he looked at her panicked expression, he

killed the engine and softened his tone. "You've got your life jacket on, we're not in deep water and, Gina, I'm here. I won't let anything happen to you. Trust me."

That wasn't the first time he'd asked for her trust. For anyone else, leaning over to put their hand in the ocean might seem easy as pie, but they hadn't witnessed the water swallowing up their parents.

But Gina also knew it was time to face her fear and not let it dictate her life anymore. On a deeply held breath, Gina, seeking his encouragement fastened her gaze on Wade then leaned over and put her hand in the water. She managed to splash it around, tamping down shivers rising up.

"I'll get back at you for this," she told Wade, without the least bit of sincerity.

"I don't doubt it," he said, with a crooked smile, watching her scoop and sift water around for a few seconds. When she pulled her hand out, he seemed satisfied. And again, he didn't pass it off and remark how easy that was for her. No, she appreciated the fact that Wade knew how hard that simple act was for her.

"Now sit back. We're heading in." He started up the motor again.

And once they docked, Wade helped Gina out of the dinghy, placing a chaste kiss on her lips. "You did good back there."

Gina felt like a child who'd won the spelling bee, a stirring of pride, relief and accomplishment. No one knew the terror she'd felt that day and, finally, with

Wade's help she was learning to accept what happened and overcome her fear. "You gave me no choice."

Wade smiled again. "I know. It's how I operate. But it worked. I think you're slowly coming around. Still want to get back at me?"

Gina looked into his beautiful deep green eyes. "I haven't decided yet."

"You can decide over dinner tonight. No work. Just play. We'll have a quiet meal at the Portofino and celebrate."

"Celebrate?"

"Our work is nearly complete here. The bid is ready and we both deserve some time to relax and enjoy."

Gina closed her eyes, imagining dim lights, soft music and a good meal. "Mmm. That sounds good."

"It will be. Come on, I'll walk you back to the hotel so you can get ready."

When he placed his hand on the small of her back, Gina stopped him. "No. I want to walk along the beach. By myself this time."

Wade looked into her eyes, studying her, then nodded. "Okay. I'll meet you downstairs in the Portofino in three hours."

Gina reached up and kissed Wade on the cheek, remarkably grateful for his heavy-handed tactics. With his help, she was finally regaining the part of herself she'd lost nine years ago.

Wade was early. He'd dressed in a casual light-silk suit and paced the floorboards of *Total Command* wishing the time would move faster. He'd shut off the computer, snapped shut his briefcase with a click and shut down his mind from work. He was ready to play.

With Gina.

He decided he'd be better off waiting at the Portofino having a drink instead of pacing the interior of the boat. So he motored into Avalon and walked the distance to the hotel as the early evening sun set on the horizon.

He was immediately greeted at the restaurant door by Peter, the maître d'. "Good evening, Mr. Beaumont. May I see you to a table?"

"Yes, thank you, Peter. There'll be just two. And I'd like a corner table.'"

"Of course," he said, "right this way."

The maître d' led him to a table in the far corner of the dimly lit room and showed him a seat. "This is fine."

"Are you enjoying your stay here on the island, Mr. Beaumont?"

Wade engaged in light conversation with Peter for the next few minutes. When Peter handed him a wine list, Wade immediately shook his head. "No need. I'll take a whiskey on the rocks. And when the lady arrives, a bottle of your finest champagne."

"Of course. I'll have your drink sent to your table right away."

Once Peter walked away, Wade scanned the restaurant in hope of finding Gina here early as well. No such luck. Then the door opened and Gina strode in, looking stunning in a delicately fitted white halter dress with enough folds and billowy flair to turn every head in the place. She wore her hair down, flowing just past her shoulders in soft waves. Wade rose immediately and took a step forward.

Gina strode directly to the bar and sidled up to a man who had his back to him. Wade stopped his approach, retreated and leaned against the back wall, sipping his drink, watching.

The man bought Gina a drink. They stood talking for a while and then they both turned slightly, so that their profiles were visible.

Blood boiled in Wade's veins the instant he recognized the mysterious man. It was John Wheatley, president and CEO of Creekside Construction, his only real competitor on the island.

What the hell was Gina doing sharing a drink and sweet smiles with him? They seemed deep in thought, with shared whispers and heads close. Obviously, she had no knowledge that he was here. Wade had arrived early on purpose and so had she. She probably didn't suspect he'd be here this early.

A myriad of thoughts ran through Wade's mind, trying to fathom why Gina would be speaking with his competitor.

And then everything became crystal clear.

Wheatley dipped into his jacket and took out a checkbook. He wrote the check, ripped it off and placed it directly into Gina's hand. She didn't bother glancing at the amount; she simply opened her purse and dropped it in. She closed the purse again without hesitation. As though she knew the amount. As though this had all been prearranged.

Wheatley and Gina exchanged a few more words, then he kissed her cheek, giving her one soulful lingering look before exiting.

Wade polished off the remaining whiskey in his glass as Gina's words struck him with full force.

There isn't anything I won't do to clear my name.

I'll do whatever it takes to get out from under all my debt.

Gina had done it again. She'd played him for a fool. To think he'd actually admired her gumption and determination. He'd liked her win-at-any-cost attitude. But he'd been blindsided. He honestly hadn't seen this coming. Yet the woman had practically spelled it out in big bold red letters. She couldn't be trusted. She had a ruthless streak in her that ran down her spineless back.

She'd conspired with the enemy. She had access to all Triple B files, all his ideas and the actual bid on the project. Wade couldn't see past his fury. But he was angrier with himself for letting down his guard. For actually beginning to believe Gina had changed. For nearly falling in love with her again.

She'd shown her true colors tonight. She was a liar and a cheat and Wade planned on making her pay. She wouldn't get away with this. As he slipped out the back door only to enter through the front again, he planned his revenge. He knew exactly what he needed to do.

Gina had put him off far too long.

* * *

Gina finished her chardonnay and was setting the wineglass on the bar just as strong arms wrapped around her waist and pressed her close from behind. Warm breath caressed her throat. "You look gorgeous tonight."

She leaned into him, closing her eyes.

Wade.

His scent alone brought shivers and Gina indulged, drinking in the feel and smell of him, man and musk. Her well-honed defenses were crumbling. She was too happy today to fight it. Things were going well, in all aspects of her life, so why not enjoy the evening with an incredibly appealing man?

"You're early," she said quietly.

Wade turned her in his arms, the flow of her soft white dress brushing his thighs. "I couldn't wait to see you again."

There was intensity on his face and in his green eyes as he cupped her chin and lifted her mouth to his. He kissed her soundly, fully, ending the kiss all too soon. She opened her eyes to find him watching her. "Let's have dinner."

He took her hand and she followed him to a table set for two in the far corner of the restaurant. He seated her and took his own seat. A waiter immediately rushed over with an ice bucket and a bottle of very expensive champagne. He set it down and Wade thanked him before turning to her. "The Portofino is known for outstanding service."

Wade wasted no time pouring from the bottle.

He filled two flutes. Bubbles sparkled to the top as he handed her a tapered glass, his smile warm and charming. "To you, Gina. I've finally come to know the woman you are."

This was a new Wade, one she hadn't seen before. Gina touched her flute to his, pleased with his toast. Had he forgiven her? Had he finally realized that she was a woman to be trusted? Could they really put the past behind them?

Slowly, step by baby step Gina was overcoming her fear of water. She had Wade to thank for that and she was grateful for his dogged persistence. He was a never-say-die kind of man and his relentless efforts had worked. That wouldn't have happened if she hadn't taken this job and come to this island.

The glasses clinked. She stared into Wade's beautiful eyes. "Don't forget Triple B. We should toast to a job well done, Wade."

Wade blinked and she thought she lost him for a moment, but then he smiled and nodded. "Right, Triple B. Let's drink to my company and your role in its success."

Gina lifted her lips to the glass. "It's a team effort."

Wade gazed at her from over the top of the glass then sipped champagne. "And you always like to be on the winning team, right?"

He spoke to her softly, but with intensity in his eyes. Gina knew how important winning this bid was for him. She agreed. "I'm hoping to be."

They finished off the bottle of champagne, dined

on Italian bread, Caesar salad, scampi and a light raspberry mocha tart for dessert as the sound of Sinatra serenaded the softly lit room. By the time the meal ended, Gina's head spun from gourmet food, expensive champagne and Wade's complete and charming attention.

She stood and sighed heavily. "Thank you for the meal. It's been a wonderful night. But I think I'm ready for bed."

Wade was by her side, taking hold of her hand. "I've been thinking that all evening, sweetheart."

Before his comment had a chance to register, Wade wrapped an arm around her waist and guided her out of the dining room, changing the subject as they made their way up to her suite.

He was close. So close. And warm. So warm by her side. Her defenses down, when he took the key-card from her hand to open the door she rested her head on his shoulder as the arm embracing her waist, tightened.

"Th-thank you," she said, "I can manage from here."

Wade shook his head. "I think you need more help," he whispered into her ear, then turned her to face him right before his lips came down on hers. He kissed her long and deep and when he was through, Gina's body quaked with raw emotion.

She didn't know which Wade he really was, the charming sexy man she'd been with tonight or the ruthless, powerful never-say-die man she'd seen this week. It didn't seem to matter. Her heart was melting, along with the rest of her body.

His breath flowed over her lips. "Let me tuck you in."

He folded her into his embrace, meshing their bodies together. His heat became her heat, his desire became her desire. She sighed, realizing she was helpless to stop the flow of passion between them. "I can tuck myself in," she said without a drop of conviction.

Wade reached up to play with the straps of her halter, brushing his fingers along the nape of her neck. "But it's more fun when I do it."

"Is it?" she breathed out.

"Try me."

She had tried him once before and she'd never forgotten. She'd given herself to him wholly and without hesitation and the night had been magical. Later when she believed he'd betrayed her, she'd run far away.

At the time, her friend Sarah didn't know what her lies had cost them. But it was too late for regrets. Maybe now, finally, they could move on.

Wade ushered her into the suite and closed the door behind them, but he didn't let her get far. He grabbed her shoulders with both hands, turned her and crushed her against him, stepping back until the door braced his body. She fell into his embrace, his strong arms circling around her.

A buzzing thrill coursed up and down her body. Her legs went weak. Wade had taken control and this time she gave in to him without resistance. "This is going to happen tonight," he said, his voice a husky whisper.

In the back of Gina's mind, she related him to his yacht, the power and sleek smooth ride that was guaranteed.

Total Command.

"Yes," she sighed, her reply unnecessary as Wade wasted no time. He lifted his hands to the back of her neck and untied the straps of her halter. His gaze left her face to watch the tapered ties loosen then fall to her shoulders. His fingers slid over the material, inching it down, further and further, until the air, warm and sultry, hit her breasts.

Wade looked at them and his breath quickened.

She wanted him to touch her, to put his mouth on her. The look in his eyes was far too tempting.

He struggled out of his jacket, then out of his shirt with Gina frantically helping as they tossed his clothes away.

Wade cupped her from behind, his hands splaying across her cheeks, tugging her closer. She meshed against him, her breasts flattened against his chest, her thighs teased by the strength of his erection.

She felt him. Wanted him. His breaths wafted over her neck, his lips nestled against her throat. He unzipped her dress, then maneuvered it down, catching her white lacy panties along the way until she was buck naked, standing before him in her two-inch heeled sandals.

"Better than I remembered," he rasped out, before spinning her around, so that they'd traded places. Gina's back was now pinned against the door. Her heart hammered hard. Wade gave her no time to think. He was on bended knee before her, stroking her calves, his hands climbing higher now, over her knees to slide smoothly up her thighs.

Sensations roared in her head, her body ached. Her mind shut down. "Open for me, baby," he said, and she did. She spread her legs and his fingers found her core. She jolted when he touched the nub that sparked flaming heat and raw, hot desire. She moaned quietly, the erotic sound reverberating in the stillness of the room.

Wade stroked her for only a second, before his mouth replaced his fingers. Gina cried out, the torturous pleasure, so long in coming, would have buckled her if not for Wade's hold on her waist, firm and unrelenting.

His mouth found her folds and parted them. Then his tongue found it's mark and Gina's temperature soared. He stroked her unmercifully while she moaned and moved, up and down, her body finding a pace and a rotation to meet his fiery demand.

He stood abruptly, grabbed a packet from his trousers before removing the rest of his clothes and in seconds, he was lifting her, fitting her to him. "Lock your legs around me, baby," he commanded, and she did. She watched him watch her, the passion in his eyes a heady elixir.

He entered her slowly, the feel of him inside her only matching the look of pure unmasked undeniable lust on his face. She closed her eyes and threw her head back, taking from him what he offered her. Slowly, as if drawing out the pleasure, he filled her.

And when he moved, she clasped him tight, squeezing out her own pleasure.

She heard him grunt then, a carnal sound of deep gratification and, from then on, he moved with quick powerful thrusts, penetrating her to her depths. He pumped harder, faster almost violently and Gina matched him, fulfilling her deepest yearnings.

He wasn't kissing her or caressing her fondly as he had in the past and Gina recognized a difference in him and the way he made love to her. But her mind and body couldn't quite sort it out. She was beyond that now anyway and she clasped her legs tighter around him, sinking into him, fully immersed in his strength and power.

She knew the exact moment when he towered over the edge. She followed him and panted with each potent deliberate thrust, until both were fully sated and spent.

Wade lowered her until her heels found the floor.

He brought her close and whispered in her ear. "Don't even think about getting dressed. I want you naked and in that bed, all night long."

They were hardly the words of love and adoration she expected. Gina pulled back and away to gaze up at him. For a moment, there was a cold bleak look in his eyes, before he blinked it away. She tried to make sense of it all, but then Wade softened his expression, his eyes turning warm and tender on her right before he kissed her. His lips were gentle and sweet and he cradled her, comforted her, gently caressing her shoulders and then her breasts finally making her feel like a woman who had just been loved.

"You want that, too, don't you, honey?" he asked, a charming smile on his face.

She didn't have to think. She was totally, one-hundred percent in love with Wade Beaumont. She reached up to kiss him soundly on the lips. "There's no place else I'd rather be, Wade."

Wade nodded, then picked her up and carried her to the bed.

The night was just beginning.

Eight

Wade made love to Gina slowly this time, enjoying the full expanse of the king-size bed. Gina relished his hands on her, leisurely seeking, exploring and caressing every part of her body. She lay back against the lush cool sheets, savoring his thorough assault and the kisses that caused a tremor to rumble through her. His mouth knew other tricks as well and she welcomed lips that bestowed pleasure at the base of her throat, her shoulders, her breasts. She offered her body and he took it all without hesitation until she felt as though they were at last truly connected.

Though Wade said little, she felt his desire, the fiery look in his eyes, the heat and passion that he couldn't conceal. She witnessed it all and wished for a future filled with that same lust and craving.

Wade reached up to place her arms above her head. He clasped her hands in one of his and held her there, her fingers scraping the headboard. He thrust into her once, holding firm, absorbing her, his eyes closing. "I wanted this...wanted you since the moment I saw you walk into Aunt Dottie's kitchen."

Opening his eyes to stare into hers, he pumped into her, again slowly. "You were the most beautiful girl I'd ever seen."

"Oh, Wade. I wanted you, too."

But Wade didn't respond to her. He continued. "I wanted a future with you, Gina, but then you ran away."

"Wade," she breathed out softly, "let's not talk about the past. Let's just think about tonight." She didn't want anything to spoil this special time with him.

He stared down into her eyes for a long moment. Then nodded. "Tonight, then," he whispered with a kiss.

Gina sighed happily and hoped this night would finally change their relationship from one of betrayal and doubt to one filled with promise and trust.

She moved her body with his, until the final culmination, collapsing him onto her chest, his breath labored and strong. She held him against her, his powerful body still hot and pulsing. When he rolled onto his back, he took her with him. He wrapped his arms around her and nestled her head under his chin.

She felt safe there and protected and she dozed peacefully for a while, tucked in Wade's strong embrace.

Gina woke up to a cool empty bed. Lazily, she glanced at the digital clock. It was one o'clock in the morning. She lifted up from the bed, searching for Wade. She found him partly dressed, wearing his trousers standing outside with arms braced on the balcony railing, looking out at the sea. A tick in his jaw beat out a rhythm as clear night stars twinkled overhead.

Quietly, Gina rose and threw on Wade's shirt. She tiptoed to the balcony and stood behind him, her heart beating fast. She was so much in love with him that she could barely stand it. But he hadn't spoken of his feelings for her and she knew that for Wade, it would take time. "Can't sleep?"

Wade spun around. The pensive look on his face vanished, but she'd seen it, just for an instant. "I'm just waiting for you."

She pointed to the middle of her chest. "Me?"

His gaze riveted to that place on her chest, then flowed over the rest of her. "I said I wanted you naked all night, but damn. You look hot in that."

A sense of relief swamped her. For a second, she'd seen a look in Wade's eyes that frightened her and threatened this newfound beginning they shared tonight. "Hot?"

He took her into his arms. She relished the feel

of him again, needing his touch. "Sexy, Gina. Gorgeous. You're a man killer, honey."

"Hardly that, Wade." Then she bit down on her lip and tilted her head to ask, "Am I killing you?"

He took her hand and led her back into the suite. "Yeah, I'm a dead man."

Wade plopped onto the bed and coaxed her to straddle him. She crawled over his thighs and looked at him with dewy, half-lidded desire, her heart and body in sync.

He reached for the shirt she wore and lowered it down to bare her shoulders. The shirt pulled open and Wade brought his hands up to rub her erect nipples with his thumbs. A low moan of ecstasy erupted from Gina's throat from the tortured explicit pleasure.

"Kill me again, honey."

Gina pulled his unzipped pants down and off and then fastened the condom before lifting over him, eager to please him, to take him inside her. Once she did, Wade's face tightened, his need and desire fully unmasked now. She moved on him, his erection tight and hard, filling her, fulfilling her and making her complete.

He coaxed her with gentle commands and she rode the waves up and down, his fingers teasing her taut nipples, then his hands lowering to guide her at the waist to set a rapid pace. Passion flowed. She took so much from his eyes, always on her: his desire, need and complete wild abandon.

The ride was crazy hot. Soul-filled and earth-shattering. She climaxed first, shuddering out of control.

"That's it, baby," he rushed out, "give me everything."

And once she did, he rolled her onto her back, taking control and thrusting into her until neither one could move another muscle.

Wade lay back on the bed, breathing hard. "You can bury me, now."

Gina snuggled up close and his arms automatically wound around her. "I'm too tired," she whispered. "Tomorrow."

Wade made a low grunt of a sound. Exhausted, he said quietly, "I don't want to think about tomorrow."

Sunshine made its way through the suite and light rays targeted Wade, hitting his face, waking him from a soundless slumber. Sleep-hazy, he nuzzled Gina's neck, her long flowing hair tickling his throat as they lay together in spoon-like fashion, with his arms wrapped snugly around her. He stroked her soft skin with gentle fingers. The scent of her and of their lovemaking during the night stirred his body once again.

She was the perfect woman for him.

He cupped her breasts, teasing the ripened orbs, then slid one hand along her torso and lower along her thigh. He could go on touching her like this, feeling her smooth sleek perfect skin and he'd never tire of it.

She stirred awake. "Mmm."

Wade nibbled on her throat and with languid movements, Gina turned in his arms. Her beautiful dark-almond eyes opened on him and she sent him a sexy smile. "Morning."

He blinked. And blinked again.

Then he remembered.

The appalling truth struck him like a bludgeoning hammer to his head.

The deceit.

The betrayal.

The check Gina had so willingly taken from his competitor.

I'll do whatever it takes to get out from under all my debt.

Her damning pronouncement slammed into him with rock-hard force. He'd almost forgotten. He'd almost been snared into her trap. He'd shared the best night of his life with a woman he had to write off—a woman who had badly burned him.

For his revenge to be complete, he had to cut her out of his life for good.

Wade winced. He hated her for making him seek revenge, for putting him in this position, for turning his life upside down again.

He'd cut her out, but the knife would slice him up just as badly. He had no choice. He had to protect himself and his company.

He had no use for a woman he couldn't trust.

Wade shoved the covers off abruptly.

Gina's eyes went wide with surprise.

He rose from the bed and looked his fill, drinking in the sight of her lying there, beautifully naked, her inky tresses falling over soft shoulders. Wade knew it would be the last time he'd see her this way.

"Wade?"

Wade pulled his trousers on and zipped them up. "Get dressed," he said harshly.

"Why? Are we late for—"

"Pack your bags. You're fired."

Gina laughed, her eyes dancing with amusement. "What kind of joke is—"

Wade loomed over her, his lips tight, his eyes hard. "It's no joke, Gina. You no longer work for Triple B."

Gina's smile faded fast. She clutched the sheet and covered herself. "You're serious, aren't you?"

Wade grabbed his shirt—the one Gina had tortured him with last night, shoving his arms through the sleeves. Damn, it smelled of her. He didn't bother with buttoning it. "Dead serious."

Gina rose and they faced each other from opposite sides of the bed, her expression not one of guilt but of puzzlement. "I don't understand."

Furious now, thinking about how she'd almost duped him again Wade spoke with deceptive calm. "I saw you last night, Gina. Accepting another bribe. This time from my biggest competitor. Don't deny it, *sweetheart*. You were at the bar last night with John Wheatley. The two of you looked awfully cozy. So don't even try to lie your way out of this one."

But Gina did begin to deny it, by continually shaking her head. "No, no."

"Yes, yes. What kind of woman are you? Hurting me last time wasn't enough?" Thinking of her multiple betrayals only fueled his anger more. "This time you weren't satisfied with destroying my heart. No, that wasn't enough. You set out to destroy my company as well. But you damn well failed. I found out and now I want you out of here."

Gina's face flamed. Her eyes turned black as coal. She took a step toward him, fixing her glare on him. "Are you saying that because you thought I screwed you over, you decided to do the same to me?"

Wade lifted his lips in a smug smile. "I guess the screwing went both ways last night."

"Bastard!"

"Bitch."

Gina closed her eyes as if trying to tamp down her fiery temper. Then she walked over to her purse and dug out the check. "Is this the check you're referring to?"

Out of curiosity, Wade strode over to her to see how much money, was enough for her to sell him out. "Yeah, that's it."

She shoved it up into his face. "Read it, Wade." Then she spoke slowly, and with unyielding determination. "Read it and know that I'll never...ever... forgive you for this."

Wade grabbed the check and looked at it, his mind going numb for a second, as impending dread crept in. "The Survive Foundation?"

Gina snatched the check from his hand and returned it to her purse. Her voice broke with unbridled anger. "When I left El Paso, I thought about ripping up your father's check. Maybe I shouldn't have taken it in the first place, but you see, I thought you had betrayed me. I thought—never mind."

"Tell me, Gina." He softened his voice, realizing that he might have just made a huge mistake, one that would cost him more than this project. "Why would you think I betrayed you?"

Gina immediately backed away from him, as if being near him disgusted her. Her voice elevated. There was fire in her eyes. "That's Sarah's secret to tell, but I will tell you this. I came to Los Angeles, brokenhearted, grieving from the loss of my parents and over losing you. But I had your father's money and I decided to put it to good use. I helped start The Survive Foundation, a nonprofit organization to aid and support survivors of accidents and those who are grieving."

Wade made a move toward her, but she put up her hand and shook her head. "Don't."

It wasn't so much her stance, but the depth of hatred in her eyes, that left him immobile.

She spoke with a rough bitter edge, one Wade had never heard before. "I only know John Wheatley and his wife because they lost a child to leukemia two years ago. The foundation helped them through their loss. I saw them both on the beach yesterday and he wanted to thank me. The check is a donation."

Wade sucked in oxygen as he took this all in.

He'd been wrong about her, misjudging her loyalty and—

"Get out, Wade."

Gina's command startled him. "What?"

"Get out of my room. Get out of my life. I never want to see you again!"

Wade shook his head. "No, I can't leave now. I'll admit that—"

Gina picked up a shoe and threw it at him. He ducked and the sandal missed his head but grazed his shoulder. "Get out!"

"Gina," Wade mustered warning in his tone, though in truth, he'd been poleaxed by her revelations.

"Don't *Gina,* me, Wade. I want you out of this room. Now! I never want to set eyes on you again. You're just like your father…coldhearted and ruthless and I'm tired of your accusations!"

Her voice wobbled and she held back tears. Wade saw the destruction on her face and the hurt. Damn it. Why in hell hadn't she told him all of this before?

Next, she picked up the flower vase from the sofa table, threatening to toss it. "I mean it."

Wade knew her hot temper. And he knew she wouldn't hesitate. He backed out of the room. "I'm going," he said, and exited.

He heard the crash, glass splintering against the door the instant he'd closed it and loud profane curses coming from inside the suite.

He braced his body against the wall, trying to absorb all that had happened already today. He'd been so wrong. And Gina wasn't about to forgive him easily.

Wade winced and massaged his temples. The only thing he could do was give her time to cool off. She wasn't about to speak to him now. And he needed time to sort this all out.

Somehow, he'd make it up to her.

And then he'd talk to Sarah.

Tears streamed down Gina's face, the unbelievable hurt going deep. Wade wasn't worth her tears. She never wanted to see him again. She'd loved him once, and up until this morning had hoped he was still the Wade she'd once known. The man she could trust who'd been caring and kind. But she couldn't love him anymore. And she'd fight it until her last breath not to feel anything for him ever again. He'd shown her his heartless, diabolical, calculating side. She'd been right in accusing him of being just like his father. He was and that spoke volumes for his character.

Gina shoved her clothes into her suitcase. More tears slid down her cheeks. "Bastard, jerk, idiot," she continued on until she couldn't think of any more ways to describe him, while she packed everything up and stormed out, leaving everything Wade had ever given her behind.

She made immediate arrangements with Catalina Express for transportation back to Los Angeles. She was too angry to acknowledge her fear of traveling over the water for ninety minutes on a three-tiered boat, by herself. She'd manage. With suitcase in hand, she ran along Crescent Avenue to the boat landing, rushing to make the earliest departure from the island. Once she handed in her ticket and stepped aboard, she felt not fear, but an uncanny sense of relief to be completely rid of Wade Beaumont and this island.

She braced herself, holding onto the railing. Once a few more passengers boarded, the boat motored up and took off. Gina faced her fear, forcing herself to look out over the ocean. She had more than an hour to endure on the Pacific and, once she reached the San Pedro dock, she'd have to face her future as well as her fears. One that did not include Wade Beaumont or Triple B.

And though the trip had been a test of her will, keeping herself composed while the Express glided over waves and headed home was far easier than forgetting the hurtful image of Wade as he loomed over the bed they'd just made love in. He'd coldly dismissed and fired her, demanding that she pack her bags.

He hadn't even given her the benefit of the doubt.

Or asked her up front about John Wheatley and the check she'd been given.

He'd deliberately seduced her, not out of love or compassion, but for revenge—to teach her a lesson.

And he'd gotten his revenge—a job well done. Gina had made it easy for him. She'd laid it all out on the line for him and he'd crushed her in one sweeping blow.

But just a few hours later, as Gina sat on her tiny sofa, opening the week's mail, her hand shook at the wedding invitation staring back at her. Another blow, this one not as shocking. But the timing and irony was almost too much to bear.

> **Mr. and Mrs. Charles Buckley request the honour of your presence**
> **at the marriage of their daughter**
> **Sarah Nicole Buckley**
> **To**
> **Roy Zachary Winston**

The rest of the words blurred as Gina's eyes misted up. After nine years, Sarah had finally gotten the man of her dreams. She'd hung in there and worked it all out.

If only Sarah hadn't told those lies nine years ago.

Then maybe Gina's whole life might have turned out differently and she, too, would have gotten the man of her dreams.

Too bad that man didn't exist anymore.

Nine

Wade slammed the phone down for the tenth time in three days. He glanced at the work piling up on his desk, the contracts he needed to go over, the payroll checks he needed to sign, but he couldn't concentrate on any of it.

Gina refused his calls. She wouldn't pick up. He got her answering machine each and every time. "Damn you, Gina."

He lifted the wedding invitation on his desk, staring at it with unblinking eyes. And the note attached. Sarah had been trying to reach him all week.

They'd finally spoken.

Wade spun around in his leather swivel chair and

stared out the big bay window. Summer gloom had set in, but even through the afternoon haze he could see the ocean, blue waters now appearing gray and dingy from the low-lying cloud cover.

Gina had crossed that Pacific. Without him. She'd faced her fears alone. He'd driven her to that. And now she refused to speak with him.

He recalled his surprise when he went back to the Villa Portofino just hours later, ready with a dozen red roses, a heartfelt apology and willing to do whatever it took to make it up to her, only to find her gone.

The hotel clerk refused to divulge any information. Wade used his influence and status, calling over the manager to extract the information. That's when he found out she'd checked out and booked a ticket on the next boat back to the mainland.

Wade hadn't seen it coming. He'd been shocked. He knew she'd been furious with him, but to actually take it upon herself to leave the island alone and fight her fear of the water, told him one very key thing—getting her back wasn't going to be easy.

"To hell with it," he muttered, standing up and jamming his hands in his jacket sleeves. He fished through the papers on his desk, until he came up with what he was looking for. Shoving the envelope in his inside pocket, he strode to the door.

One way or another, Gina was going to speak to him.

And it was going to happen tonight.

* * *

Gina brought her dinner dish to the kitchen sink and thanked her landlord and friend, Delia, once again. "The meal was delicious, Dee. Thank you. I needed this."

"I know you did. And I'm glad you finally agreed to our invitation. Marcus and I have been worried about you."

Gina tightened the elastic band on her ponytail and shrugged with a heavy sigh. Her landlords had been such wonderful moral support lately. Once she'd returned from Catalina, they'd spotted her sullen demeanor immediately and tried to cheer her up with home-baked cookies, hand delivered mango margaritas and invitations to dine out with them. She hadn't been in the mood for any of it. But, finally, tonight she'd accepted their dinner invitation and told them the whole story, from El Paso to Catalina and everything in between. "I'll be fine…soon."

Delia took the plates and rinsed them then handed them one at a time to Gina, who was arranging them in the dishwasher.

"You know, it's okay for you not to be…fine. I mean, don't knock yourself out convincing yourself everything is wonderful when it's not. Allow yourself time."

Gina wiped her damp hands on her jeans. She'd been slumming it lately, dressing down and laying low while searching the classifieds for the past few days. The job hunt was not going well. Gina's heart wasn't in it. "Time for what?"

Delia only smiled, her eyes insightful. "Just time, honey."

Gina wished she had the luxury of time. But she needed to move on with her life and the sooner the better.

"Oh and don't you worry about the rent this month. Marcus and I don't want you stressing about it."

"I have rent money, Dee. I'm not broke." Her heart had broken, but fortunately her tiny bank account hadn't, not just yet.

"No, but you have that wedding this month, don't you? It'd do you good to see the Buckleys again. Don't you think so?"

Gina had forgiven Sarah for her unwitting crimes years ago and she was happy for her, but attending anyone's wedding right now was the last thing she wanted to do. Yet she wanted to be there for Sarah and the Buckleys. "Yes, they've always been kind to me. I wouldn't miss seeing them. Sarah and I, well, we've had some drama in our lives, but we're still good friends. She's asked me to be in the wedding party."

"The change of scenery will do you good."

Marcus popped his head in the kitchen doorway. "Care for coffee outside, ladies? Stars are out tonight."

"That sounds nice, sweetheart," Dee said to him, then turned to Gina. "Coffee?"

Gina smiled and shook her head. "No thanks. Not tonight."

Marcus strode into the room to place his arm

around her shoulder. "I can't coax you into decaf? It won't keep you awake, I promise."

Gina chuckled. She wished caffeine were all that was keeping her from sleep these past few nights. "I really should be going. I'd like to do some reading."

Marcus squeezed her shoulders tight. "You hang in there, Gina." He kissed her forehead and Dee gave her a big hug.

"I'll bring over that book I was telling you about," Dee said, slanting her husband a look. "Marcus misplaced it, but I know it's somewhere in the house. I'll look for it again."

"Thanks, I'd like that. Dinner was great."

"We'll do it again soon."

"Ciao, my friends," Gina said to both of them as she walked out the back door and across the lawn to her humble but homey little guesthouse.

Once inside, she settled in, propping her feet up on the sofa with a glass of iced water and a handed down copy of *Vogue*. She glanced at her answering machine, relieved to see no new messages. She'd hoped Wade had given up calling her. Having her nerves go raw each time the phone rang was an added strain she could do without.

Gina opened the magazine and glanced at the pages. She liked to keep up on fashion, comparing the newest creations on the shelves to those in her head and finding that she always liked hers better.

One day, she'd have her own company. She hadn't given up on that dream.

When the knock came, Gina bounced up and opened the door wearing a smile. "Dee, you found the book already!"

But it wasn't Dee standing there holding a copy of *The Devil Wears Prada*. No, it was another *devil* entirely, one with bold green eyes and a solid steadfast stance. Her first thought was that she'd missed him. But she killed that thought instantly, her second thought being that she hated him. Still.

And her third thought was that he looked so darn handsome, standing there, wearing tailored Armani and a sincere expression that he took her breath away. "Whatever book you need, I'll get it for you."

"What I *need* is for you to leave," she managed quite elegantly and began to close the door.

Wade's arm jutted out, preventing that from happening. His expression fierce now, his eyes raging, he said. "We need to talk. Now. I'm tired of you refusing my calls."

Gina played innocent, just to annoy him. "Oh? Did you call? I don't recollect."

He pushed the door wide open and moved past her, letting himself in. Gina looked out at Marcus and Delia having coffee across the lawn in the patio. Marcus immediately stood, his gaze pensive as he was about to approach. Gina shook her head and gestured that all was okay.

She had to deal with Wade sometime. She knew he wasn't the kind of man to let things drop. No, he always had to have the last word.

"No more games, Gina."

"Spoken from the expert," she blurted as she took her seat on the sofa and opened the magazine again, flipping through pages she really didn't see.

He looked around. "This is nice."

"Hardly a beachside resort," she answered casually.

Wade sat down next to her and took the magazine from her hand. He set it down on the small table next to the sofa. "You're forgetting I came from humble beginnings, too."

Gina rubbed her hands up and down her jeans and then fidgeted with her ponytail. She knew her appearance wouldn't win awards, yet the look in his eyes told her it didn't matter. He caressed her with that look and made her nervous. "What do you want, Wade?"

He smiled and stared at her for a long moment. "I know the truth. I spoke with Sarah."

"And?"

Wade leaned back against the sofa cushion, making himself comfortable. "And I'm pissed. Royally pissed."

"That makes two of us." Gina sent him a wry smile.

Wade shook his head. "I had no idea. All this time, I had no idea that Sarah used me as a shield for Roy Winston."

"She was in love with Roy and she knew her parents would go ballistic if they found out. They'd warned her not to get involved with Roy. He was bad news."

Wade agreed. "He *was* bad news. He'd been suspended from high school, what, three or four times. His parents were the town drunks."

"After college, when we came back to El Paso, I remember the Buckleys telling Sarah that nothing had changed with the Winstons and Roy had gotten arrested for a barroom brawl."

Wade nodded solemnly, "Yeah, I remember that. I was there. Roy got a bad rap. Five of us were there, but the sheriff chose to arrest only Roy. He was known as a troublemaker in town, so naturally they blamed him, but all of us were just as guilty."

Gina went on, "So when Sarah thought she was pregnant, she panicked. She loved Roy, but knew her parents would never accept him. Mr. Buckley had just been diagnosed with a heart condition. Sarah feared it would send her father over the edge. She named you as the father of her baby. She knew her parents liked you, at least. They would accept it. But she didn't know that we had gotten close. If you remember, Sarah had been gone that week with her mother. I never had the chance to tell Sarah my feelings for you.

"She was only trying to protect her family. And Roy. When she told me you had fathered her baby, I was in shock. We'd just been together and I thought…"

Wade pursed his lips and leaned forward, bracing his elbows on his knees. "You thought the worst of me. The very worst."

Gina bounded up abruptly and lashed out. "What

else could I think? My best friend confided in me that you, the man I'd fallen in lo—the man I'd just had sex with for the very first time in my life, was going to be her baby's father."

"Sit down, Gina. And calm down."

"No! You don't know the hell I went through. I was so lost…so vulnerable. I couldn't tell my best friend. I'd begun to hate you and then your father showed up with the bribe. It was a way out. I couldn't stick around El Paso anymore. Not thinking you and Sarah were going to have a child together. So I took the money."

"I hated you for that."

"I know. I wanted you to. It was the only way I could think of to make sure you stayed in El Paso with Sarah. But I used your father's money for a good cause. I'm not sorry I took it. But I am sorry about the circumstances."

"And the irony of all this is that Sarah is marrying Roy," Wade said.

Gina took in a breath, amazed at how things had worked out. "He left El Paso right after that barroom brawl incident and turned his life around. He's successful now, owns his own body shop and is doing well. He came back for Sarah. He'd always loved her."

Wade stood and paced the confines of her room. "Sarah was never pregnant."

"No, she wasn't. It was a false alarm, but I only found that out later on. I'd lost contact with her. Deliberately. But she tracked me down and told me the truth a few years later. And I told her the truth about us. She was mortified, so sorry about all of it. She'd been so wrapped up with hiding her secret about Roy that she hadn't a clue about how we felt about each other. She wanted to find you and tell you the truth too, but I stopped her. What good would it do? By then, you were working in Houston with your father and I was involved with—"

"Another man."

"Yes. That's right." Gina hoisted her chin. "I'd moved on."

"So did I. But I never forgot you."

Gina let out a rueful nervous chuckle. "Right, plotting a way to hurt me. Well, it worked. Congratulations. You got your revenge, didn't you, Wade?"

Wade's voice elevated slightly, "I thought you were out to ruin my company."

Gina faced him now, coming to stand toe to toe with him. She looked at his face and condemned him with the truth. "You used me, used my body. You took something precious and made it ugly. How little you must think of me to believe that I'd sleep with you right after accepting a bribe to ruin you and your company. I don't know why you're here, but I'd like you to leave." She strode past him to open the front door. "There's nothing more to say."

Wade's green eyes flashed with indignation. She'd angered him and she was glad. It was about time someone put Wade Beaumont in his place.

Wade stood still for a moment, staring at her, then removed an envelope from his coat pocket. He set it down on the table. "We won the bid on the Catalina project. Your bonus is in there, along with your paycheck."

Gina nodded, glancing at the envelope, but said nothing. She'd earned that money—the hard way.

Wade strode to the door quickly and stopped to look deeply into her eyes. "You should have told me the truth, right from the beginning."

With that, Wade walked straight out of her life, without so much as a glance back.

Wade stared out as night fell on the Pacific Ocean. He leaned against his deck railing watching the tide creep in then recede back into the darkness of the sea. Only a few stars illuminated the sky, the night as black as his mood.

"You haven't touched your champagne, little brother," Sam said, coming up to stand beside him. He sipped from his glass and leaned against the railing. "Or would you rather have a cold beer?"

Wade shook his head. "No."

"I flew all the way out here from Texas to help you celebrate. Hell, it isn't every day a company wins the biggest bid in its history. You did it, Wade. You should be proud. Instead, I find you here looking like death warmed over."

Wade let out a self-deprecating laugh. "That's one way to describe me. Others might say you're being too kind."

"Others? Or only one other, as in Gina Grady?

"That's the only *other* that matters," Wade admitted.

"Ah," Sam said, sipping his Dom Pérignon. "So how is my old friend?"

"Intelligent, sweet, dedicated and gorgeous."

"Sounds like the Gina I remember."

Wade finally succumbed. He gulped his drink, emptying the glass in five seconds flat. "She's not a fan."

Sam chuckled. "So she's got more brains than most women. She didn't throw herself at your feet?"

Wade muttered a curse, directing it right at Sam.

He chuckled again. "Kidding. Hey, what's really up? I come here expecting a party, and you look like—"

"Death warmed over?" Wade finished for him.

"I was about to say, like you lost your best friend."

Wade grabbed the bottle and poured another drink. "Maybe I did. I made some mistakes with Gina. Now she doesn't want to have anything to do with me."

Sam's smile faded. "You're serious about her?"

Wade nodded.

Sam reflected, this time on a serious note. "I thought you two were a perfect match, even back in El Paso. That's why I recommended her for the job here in L.A., little brother. I thought, you two would pick up where you left off. I take it there's problems?"

"You don't want to know," Wade said, sipping his drink again, this time slowly and savoring the taste, letting it glide down his throat.

"I do want to know. I'm here. Lay it on me."

Wade turned to Sam. "It's a long story."

Sam smiled and put his hand on Wade's shoulder. "I'm not going anywhere."

They sat in the deck chairs for the next thirty minutes, polishing off the Dom, while Wade explained to Sam his situation, leaving out some of the more intimate details.

And after hearing him out, Sam leaned back in his chair, staring up at the stars. "Well, the easiest thing to do is forget her. Move on. Concentrate on the project."

He eyed Wade then, with an arched brow.

Wade scoffed, "Not possible. She's hard to forget. If I couldn't do it in nine years, I certainly can't do it now."

Sam smiled. "Okay, that was the first test. You passed, by the way."

Wade didn't smile back. "So I get an *A*. Any other bright ideas?"

Sam leaned in, and spoke directly at him, in all seriousness. "You going to Sarah's wedding?"

Wade inhaled sharply. "I haven't decided yet."

"Can't forgive her?"

"Hell, she wants me to be in the wedding party. She apologized up, down and sideways. I can't really blame her. I understand about Roy. What happened, well, it happened. It was nine years ago. I told her I'd think about it."

"If I were you, I wouldn't think too long. Gina's going and she's in the wedding."

"How do you know that?"

"Because Caroline called Sarah to say we can't go to the wedding and Sarah told her all about the wedding plans. We promised to visit soon; it would be good to see Uncle Lee and Aunt Dottie again. Besides, we have news of our own."

Wade's head snapped up. "What news?"

Sam's mouth stretched into a big grin. "We're going to have a baby. Caroline's pregnant."

Wade bounded up from his seat and Sam rose, too. He hugged his brother and myriad emotions streamed in. Happiness for his brother and the second chance he'd gotten with Caroline and her little daughter Annabelle, but then a shot of envy filtered in as well. For the first time in his life, Wade wanted what Sam had. A wife and family. And he wanted Gina to fill that role. "Geez, why didn't you say so sooner?"

Sam laughed. "She'll be pregnant eight more months. There's no rush. I wanted to tell you in person. And we're going to visit her folks in Florida to tell them the news firsthand, too. That's why we can't make Sarah's wedding."

Then Sam took his shoulder, his smile fading some. "Remember when you came out to Hope Wells and saw me with Caroline at her stables? Then later, when I left her, unable to face losing my own child, you made me see that I had a second chance in life. You made me take that chance. And now, not only did I adopt little Annabelle, I'm going to be a father again. I've got a wonderful wife and family and this time I'm doing it right. We all make mistakes, Wade. Go after what you want."

Wade hesitated, scrubbing his jaw. "I've already had a second chance with Gina. Seems the stars aren't aligned with the two of us. She's accused me of being like our father—ruthless, cold, hard-hearted. And you know, I'm beginning to believe it myself."

"That's crap, little brother. You're not your father's son. You never have been."

"She walked out on me so easily the first time. Seems that the people I care about most, don't give a sh—"

"Gina does. I guarantee it. She cares for you. From what you said, she didn't so much run away from you as the situation. Okay, so you blew it the second time. Call it even. Take another chance. The third time's the charm, they say. Go to that wedding. Make her see the real you and not some replica of Blake Beaumont."

Wade scratched his chin, pondering.

Sam prodded, "If you don't, you'll regret it the rest of your life."

Wade knew that Sam was right. He had to go to that wedding. He'd never been one to back down from a challenge. And Gina posed the biggest challenge of his life. He'd falsely accused her and hurt her deeply. Turning her feelings around would take nothing short of a miracle. "She can't stand the sight of me."

Sam chuckled, seemingly sure that Wade could pull this off. "That's the best way to start. You can only improve from there."

Wade had to smile at his brother's optimism. "I'll call Sarah. Let her know I'll be coming to her wedding after all."

Ten

Gina packed her bags, telling herself she needed this time away. Sarah had been thrilled that she'd accepted not only the invitation, but a place by her side up at the altar as a bridesmaid. She'd put this wedding together in a matter of weeks, wanting to marry Roy as soon as possible. She'd wasted enough of her life and she was ready to finally begin her future with the man she loved. Gina understood that all too well.

She'd wasted time on Wade, but her future was destined to play out much differently.

On a sigh, she snapped close her suitcase, took one look around, making sure she hadn't forgotten anything, then picked up her traveling case. She slung it over her shoulder and wheeled her luggage to the front door.

Sarah had her bridesmaid dress waiting for her in El Paso and had coaxed her into coming a week early to be a part of the pre-wedding arrangements, seeing to the decorations, favors, music and of course, to attend the rehearsal and dinner afterward.

Sarah's happiness was contagious and Gina couldn't say no. Besides, Sarah insisted that her dress would need an alteration or two. How could she argue with that? So she locked up her house and walked outside to meet Delia who had quite generously offered to take her to the airport.

When she got halfway down the long drive, Delia stepped into view, her usual jovial face, looking tentative.

"Hi, Dee. Anything wrong?"

Dee took the handle of Gina's luggage and began walking along the path towards the front of the house. "I hope not, honey.

"I hope not, too. What's up?" Gina asked, her curiosity escalating. Dee was the most laid-back, honest person she knew. Usually, she didn't skirt around issues or appear apprehensive. Right now, she was doing both.

"I hope I made the right decision."

Again, Gina hadn't a clue what she meant.

Dee opened the large swinging gates beside the front of the house that led to the street and both walked out.

Then Gina stopped.

And couldn't believe her eyes.

Wade stood at attention beside a stretch limousine, wearing jeans and boots and enough cowboy charm to set her heart racing.

She turned to Dee. "What is he doing here?"

"Apparently, taking you to El Paso."

"What?" Gina's temper flared. She glanced at Wade, who was about to approach when Dee halted him with a stopping hand.

Dee halted him with a stopping hand?

"What's going on, Dee?"

"He called about a week ago. We met him for dinner and he explained what he wanted to do."

"We? You and Marcus? He's got you on his side now?"

Dee shook her head. "No, we're on your side. We always have been. But he's sincere. And he cares for you. Marcus and I, we talked about this and think this is the right thing to do. You two need time to talk, to clear the air. You both need another chance. He wants to take you to El Paso."

Gina's eyes nearly bugged out. "He's kidnapping me?"

Dee grinned. "Romantic, isn't it?"

This time Gina rolled her eyes.

Dee turned so that her back was to Wade who stood twenty feet away. She spoke softly, "He's in love with you, honey."

Gina didn't believe it for one second. No one could convince her of that. "He didn't say that to you."

"No. He didn't have to."

Gina glanced at Wade who was wearing dark sunglasses. She couldn't make out his expression.

"God, Dee. He could have just asked me. See, this is what I mean about him. He's so calculating. He even got you involved in this."

"Gina," Dee began with all seriousness, "any guy who would go to this much trouble for you can't be all bad. He talked to us for hours and we both came away knowing that this guy really cares about you. And besides, we both know that if he had asked you, you would have turned him down flat."

"That's right. He could have respected my wishes. Well, I'm not going to El Paso with him."

"I'm afraid you are," the deep voice resonated from just behind Dee. Both women looked up at Wade. He wasn't smiling. "We both have to get there today. We might as well travel together."

Gina shot back. "I have my own ticket, thank you very much."

"Do you?" he asked, turning to look at Dee.

Dee appeared as though she wanted to slink into the sidewalk. "Honestly, Gina, I didn't think you'd fight this so hard. I thought you wouldn't mind if I cancelled the reservation I made for you."

"What?" Gina couldn't believe this. Dee, the traitor, had fully succumbed to Wade's charm. He could pour it on when he had to. "You cancelled my reservation?"

"Sorry," she said, "but I wanted to save you the money."

Wade took hold of her luggage handle and grabbed

the traveling bag from Gina's shoulder. She'd been too floored to stop him. "I've got a chartered plane waiting for us. I'd like you come with me, Gina."

"Why, Wade? Why do you want me to come with you?"

Wade removed his sunglasses and peered into her eyes. "I miss you."

It was such a clear, honest, simple statement that she couldn't quite stop her heart from accelerating. She'd missed him, too, the Wade she'd fallen in love with. She glanced at Dee, who smiled with hope in her eyes. Gina felt somewhat defeated. She could fold her arms across her middle and declare that she wasn't going. But that would seem childish. And even though she fumed at Wade's tactics, she couldn't deny that he *had* gone to some trouble for her. Riding to the airport in a limousine and flying on a chartered plane to El Paso might not be so bad after all. Besides, his latest admission nearly knocked her to her knees.

He missed her.

"I have a fitting at three o'clock at the bridal salon, so we might as well get going."

Dee smiled in relief.

For a second Wade's mouth crooked up before he took her luggage and handed it to a chauffeur who seemed to have appeared out of nowhere.

The same way Wade had.

Gina tried to relax in the plush leather seat on the Falcon 50, Wade's chartered plane. She had to admit that traveling this way sure beat the lines, the crowds and the coach seat that had been waiting for her at LAX.

Wade sat in the seat facing her, a small polished teak table between them set with a vase filled with white lilies.

Classy.

Gina glanced out the window, peering down at the tiny dotting of houses below, fully aware that Wade's eyes were on her. She felt his perusal and it heated her and made her think of the night they'd spent together in Catalina. She wondered if he was thinking the same thing.

Finally, she faced him. "You're staring at me."

Wade smiled. "I like what I see."

His voice mellow, his eyes warm on her, Gina couldn't help but be affected. "I wish you wouldn't."

Wade leaned way back in his seat. "Why?"

He was making her uncomfortable but she wouldn't admit it. "Don't you have something to do?"

"We could eat something. Coffee? Or breakfast? What would you like?"

Gina's stomach was in knots. "I couldn't eat a thing. Thank you."

He nodded and watched her. She blinked and blinked again, only to see him smiling again.

She'd been with him for six days on that island and she hadn't seen the man crack more than an occasional grudging smile, yet here he was looking at her, smiling like a schoolboy just given an *A* on his report card.

"Do I make you nervous, Gina?"

Oh, yes. "No. Of course not."

He nodded again. "Want to talk?"

She shook her head. "Not particularly."

He nodded once again and continued staring at her.

"There must be something you could do," she said, keeping the irritation out of her voice.

"Yeah, work. But that wouldn't be polite, would it?"

But staring at her with those gorgeous green eyes *was* polite? "Oh, I wouldn't mind. Go right ahead, Wade. Really, you must have a ton of work to do, now that you've won the Catalina project."

Wade reached over the seat and brought his brief-case into view. He set it down on the seat next to him and pulled out a stack of papers. "I'd rather look at you," he muttered.

Inwardly, Gina smiled, but she reminded herself not to fall victim to his charm. "You'd get further with those papers."

He glanced up. "That so?"

She didn't hesitate. "Yes."

Wade's eyes flickered, but he seemed to hold back a comment then he spread the papers out, sorting through them. "You know, you and I made a good team. Technically, you're still on the payroll. I could use help here."

Gina clamped her mouth shut, to keep it from falling open. She was still on the payroll? "You fired me, remember?"

Wade stopped sorting through the paperwork, to look deep into her eyes. "That was a mistake."

"Doesn't matter. I would have quit, anyway," she shot back quickly.

"But you didn't quit and your next check is in the mail."

Surprised, Gina's nerves teetered on end. She'd thought she was through with Triple B for good. But apparently Wade had had second thoughts. She glanced at the Catalina papers—projections, finance reports, estimates—and admitted, for what it was worth, that she had enjoyed the work. "You mean you don't think I'd try to foil your project, in some dastardly way?"

Wade cast her a look of disgust. "No, I know you wouldn't. Can you give me a break?"

"Why, did you give me one?" Oh, that came out more harshly than she intended, but the sentiment remained.

"No. I didn't. But you wanted me to believe the worst about you the first time."

"And the second time? In Catalina?"

"That was a mistake on my part. And I apologize."

Humbled now, Gina realized she had never heard Wade Beaumont apologize for anything, to anyone. "Still, I can't work with you. You don't trust me."

"Yes I do. I'd trust you with my life."

The sincerity of his words filled her head and warmed her heart. But how could she learn to trust him again?

Instead of dealing with it, she grabbed a stack of papers and bent her head, looking them over. "What do you need me to do?"

* * *

When the plane landed at El Paso International Airport, Wade escorted her off, carrying their luggage. A taxi stood waiting for them and soon Gina was back on the streets of El Paso as all sorts of memories rushed in.

"Have you ever been back?" Wade asked.

She shook her head. "No. Sarah and I have met a few times over the years, but always on the West Coast. I haven't seen Chuck and Kay Buckley since I left nine years ago."

Wade sighed. "I'd only seen them a few times, myself. Now, I understand why they'd been distant to me those times I did see them. But Sarah has owned up to the truth to everyone now. Her conscience is clear."

"And what about your aunt and uncle? Do you see them?"

"I would like to see them more. Starting up the company on the West Coast prevented that. But I've gone back for a few quick holidays trips and I've flown them out a few times to visit me."

Gina gazed through the window as they headed out of town and the city landscape rolled into a more rural one. Large fallow fields came into view alongside the fields that grew Egyptian cotton. Roadside poppies dotted the highway and, off in the distance, Gina noted the reddish hilltops of Franklin Mountain where she'd gone hiking with Wade, Sarah and Sam once. Fifteen minutes later, the cab pulled up to the Buckleys' small ranch house.

"Looks like they've painted the house, but everything else seems pretty much as I remembered."

"Things don't change much in small towns," Wade said, helping her out of the taxi and grabbing her luggage.

"Oh, I'll get that," she said, but before she had a chance to retrieve her things, Sarah raced down the steps, her shoulder-length blond hair bouncing as she approached with a big smile.

"Oh, you two came together," she said, hugging Gina immediately, "that makes me happy."

Sarah turned to Wade, her smile more tentative and a look of complete remorse on her face. "I'm forgiven, right?"

Wade looked at Sarah for a moment and Gina's heart ached for her. Gina knew firsthand his heartless wrath and she hoped for Sarah's sake Wade still considered her a friend. She didn't want Sarah's joy being marred one tiny bit, not when she'd finally made peace with everyone and was marrying the man she'd always loved.

When Wade put out his arms, Sarah climbed in and the two hugged for a long moment. "I wouldn't have agreed to be in your wedding otherwise."

Sarah pulled back and looked at both of them. "Thank you for your forgiveness and for agreeing to be in my wedding. It means a lot to me. And to Roy. You'll have to get to know him again, Wade. He's great."

"Obviously he is if you're marrying him."

Sarah's blue eyes lit. "I can hardly believe it after all this time."

"It's always been Roy, and you were smart enough to realize it," Gina said.

"Thanks." Sarah squeezed Gina's hand. "I'm so glad you're here. Mom and Dad can't wait to see you again."

"How are your parents?" Gina asked.

"They're fine. They've finally come around and have accepted Roy. Come inside, both of you."

Wade shook his head. "I'm anxious to see Uncle Lee and Aunt Dottie, but I'll come by tonight after supper. Besides, I hear you're all going to the bridal salon soon."

Sarah darted a quick glance at Gina. "That's right. We have a fitting in a few hours! Oh, this is wonderful having you both here."

Wade took Gina's suitcases to the front door. "I'll see you later," he said then strode past them, toward the taxi. Before getting inside, he stopped and looked at Gina. "I'm glad you decided to join me on the trip."

Gina nodded, biting her lip, and Sarah waved farewell but as soon as the taxi drove off, Gina muttered, "You didn't really give me a choice."

Sarah looked at her then laced an arm through hers as they walked to the front door. "Gina, you are definitely going to have to fill me in on what's really happening with the two of you. As soon as you say hello to my folks, you're spilling the beans."

Gina had to smile.

She didn't know why exactly, but it felt good to be back in El Paso.

"I've missed your pot roast, Aunt Dottie," Wade said, filling his plate a second time. "No one makes it better."

"It's your favorite," she said, passing him the mashed potatoes. He scooped another clump onto his plate and dug in. "I didn't forget."

Wade finished his next bite. "You're still set on fattening me up."

She laughed, the simple, sweet sound, reminding him of good times sitting around this table, with Sam by his side. Aunt Dottie always had a smile and a kind word.

Uncle Lee tapped his flat belly. "See this? The woman's put me on a diet. I only get pot roast when you or Sam come to visit."

"You look great," Wade said, looking over at his father's brother and seeing no resemblance. Uncle Lee had a kindly face and a loyal nature. He loved his wife, his home and his family above all else. "Aunt Dottie takes good care of you, so no complaining."

"You tell him, Wade," his aunt jested.

"I'm not complaining," he said grudgingly, looking over at Wade's plate of food, "but I wouldn't mind a second helping myself."

"Go on, Lee," Dottie said, "I'm not stopping you."

Uncle Lee reached over and forked another piece of pot roast onto his plate. "There's nothing better than the love of a good woman."

Lee winked at his wife and Dottie grinned before setting her gaze on Wade. "Speaking of a good woman, you said that you brought Gina with you. How is that girl?"

Uncle Lee chimed in, "Still pretty as sunshine? Giving you heart palpitations?"

Wade chuckled, then sipped his iced tea. "She's fine. Gorgeous as ever and won't have a thing to do with me."

Aunt Dottie put her hand over his in a consoling manner. "Now, dear. Don't let that stop you. Weddings have a way with people and she might just come around while she's here."

Wade finished his meal, tossed his napkin and pulled back from his chair. "I'm not only banking on that, I'm going to make it happen."

"So Gina's the one?" she asked, darting a quick glance at her husband.

Wade nodded while taking his plate to the sink. "Now it's time to convince her of that. Mind if I saddle up Rio? I'm going over to the Buckleys tonight."

"Not at all, that boy needs the exercise. And say hello to Kay and Chuck for us," his uncle said.

"Will do." Wade bent to kiss his aunt's cheek. "Thanks for supper."

Uncle Lee smiled up at him. "It's good to have you home, son."

Wade no longer flinched when his uncle called him "son." For years, he resented it, but as he grew older, he realized that it felt natural. He wasn't his father's son, but Lee Beaumont's son and he was out to prove that to Gina and the rest of the world if he had to.

Fifteen minutes later, after greeting the Buckleys, Wade stood in their modest living room with Stetson in hand, completely captivated by Gina from the moment she entered the room wearing a pale-pink flowing bridesmaid dress. Her face bright, her deep-brown eyes dancing, she twirled around, unaware that he watched her.

"See, the dress only needed a tiny alteration," Sarah said. "I won't say where, but Gina's bustier than the rest of us girls!"

"Sarah!" Gina playfully admonished her friend but her smile remained.

Wade's gaze riveted to that particular part of her anatomy and memories washed over him, of touching her there, putting his lips to her breasts and tasting her, loving her and making their world spin out of control.

When finally, he looked up she met his eyes…and knew what he'd been thinking.

"You look pretty, Gina," he said.

She took a swallow. "Thank you."

The mood was broken when Roy Winston entered the house and everyone was re-introduced. Wade had to admit that Roy had changed. He, too, had been a product of his parents' discord while growing up, but he'd worked himself out of that fathomless hole and came back to El Paso a new man, one who knew what he wanted. Wade had never seen Sarah or Roy so happy.

Gina went into the bedroom to change out of her dress, while the rest of the group retired to the back porch. She returned wearing blue jean shorts and a red-and-white polka-dotted midriff-exposing blouse, looking every bit an exotic version of Daisy Duke. As the evening pressed on, Wade couldn't help glancing at her every chance he got and when the evening was about to end, he took his shot, blocking the doorway as she started to head inside the house.

"It's a nice night. Take a walk with me."

She began shaking her head. "That's not a good idea."

"Come on, Gina. I'll have you back here in twenty minutes."

"I'm a little tired, Wade. It's been a long day. And tomorrow I'm spending the day working on wedding favors with Sarah and her mother."

"All the more reason to take a walk with me. I won't be seeing you tomorrow."

Gina sighed. "Wade."

"I've got something to show you."

"I bet you do," she rushed out, with a hint of playful teasing in her tone. Wade was encouraged.

"We can take Rio, if you're not up to walking."

"*Rio?*" Gina's face lit at the mention of the gelding's name. He'd once been her favorite. "I'm glad to hear he's still around."

"He isn't as feisty as he once was, but he's healthy. Come on, Gina. What do you say?"

Gina debated for several seconds, keeping him waiting. Wade wasn't a patient man, but he was learning and Gina was worth the time. "I want to be in bed in twenty minutes."

Wade stifled a witty reply. Nothing would make him happier, but he knew Gina wasn't including him in her bedtime plans.

He took her hand. "Let's go."

Eleven

"Tell me about your designs," Wade said, as they walked along a path leading to the Beaumont ranch, Rio clip-clopping along beside them.

"They're unique." Gina never minded speaking about her passion. She still had her old designs in her head and loved thinking up new ones. She had begun a new file, recreating the designs she'd lost and adding sketches of the new ones she created. "Most are still in my head, thank goodness."

"What makes them unique?" Wade asked, his attention directed solely on her. She couldn't look at him now, not when he seemed to bank on her every word. In those western clothes and tan Stetson, he looked very much like the old Wade Beaumont. But she'd been fooled once before, this time she would protect her heart. She kept her focus straight ahead as the sun made a hasty retreat, cooling the warm evening air.

"My designs were all made with gemstones. A piece of jade or turquoise held the garment together in distinct ways, either at the front or the back, sometimes on the straps. In the beginning, I worked up several pieces, sewing them by hand and adding whatever stones I had or could buy inexpensively. But I wanted higher-quality gems like amber and topaz. I learned a lot about stones, hoping to work with a larger variety one day.

"Because the gems were all different colors and all of different quality, each piece of clothing was one-of-a-kind. I sold a few to high-end boutiques and soon I was getting requests. But the gems were costly and I began formulating a plan to start my own company."

"GiGi Designs, right?"

Gina nodded and she couldn't help but smile. "Everyone thought the name stood for my initials, Gina Grady, but actually, I had designed a logo and the tag that I fastened to the clothes read, Gina's Gems."

Gina glanced at Wade and caught him smiling. "Catchy."

"I think so, too," she said, diverting her gaze from Wade's beautiful smile and tantalizing mouth, while trying to block out the look of admiration on his face.

Rio snorted and Gina laid her hand along his long neck, stroking him absently as they continued walking along.

Wade looked straight ahead. "We're almost there."

There was a cropping of tall mesquite trees bordering the Buckley and Beaumont spreads, a long row of them appeared to be the dividing line. Wade led her to that area, dropping the lead rope from Rio. Apparently the horse knew the terrain. He wandered off only a few feet away. "You should have your company, Gina. Sounds like it was what you were meant to do."

"I will one day. I'm sure of that."

Wade took hold of her hand. "Come here," he said, guiding her to an area just beyond the trees. She viewed a large open crate and peered inside to find a mama border collie with five pups lying by her side on a quilt; two of the small pups were nuzzling on their mother voraciously, the others were fast asleep. "Oh, my. They are so sweet!" She turned to Wade, but his eyes were on the pups. "Is that your Lily?"

Wade shook his head. "No, Lily's gone now. Sugar is her daughter and now she's got pups of her own. I brought them out here for some peace and quiet today. I think Sugar likes it here. I'll bring them back to the barn later tonight."

Lily had been Wade's dog growing up. She'd been so gentle and sweet and a great herder. Wade had loved her.

She watched him bend to pet Sugar and the mama

looked up at him with adoring eyes. "That's a good girl," Wade said, stroking her coat lovingly. "You're a good mama, aren't you?"

Gina bent, too, and together they watched the little pups. "How old are they?"

"My uncle said she gave birth three weeks ago."

Gina watched the black-and-white little bundles as they woke, one right after the other, some scrambling for a spot by their mother, ready to suckle, others climbing over each other in the crate. One looked scrawnier than the rest and, instead of the common black-and-white coloring, had a coat of red and brown and white. Gina couldn't help picking that one up.

"Is that the one you like?"

Gina nodded. "I'm a sucker for the underdog."

Wade looked into her eyes for a moment then patted the little pup's head. "I'm thinking of taking one."

Surprised, Gina kept her expression even, hugging the pup a little tighter. "Really? I wouldn't think you'd have time for a dog."

"I'd make time. I'm ready for a commitment. So, you like this one the best?"

"They're all adorable, Wade. The choice is yours. Doesn't matter which one I'd pick."

Wade cocked her half a smile. "Oh, but it does matter."

I'm ready for a commitment.

An unexpected thrill coursed through her body and Gina shoved aside the heartwarming thoughts that accompanied that feeling. She wouldn't let her mind wander down that path.

She reminded herself of Wade's ruthless, calculating behavior towards her. She didn't trust him.

Puppies or not, Gina couldn't fall victim to him again. She put the tiny puppy back into the crate. Immediately, he nudged aside one of his siblings, to get to the mother. "He's a fighter."

"You're a good judge of character," Wade said, watching her with those intent penetrating eyes.

"Am I? Seems to me I messed up a few times in my life."

Wade nodded, a serious expression crossing his features. He spoke softly. "I've done the same, Gina. But I plan to remedy that."

Gina closed her eyes briefly, blocking out the sincere tone in his voice. Then she rose. "I think I'd better get going now."

Wade didn't hesitate. "Let's ride back." With a protest ready on her lips, Wade added quickly, "I promised to get you home in twenty minutes. It's faster this way."

She watched him mount Rio, those long legs lifting up and over the saddle, before he settled himself on and reached down for her hand.

She could either take the long walk back with Wade, with thoughts of commitments and puppies plaguing her every step, or she could be home in a few minutes, the downside being she'd have to share a saddle and the close proximity with him.

"Don't be afraid, Gina," Wade said, leaning down,

coaxing her with those deep-green eyes and an open expression on his face.

But Gina was afraid. She didn't want to lose her grip on the anger and resentment she held. She opted for the fast ride. She took his hand and he lifted her up, placing her in front of him on the saddle.

He wrapped his arms around her waist and handed her the reins. His breath was warm and rousing as he whispered in her ear, "You're in control now, honey."

Gina laced her fingers through the reins, nudged Rio forward, her heart beginning to melt like butter on a hot griddle.

"Glad you realized that, Wade."

His soft caressing chuckle from behind sent shivers.

She felt anything but in control, in truth, she thought she was *losing* all control.

Fast.

Gina spent the next two days with Sarah, working on wedding favors, seating arrangements and going over the plans for the ceremony. She hadn't seen Wade, but heard from both Roy and Mr. Buckley that the men had had their tuxedo fittings and then had gone out for drinks afterward.

Roy wanted no part of a bachelor party, but secretly Gina had joined troops with the two other bridesmaids to throw Sarah a quick bridal-shower luncheon. And Dottie Beaumont had offered up her home.

Gina sat beside Sarah with Kay Buckley and Dottie in the parlor along with several of Sarah's friends from the high school where she was now employed as a college counselor. Both Roy and Sarah had settled for a life in El Paso, working in jobs they loved.

After they'd finished a lunch catered by one of El Paso's finest eateries, cake was served and the gifts were opened.

"Let's see," Gina began, looking at the list she'd marked down, keeping track of which guests gave which gift. "You have three sets of sexy lingerie, apple nectar body oils and lotions, a bottle of French perfume to go along with a full case of French wine generously given to you by principal Carol Donaldson and a half dozen Waterford wine goblets donated by the rest of the staff. I say forget the wedding and skip straight to the honeymoon!"

The ladies laughed and Sarah smiled. "I don't think so. I've been wanting this wedding for a long time, but Roy would surely take you up on it, Gina."

"Sounds good to me," Roy said, coming in the front door, his eyes only on Sarah. "I can't wait to get to the honeymoon part."

Wade came in next, looking handsome in a crisp pair of jeans and a forest-green shirt, the color highlighting the deep hue of his eyes. He searched and found Gina instantly, his gaze focused solely on her face.

Gina's breath caught. Her throat tightened. She didn't like the effect Wade had on her, but she couldn't deny that she'd missed him. Just seeing him now, with all the other single females in the room, gazing at him as if he were a sweet creamy dessert they'd like to devour, put her nerves on edge. Wade, the wealthy, handsome prodigal son, returning to his childhood home, made a great catch for a local girl.

"You boys crashing the party?" Dottie asked, her gaze flowing from Roy to Wade. Gina saw the love and admiration she had for her nephew in that one solitary look. Wade may not have had a mother or a real father, but Lee and Dottie Beaumont had loved him like their own son. He'd been fortunate to have them in his life, *all* of his life. Gina had missed that. She'd missed that unconditional love and the looks of admiration she'd once received from her parents.

Wade glanced her way again and she blinked, uncomfortable with the warmth in his eyes, the softness in his face.

"This is a shower, so I'm here to shower my bride with a gift of my own. Thanks to Wade and his help the past few days, I was able to finish it on time. Come on outside. Your wedding present is waiting."

"Roy, what did you do?" Sarah asked quietly, but with a note of pleasant surprise in her voice.

"Come outside, sweetheart. I can't bring it in."

"Well, for heaven's sake, I'm going outside," Kay Buckley said to the women, "I just love surprises!"

The rest of the women followed.

Gina was the last to rise, making a final note on

her gift list. When she reached the door, Wade was waiting for her.

"Hi," he said, his eyes set on her.

Gina took a swallow and stood rigidly. She spoke with formality, "Hello, Wade."

He chuckled and drew her into his arms, his hands wrapping around her waist, tugging her close. Before she could protest, his lips met hers in a quick, almost chaste, kiss.

Gina backed up and stared at him. "Why did you do that?"

Wade's mouth quirked up quickly. "Couldn't help myself. Haven't seen you in two days."

Another chink in her armor fell away. She pulled in a deep breath. "Wade, you shouldn't…I mean, we can't…I don't think it's—"

He put a halting finger to her lips. "Shh. You think too much. Come on," he said, taking her hand and leading her outside to the front driveway. "You have to see what Roy's done for Sarah."

And as soon as she spotted the car, gift-wrapped with a giant wedding-white bow, memories flooded in of that summer, driving around in Sarah's old, but very classic 1966 Ford Mustang. This car wasn't the original, but Roy had outdone himself renovating a replica of the model.

By far, the cherry-red convertible with tufted leather seats had been Sarah's favorite possession and she'd driven it until the darn car had no more drive left.

"And my thanks go to Wade here," Roy was

telling the bridal-shower ladies, "for donating and flying in the finishing parts, not to mention helping me work on it these past two days to get the renovation done before the wedding."

Those female eyes again shifted to Wade, then moved down to their joined hands, each one of the women giving Gina a look of envy. For once, Gina was glad she hadn't broken the connection. She glanced up at Wade. "You did that for Roy and Sarah?" she asked, her voice elevated. She couldn't conceal her surprise.

Wade gave her a quick nod.

"It was very kind of you."

Wade drew his brows up. "That *almost* sounded like a compliment."

Gina shook her head. "Sorry, but you confuse me."

Wade let go a heavy sigh. "I'm making it my mission in life to unconfuse you."

With that, he leaned in and kissed the side of her head, brushing his lips into her hair.

Which only confused Gina all the more.

"Sarah, don't pair me up with Wade, okay?"

Sarah's soft-blue eyes went wide with surprise. "Why not?" They stood in the church vestibule and were only minutes away from the wedding rehearsal. Gina knew this was asking a lot of her friend.

"Because I don't want to walk down the aisle with him. Can't you send me down with Paul?"

Sarah shook her head. "I'm sorry. You know

Paul's the best man. He's been Roy's good friend forever. And, well, I *had* to ask Joanie to be my matron of honor," Sarah explained. "I was maid of honor in her wedding just last year. It's only right. Otherwise it would have been you, Gina."

"Of course she should be your matron of honor. I know you two have worked together for years at the school and Joanie has been a good friend." Gina didn't want to make the bride feel guilty, yet she suspected something else was going on here. "What about Tim?"

"You mean, break up Tim and Tanya? They'd kill me. Those two are inseparable and their wedding is coming up in six months. Wouldn't want to cause any trouble in paradise."

Gina narrowed her eyes at Sarah. "You're matchmaking, aren't you?"

Sarah twirled a finger around one long blond strand of hair. A definite sign of guilt, as Gina recalled from their early days at UCLA when Sarah had tried setting her up on blind dates. This time, Sarah didn't try to conceal her plans. She shrugged. "Why not? I have a lot to make up for. If it weren't for me…you and Wade—"

"Wade and I wouldn't have ended up together, Sarah. So, you don't have to feel guilty. Sooner or later, I would have seen him for the kind of man he truly is."

"Oh, you mean, sweet, good-natured, gorgeous and *sexy as sin?*"

Gina's eyes popped open wide. "How would you know that?"

Sarah grinned. "He is, isn't he? God, Gina. The way he looks at you, can't you give him a break?"

Gina let go a deep sigh. "We tried, twice. Both times ended in disaster. And don't say the third time's the charm. That's just a cliché and it's not true."

Sarah lowered her lashes and shook her head. "Sorry, but I disagree. And there's nothing I can do about the wedding party. It's all set. You and Wade are a couple, at least for my wedding." But when Sarah looked up, there wasn't regret in her eyes, but sheer, unabashed hope.

Gina peered down the corridor and found Wade with Roy and the other wedding ushers waiting for the minister to begin the rehearsal. He glanced her way and their gazes locked for a long moment. Gina wondered if she was looking into the face of the sweet, caring, honorable man she had once loved. Was Sarah right? Everything inside screamed at her to be careful, to watch her step, to keep her guard up, while the power of those keen green eyes told her to do just the opposite.

When the organist began to play the traditional wedding march, Sarah's excitement bubbled over. "Here we go," she said, taking Gina's hand. "I'm so happy right now, I can barely stand it. I want the same for you, Gina. Every girl should get the man of her dreams." With that, Wade approached taking long confident strides. "Looks like yours is coming for you now."

Gina closed her eyes briefly, wishing she didn't feel

exactly the same way. Only she wasn't bubbling over with joy like Sarah at the thought. No, she gazed at the handsome, appealing man standing before her now with trepidation, wondering about her unknown future.

"Are you ready to walk down the aisle with me, honey?"

It was a loaded question and one to which Gina could only grunt an unintelligible reply.

Wade laced her arm through his, an unmistakable twinkle in his eyes and a rare but striking smile on his face.

Gina turned to face the long narrow aisle leading to the altar. She imagined what it would be like tomorrow in the tiny romantic chapel in the canyon with family and friends filling the pews, bouquets of pink lilies with streaming large white satin bows lining each aisle, the minister welcoming the wedding guests and Sarah speaking vows of love and devotion.

Sarah and Roy had had a bumpy journey to the altar, but they'd found their way. Gina didn't think it was possible for her and Wade.

Before they took their first steps down the aisle, Wade leaned over, whispering in her ear, "Trust me, baby. We'll be good together."

The warmth and power of those words seeped into her, knocking loose even more chinks in her quickly crumbling armor. But Gina was a survivor, someone who had learned how to protect herself through the most difficult of times. She wouldn't make it easy for him. After the wedding, Gina didn't doubt that they would go their separate ways. "Trust you, Wade? If only I could."

But instead of putting him off, her statement only brought his lips up in another deep and stunning smile.

Twelve

"Wade, let me straighten that tie," Aunt Dottie said, standing close behind and catching his reflection from the bedroom mirror. She'd kept the room he had shared with Sam pretty much intact, complete with baseball trophies, school pennants and family pictures on the wall. Wade was glad she hadn't changed anything. He'd always thought of this place as home, even after he'd moved to Houston with his father and later relocated out west to California.

When she was through with the tie, she faced him and patted his shoulders like she had when he was a small boy. "You're a handsome devil, Wade Beaumont, all grown up now, running your own business." Her eyes were soft on him. "In that tuxedo, you'll turn every female head."

"Thanks for the help. And I only want to turn one female head today."

"That little gal giving you trouble?" Uncle Lee asked, stepping into the bedroom, looking as uncomfortable as a man could get wearing a three-piece suit.

Wade faced the mirror to run a comb through his hair. "She's stubborn."

Aunt Dottie said, "I like to say she's strong in character."

"Hardheaded," Wade rebutted, setting down the comb.

"A woman who knows her own mind," Aunt Dottie reasoned.

Wade nearly snorted, "Driving me out of mine."

"But worth every minute of it." Aunt Dottie tipped her chin for all the independent women in the world.

"I wouldn't be going through this if she wasn't."

Uncle Lee sighed, coming to stand beside him. "You know I felt the same way about your aunt a few decades ago. I had to wear her down."

"Hmph." His aunt smoothed out the wrinkles in her soft floral dress.

"Charmed her." His uncle's eyes lit with amusement.

"And tell Wade what you did when that didn't work," she said, fussing with her updo.

"I swept her off her feet," he said, with a decided puff of the chest.

Aunt Dottie walked over to lace her arm through her husband's. She looked at him lovingly. "More like you kidnapped me, Lee. Drove me over the state line and—"

"You went willingly, Dot, as I recall."

Wade had heard this story countless times in the past, but he didn't mind hearing it once more. Seeds of inspiration were beginning to grow in his mind. Wade wasn't going to let Gina get away this time.

"I did go willingly, Lee. Haven't regretted it a day in my life."

Lee squeezed her hand, then brought his gaze up to look into Wade's eyes. "Son, if you've got your sights set on a strong-minded woman, then you've got to outthink her."

"It's in the works, Uncle Lee."

Wade grabbed his wallet and the keys to his rental car, one he'd picked solely for tonight. "You look pretty Aunt Dottie." He kissed her cheek and smiled. "I'll see you both at the wedding."

"You're sure you don't want to drive with us into town?" his uncle asked.

Wade grinned. "I need my own car if I'm going to do any kidnapping tonight."

With that, Wade left the two of them standing there speechless, their mouths ready to fall open.

"Sarah looks breathtaking," Gina said, watching her friend greet the wedding guests at the reception in the Canyon Ballroom, a lovely intimate room adjacent to the church. She'd managed to get through the ceremony with Wade by her side every second, before, during and afterward. The only time they separated was at the altar, when the ladies stood up for the bride and the men positioned themselves next to a very eager groom.

Wade wrapped his arm around Gina's waist and leaned in close. "*You* look breathtaking," he whispered. "You're the most beautiful woman here."

Gina's toes curled. His nearness, his demeanor today, the caressing way his eyes traveled over her body, warmed her in ways she didn't think possible. She cast him a quick glance. Wade had never looked more appealing, wearing that black tuxedo like a second skin, confidant, sure and so handsome that he stole her breath.

The bride and groom had their opening dance, then Sarah danced with her father and Gina couldn't help but envy her. With Gina's future so unsure, she wondered if ever she married, who would walk her down the aisle? Who would take her into his arms lovingly and sweep her away in that father/daughter dance. It was times like these when Gina missed her parents the most.

Wade's uncle Lee came to stand beside her. He wrapped an arm around her waist. "You and Wade make a fine couple," he said, with a wink. "Walking down that aisle together, gave me notions, girl."

Gina had a protest on her lips to say she and Wade were not a couple, but Uncle Lee's eyes shone just too bright, his face was too sincere and Gina found she didn't want to disappoint the man. "Thank you," she said, and when she met Wade's eyes, she found his approval.

They danced once, the obligatory wedding party invited up to share the dance floor with the bride and groom, as pictures were snapped and then they retired to their seats for dinner.

The round table seated the entire wedding party and when the meal was through, Wade took Gina's hand, placing it on his thigh. Every time he smiled at her with those green eyes, Gina felt herself losing her grip.

"I won't be coming back to work at Triple B, Wade," she began. "Even though you said I still have a job there, it's not what I want."

"I know and I agree."

That surprised her. "You do?"

He nodded, his eyes still soft on her. She'd thought her announcement might have angered him. "You should pursue your own dreams. You should start your own company."

Gina felt somewhat validated. "Thank you for that."

"For what? Realizing that you're a capable woman with a lot to offer. That you have talent and drive and that you deserve a chance, a real chance at doing what you love to do."

Gina smiled, unsure of his intentions. "Are you trying to charm me?"

"God I hope so. Is it working?"

Gina chuckled. She'd never seen Wade so forthright, so open. And while it frightened her, she couldn't help but enjoy his company this evening. "I'm not sure how I feel right now."

When the band began a slow country ballad, Wade rose. "Dance with me?" he asked, offering up his hand.

Gina thought better of it, she knew she wasn't immune to Wade, but as she glanced around the joy-filled room, she couldn't help but want to share in the festivities a little. She took a leap of faith and placed her hand in his.

"Why not? I love this song," she said as Wade guided her to the edge of the dance floor.

"And I love any excuse to hold you in my arms," he said, bringing her in close enough to smell his familiar musky scent. He wrapped his arms around her tight and between the musk and intimate proximity, the reminder of that one blissful night they spent in Catalina rushed into her thoughts.

She closed her eyes and absorbed the music, the heat of the night and the thrill of being in Wade's arms again. Wade's lips teased her temples as he kissed her gently there, whispering in her ear. "I've named the pup, GiGi. I want her to be ours."

Gina popped her eyes open. "Ours?"

Wade smiled. "Yours and mine. That's what ours means."

"But how? It isn't possible. We can't—"

Wade put a stopping finger to her lips. "We can. Anything's possible."

Gina opened her mouth to debate the issue, but Wade's lips met hers in a soul-searing kiss that nearly wiped all rational thought from her head. When she finally opened her eyes, completely breathless, she stared up at him.

"Let's get out of here. I want to be alone with you."

"We can't leave," she said through tight lips. "We're in the wedding party."

"We've taken more pictures than they'll ever need and have done everything we were here to do.

"They haven't cut the cake yet."

"They won't miss us, sweetheart. And once they have cake, the guests will start leaving. We've done our part. Come away with me."

Gina resisted benignly, "Where?"

But Wade had already begun tugging her toward the door. "You'll see."

"You've got to be kidding," Gina said, standing beside Wade's rented convertible Porsche in front of a small lake that bordered the Beaumont ranch, holding a white thong swimsuit that looked suspiciously like the one she'd discarded on Catalina island.

They'd taken a wind-blown drive, letting the breeze and soft rock music steal them away. Now, Wade stood by the car, unfastening his tie. "It's hot, honey. I'm going in for a dip."

"And you expect me to go in with you?" Gina's voice elevated to the incredulous level.

Wade came forward and lifted her bottom onto the hood of the expensive silver sports car. He trapped her between his large hands. He leaned forward, his eyes intense, but his voice a simple soft caress. "I love you, Gina. Get used to hearing me say that. I love you. But I know you can't love me back until you truly trust me."

Stunned, Gina couldn't respond.

I love you, Gina.

"I've never said those words to another woman. And I've been trying so damn hard to get you back. I want you in my life. But first—"

"I have to trust you," she said softly, finally finding her voice.

"That's right. I'm hoping this helps," he said, removing something from his tuxedo jacket. He placed it into her hand and closed her palm with his. "This was my mother's. It's all I have left of her and I want you to have it."

Gina opened her hand slowly, then gasped when she saw the brooch, a sea of tiny flawless diamonds and in the center the most perfect gem she'd ever seen. Jade.

"To start up your gem collection for your company."

"I can't take this," she said, genuinely touched. "Really, Wade. This is…this is so sweet, so kind, but I can't." And as she glanced once again at the exquisite stone, she noted, "It's the perfect match to your eyes."

"I have my mother's eyes. My father gave it to her just months before he lost her."

"He must have loved her a lot. Maybe that's why he was so—"

"Shh. I don't want to talk about him. I want you to keep it."

"But it's yours."

"That's right. And you're going to be mine."

With that, Wade smiled and began undressing one bit at a time, leaving a trail of clothes all he way down to the moonlit lake waters. She watched him dive in and come up from the water, his eyes piercing and passionate. "Trust me, Gina."

It was a request.

A plea.

And an invitation she couldn't ignore.

He loved her.

She felt the clarity of that truth, deep down in her heart. She believed him and as astonishing as that seemed, she felt the rightness of it all, finally, simply.

It was that easy.

Gina scrambled out of her clothes and slipped on the thong while Wade was busy underwater. She approached the lake now, meeting her fear, understanding it for what it was and finally being able to overcome the dread that had always plagued her.

Wade came up from the water and stood, half in, half out, a mythical god with the lake dripping from his skin, beckoning her with his eyes and one out-stretched hand.

She stepped in and reached him, taking his hand. "I trust you, Wade," she said, knowing in her heart, he would never do anything to misplace that trust again.

Wade kissed her then, his mouth cold from the swim, but she felt his heat reaching out, touching her.

And together, they moved through the water.

* * *

Later, dripping wet and cold, their clothes thrown on haphazardly, they ran hand in hand into the Beaumont barn, their laughter rousing the sleeping pups.

Gina glanced at the precious litter, too happy to worry about their ruined sleep.

Breathless and burning with desire, she stared into Wade's hungry eyes.

"This is where it all began," he said.

Gina glanced at the wool blanket hanging up along a stall and the stack of hay that had once been their bed. She'd given Wade everything that night. "I've never stopped loving you, Wade. You were always there. I couldn't get rid of you, though I tried. You were my first."

Wade took her into his arms. "I plan on being your last. Until the day I die."

Gina nodded, swallowing the lump in her throat. "Okay."

Wade smiled. "Okay?"

Gina smiled back.

"We already have a family. You, me and GiGi. Wonder how she'll like my house on the beach."

"She'll love it," Gina said, peering down at the pup with the unusual colors.

"Will you?" he asked, reaching around to unzip her ruined bridesmaid gown.

"I think so," she said softly, staring into his eyes.

"And will you let me be your partner, in business and in life?"

He slipped the zipper down, notch by notch, then reached up to expose her shoulders. He kissed her there, making her head swim with delicious thoughts.

"I will, but you won't boss me around."

Wade kissed her lips. "You won't let me."

Gina smiled then and wrapped her arms around his neck, tugging him in to mate their mouths. She kissed him soundly, freely, giving him her trust, her love and her heart. "I'm glad we've got that straight."

Wade slipped her dress off, letting it puddle at her feet. She stepped over it, standing fully unclothed before him.

"I wanted you for my wife the minute I laid eyes on you," he said, quietly, reverently, his gaze gently scanning her body.

Gina removed his shirt, unzipped his pants. "You're a fast worker, sweetheart. Only took you nine years."

They stood naked before one another.

Then together they lowered down onto the hay.

They joined their bodies, bonding themselves for the future, in the barn, on a soft patch of straw, where they'd first found each other.

"Some things are just worth the wait."

* * * * *

HOUSE CALLS
by
Michelle Celmer

MICHELLE CELMER

lives in southeastern Michigan with her husband, their three children, two dogs and two cats. When she's not writing or busy being a mum, you can find her in the garden or curled up with a romance novel. And if you twist her arm really hard you can usually persuade her into a day of power shopping.

Michelle loves to hear from readers. Visit her website at: www.michellecelmer.com, or write to her at PO Box 300, Clawson, MI 48017, USA.

To my children,
who never fail to amaze, bewilder, confuse and
delight me – and always make me proud.

One

At the sound of a car door slamming, Pete Morgan wheeled himself across the library to the window overlooking the circular drive, but he was too late to see the occupant of the dark blue SUV parked there.

What difference did it make? He'd only gone to the window out of habit. It wasn't as if he got many visitors these days. Or wanted any, for that matter.

The flowers and get-well cards had stopped arriving soon after he was released from the hospital, and after weeks of enduring the seemingly endless looks of pity from friends and colleagues, he'd begun turning visitors away. It had taken a few weeks, but people finally got the hint and stopped coming altogether. Now he spent his days alone in his private wing of the house. The solitude it provided suited him just fine.

He stared out the window, trying to recall when he'd last

been outside. The afternoon sun looked warm and inviting and a gentle breeze swayed the trees bordering the ten-acre estate. Occasionally he yearned to get out. He missed the sting of the sun on his back as he sliced across the lake on water skis, the burn of his muscles as he scaled the jagged face of a mountain, the wind in his hair as he biked the trails at Stony Creek State Park. Those had been the days he'd lived for, the days he'd felt truly free.

Those days were over.

He stared out the window, remembering all that he'd lost—all that he would never get back. When he heard the door open, it might have been five minutes later or it could have been an hour.

"Peter?" a voice said stiffly, as though the mere mention of his name caused enormous regret.

He didn't bother turning to face her. He knew what he would see if he did—disappointment, pity. He wasn't in the mood.

"What do you want, Mother?"

"Your father and I would like to have a word with you."

Glancing over his shoulder, he saw that his father stood next to her in the doorway—towered over her was more like it. Charles Morgan, a force to be reckoned with. There had been a time, long ago, when Pete had respected his father's powerful presence, feared it even. Not anymore. He'd grown immune to him a long time ago. "I'm afraid you'll have to call my secretary for an appointment. I'm booked solid this afternoon."

The pinched, irritated look he received from his father gave Pete tremendous satisfaction.

"I don't find your sarcasm amusing," he thundered. "You will apologize to your mother this instant."

"Or else what?" He swiveled to face them. "You'll ground me? You'll take away my driving privileges? News flash: I'm not going anywhere."

"I've had enough of your attitude." A vein pulsed at his father's temple. "You've spent weeks wallowing in self-pity when you should have been working to rehabilitate yourself."

"What you think is of no concern to me. If you insist that I stay here, you're just going to have to learn to live with me this way." Pete tossed the medical journal he'd been reading on the table next to the couch and spun back to the window. "Maybe I'm happy the way I am."

"Nonsense," his mother said, her voice softer but no less disapproving. "You're a doctor. You won't be satisfied until you've made a complete recovery."

"Has it occurred to either one of you that I may not make a complete recovery? Have you forgotten that my leg was nearly blown off?"

"Morgans are fighters," his father replied, as if his word was law. As if that reversed the damage Pete had sustained. Talk about arrogant.

"You'll learn to walk again," his father said. "Starting today."

He sensed his mother crossing the room, and in his peripheral vision saw her lift a hand to his shoulder, then pull away before she touched him. Touching had never been a big hit at the Morgan estate. His father had always believed in tough love. Affection hadn't factored into the program. Obviously that hadn't changed in the years he'd been away.

"Peter—" she said gently, before his father's voice boomed behind her.

"We're wasting our time here. He won't listen."

He sensed her pause, as though she might actually defy her husband and speak her mind for the first time in her life, but her hand dropped to her side and she backed away. Their retreating footsteps told him the conversation was over.

"Suppose I don't ever walk," he said aloud, wheeling back to the window. "What then?"

"Suppose you stop acting like a big baby and at least try."

The comment came from neither of his parents and Pete swung around, startled to find that he wasn't alone. "I beg your pardon?"

She stood across the room, her back to him, a compact little package of luscious curves and softness poured into a snug pair of blue jeans and a clingy red shirt. She gazed up at the bookcases spanning the north wall. "You know, I don't think I've ever seen so many books in one place." She laughed to herself. "I mean, I've obviously seen lots of books at the library and the bookstore, but not in someone's house. I wonder if they've all been read?"

She pulled a leather-bound copy of *The Hobbit* from the shelf, running a hand over the worn binding. That had been one of his favorites. He'd read it so many times he was sure if he gave it some thought, he could recite it word for word from memory.

"I love the smell of paper and leather, don't you?" She raised the book to her nose and inhaled. "Hmm, it reminds me of weekends at my grandfather's house. He owned lots of books, too. But not this many."

Pete wheeled himself closer, mesmerized. Something about her was so familiar, yet he hadn't even seen her face. "Who are you?"

She carefully returned the book to its place on the shelf. "Considering that little tantrum you just pulled with your parents, I suppose you could say I'm your worst nightmare."

As she turned to him, Pete had to remind himself to breathe. Worst nightmare? Hardly. She looked more like a wet-dream fantasy. Short dark hair hung in soft ringlets around a lovely heart-shaped face—

Lovely? Good God, where had he dredged that up from? He wasn't the kind of man to use a word like *lovely,* though he had to admit the description fit. She was sharp, too. He could clearly see the spark of intelligence in her eyes. They were round and dark and shone with a cockiness he used to see when he looked in the mirror. She also looked very familiar.

"Do I know you?"

"You know that taking your anger out on your parents isn't very constructive," she said. "You should channel those emotions into your recovery."

He frowned. "What are you, a shrink?"

"God, no," she said with a short burst of silvery laughter. "I'm going to teach you how to use that new knee. I'm Maggie Holm, your physical therapist."

Maggie followed her newest patient as he wheeled himself out the door, amazed by the speed with which he made his getaway. He sure could move fast when he had something to run from. It had been difficult not to exhibit the surprise she'd felt at the drastic physical changes since she'd last seen him in the hospital cafeteria line. At that time, they'd only said a brief and perfunctory hello. But throughout her lunch break she'd sneaked glances at him every so often, at the meticu-

lously sculptured physique he must have worked years in the
weight room to perfect. He was, in every sense of the word,
a hunk.

And nice. He'd never carried himself with that air of au-
thoritative arrogance so common to doctors. Pete was friendly
and easygoing. There was hardly a time when he hadn't been
smiling.

He wasn't smiling now. Today, if she'd seen him on the
street, she might not have recognized him—sort of like he
hadn't recognized her. Not that many men had given her a second glance back then. Not with the spare forty pounds she'd
been hauling around. They'd both changed considerably.

His changes weren't necessarily for the better.

The Pete who sat before her today wore a wrinkled T-shirt
and loose sweatpants, and his wavy dark hair was more than a
little shaggy around the ears. Absent was the perpetually cheer-
ful demeanor she remembered and the larger-than-life aura
he'd once radiated like a beacon. Deep lines creased his forehead and brow, making him look years older than thirty-one.

She followed quietly behind him, gauging the amount of
muscle mass he'd lost in the four months since the shooting.
Though his physique was still above average on a normal
scale, he'd lost more than a few inches in his upper body
alone. That had to be a blow to his ego. She nearly cringed at
the thought of what the inactivity had done to his legs, and at
the grueling work ahead. Even worse—given his rotten attitude—she had to determine the proper method of motivation.

A cattle prod came to mind.

He glanced over his shoulder at her and smirked. "Are you
still here?"

She regarded him with a pleasant smile. "I'm sorry, did you want me to leave? I thought you were giving me a tour of the house."

He stopped and turned. "Look, I appreciate that you have a job to do, but you're wasting your time here."

"I disagree," she said.

"You do?" His eyebrows quirked up and for a second she saw a glimpse of the old Pete, the one hiding behind the sarcasm. *Phew.* At least he was still in there somewhere. Now she just had to find a way to draw him out, to turn his anger around and use it constructively.

She chuckled to herself. She did sound like a shrink, didn't she?

"Yes, I do," she said. "I'm going to get your stubborn behind out of that chair."

His jaw tensed. "Suppose I don't want to walk?"

She shrugged. "That's never stopped me before."

He wheeled around and continued down the hall.

She followed him. "I've seen your file. Total knee replacement. You've lost bone, making your left leg slightly shorter than the right, and you've suffered some minor permanent nerve damage. I've seen worse. I've had sixty-year-old women with both knees replaced and you can hardly tell. Don't tell me you have less stamina than a sixty-year-old woman."

His back straightened just a little at the jab. "This is not about stamina. I'm never going to have full use of my leg."

"No, you won't."

He glanced back at her, a look of surprise on his face.

"What? Did you think I was going to lie and say you would

make a total recovery? I'm a good therapist, doc, but I'm not that good. Not to mention that your attitude sucks."

He hung a right into a large suite at the end of the hall. She sidled in behind him before he could slam the door in her face. She was sure that was exactly what he had been planning to do.

Gazing around the room, her eyes widened. Yow! What a spread. The sitting room alone was larger than her entire apartment. Hell, it was probably larger than the entire first floor of her parents' house. The room was extravagantly decorated in rich shades of green and mauve, ostentatious Oriental rugs covered the polished wood floors and heavy velvet drapes hung in arched windows that kissed the peak of the cathedral ceiling. It was a bit on the gaudy side—as in gag-me-with-a-fork gaudy—and she couldn't help thinking how out of place Pete looked there. She'd pictured him in something a little less…well, *ugly.*

She wandered toward the adjoining bedroom and peered in. It was even worse. The same ugly drapes were drawn, making the room dark and foreboding, like an oversized tomb. The cherry furniture looked antique, with the exception of the hospital bed that stuck out like a sore thumb. It sat low to the ground with a bar overhead to help him lift himself in and out.

Completely unnecessary, she thought. His legs were probably stiff and weak, but there was no good reason why he couldn't use them to hoist himself in and out of bed.

She glanced over and saw that Pete was watching her. "May I?" she asked, gesturing to the bedroom.

"Would it do me any good to try and stop you?"

"You could try," she said. "But I'm pretty fast."

He shrugged. "I don't know what you expect to find in there."

Neither did she. But it wouldn't hurt to look.

She stepped inside. As far as she could see, no personal effects had been set out to give the room character. In fact, it reminded her an awful lot of a hotel room. That alone spoke volumes about his frame of mind. Though he showed no interest in getting on with his life, he lived in an environment that looked awfully temporary.

She checked the bathroom next. Every conceivable amenity had been added to make it wheelchair-friendly. The sink and counter were wheelchair height and a shower seat sat in the stall. The whole suite would be just dandy for a paraplegic, or a man who'd had both legs amputated. Pete was neither.

By trying to make his life easier, his parents had given him no incentive to fight.

Unfortunately, that wasn't uncommon. Parents, no matter how good their intentions, just seemed to have a way of messing their kids up.

Like her parents' approach to dealing with their fat, out-of-control daughter. The disapproving looks when she reached for that second roll at dinner. Allowing her half the food they let her thin older sister pile on her plate, then wondering why she would sneak into the kitchen in the middle of the night and gorge herself. The lone bag of raw vegetables and bottle of water she'd find in her school lunch every day when the other kids had peanut butter and jelly with chips and granola bars.

The absolute worst, most humiliating form of torture her parents had dished out had been the summers spent at fat camp. She used to dread the end of the school year, knowing she would be shipped off to that horrible place. And then there was the even more ghastly experience of coming home at the end of summer and seeing the disappointment on her parents' faces when she hadn't magically become thin and beautiful like her older sister Molly.

"Another five hundred down the drain!" her mother would bluster in front of God and everyone. "Margaret Jane, I swear you're going to be the death of me."

She felt a familiar jab of resentment and knocked it back down. Now was not the time to mentally rehash her very dysfunctional childhood.

She walked out of the bedroom, and Pete was sitting by the window with a faraway, almost yearning look on his face. His parents were right about one thing—he wouldn't be happy until he was up and moving again. He just had to learn to accept his disabilities, to accept himself as imperfect. For a man like Peter, a man who had once personified perfect, that could be difficult.

She stepped up behind him, gazing out upon a picture-perfect garden. A cobblestone path wound its way through lush flower beds exploding with vibrant color; trees swayed lazily in the gentle summer breeze amid acres upon acres of rolling green grass.

"It's beautiful," she said.

"I guess."

"Do you get out there much?"

"The path is too narrow for the chair."

"I noticed a pool on the other side of the yard. Swimming would be good for your leg."

He looked up at her, his expression blank. "Seen enough?"

"Of what?"

He spread his arms out toward the room. "Of this—my life. If you're finished, you can go. I don't mean to be rude, but it's time for my nap."

"You don't mean to be rude? Isn't that *exactly* what you mean to be?" she asked, and he shrugged. "Knock yourself out, doc. I'm pretty tough."

He glared up at her, eyes like daggers. "Get out."

She folded her arms over her chest. "Okay, tough guy. Make me."

Two

The anger on Pete's face slipped for an instant. "Come again?"

"I said, make me. What are you going to do, pick me up and throw me out? You can't walk, remember?"

"That's very cute," he said. "Is that some sort of warped reverse psychology? Am I supposed to jump up and miraculously walk across the room now?"

She slammed her hands down on the armrests of his chair, caging him in, getting right in his face—and boy, did he smell good, just like she'd always imagined he would. A clean, masculine scent.

"Look, doc, for all I care, you can rot in that chair. I'm doing this for your parents, who I realize are not what you would call warm and fuzzy, but who seem to genuinely care about you. They think you'll make a full recovery, which, let's face it, we both know isn't gonna happen. You'll have a limp, possibly to the point of needing a cane to negotiate certain situations, or it may barely be recognizable. And of course you can look forward to more surgeries and physical therapy in the future, since that knee is only good for about ten years—fifteen if you're lucky.

"How you do all depends on how hard you're willing to work. Then again, maybe you won't work at all. You'll sit in that chair feeling sorry for yourself until every muscle has atrophied beyond repair and you never walk again. It's your choice."

His face remained stoic, but his Adam's apple bobbed as he swallowed.

She straightened to her full five feet four inches, but didn't back away. She could tell that her presence made him uncomfortable. At well over six feet tall, he probably wasn't used to people towering over him. In many respects, it had to make him feel overpowered, if only subconsciously. It was very likely part of the reason he insisted on pushing everyone away.

That wouldn't work with her. She excelled at making a pest of herself.

A nerve in his jaw jumped and for a second he looked a lot like his father. "Did anyone ever tell you that your methods suck?"

She couldn't help but crack a smile. "Honey, I haven't even started. When I'm finished with you, you're going to either love me or hate me."

"I think I hate you already," he muttered.

"Hate me all you want, doc. As long as you bust your butt to get better. You've got people rooting for you."

"What people?"

"At the hospital. The people who used to be your friends."

"You work there?" A speck of recognition lit his eyes.

"In the PT department."

"I thought I recognized you." He took her in from head to toe. "But, didn't you used to—"

"Be enormous?" she interjected.

Pete rolled his eyes. Why was it that all women had such a warped self image? She may have been a little on the thick side, he honestly couldn't remember. What he did remember was her eyes. They were so bright and full of life. That he'd forgotten her was an indication of how empty his own life had become. "I was going to ask if you used to have long hair."

"Yep, down to my butt," she said, fingering the short dark spirals at her nape. "We should get started. We have a lot of work ahead of us. Your parents gave me a tour of the exercise room and showed me the equipment they've rented. It should be adequate."

Boy, she was stubborn. Hadn't he already told her he didn't want her help? Hadn't he asked her to leave? "I don't think you heard what I said."

She stepped behind him and grabbed the handles of his chair, leaning close to his ear. "Oh, I heard you. I'm just ignoring you."

Her warm breath tickled his ear, making it difficult to concentrate—until she started pushing him toward the door. Beautiful or not, she was ticking him off.

He grabbed the wheels, grinding them to a jerky halt. "Look, Maggie…."

"No, *you* look." She circled the chair, propping herself on his armrests again, getting in his face for the second time that day. If she were a man, he probably would have decked her by now. And if she were a man, he wouldn't be having such a hard time *not* looking down her shirt, which was fairly low-cut and just happened to be at eye level. Her chest was full and lush and lightly freckled across her cleavage. It was just...*wow*.

He couldn't stop himself from enjoying the view.

"I'm going to get you out of that chair, whether you like it or not," she said.

He tried to keep his gaze locked on her face. "So I can limp around and make a fool of myself? I don't think so."

"You don't mean to suggest that anyone with a limp is a fool? The thousands of men who come home from war with debilitating injuries are fools? Children born with crippling birth defects are fools?"

"That's different," he mumbled. He could see exactly what she was trying to do, but she didn't understand—anything less than perfect wasn't good enough. Not for him. Not for his parents.

And certainly not for Lizzy, his *ex*-fiancée.

"What do you plan to do with the rest of your life, doc? What about all those years you spent in college and medical school? Would you really throw all of that away because you're afraid?"

He narrowed his eyes. "Let's get one thing straight. I'm not afraid. I just don't do things halfway."

"Halfway?"

He looked away. "You wouldn't understand."

She arched her neck, forcing him to look at her. She had

the darkest eyes he'd ever seen, and so deep he could get lost in them. "Try me."

"I worked in the ER. The pace is fast and reaction time is critical. If I were to rejoin my staff in anything less than perfect physical condition, I would be compromising the integrity of the entire team. I can't, with a clear conscience, limp around the ER just hoping that I won't slow everyone else down."

Her eyes narrowed slightly. "And your colleagues, they've expressed their concern to you?"

"Not exactly. They would never come right out and say that to me, but I know what they're thinking."

"Really?" She looked intrigued. "Forget medicine altogether. You should look into a job at one of those psychic hotline places." She leaned closer, until it was almost impossible *not* to look at her breasts. They were just so right there in his face. "Tell me, doc, what am I thinking right now?"

He cleared his throat. "Given your track record today, I'd have to guess it's either rude or sarcastic."

Smiling, she backed away and he heaved a silent sigh of relief. He may have been a cripple, but he was still a man— a man who hadn't had the pleasure of a woman's company in four months. Four very *long* months.

"Actually, I was thinking that you smell great. It's that clean, crisp cologne that makes me think of camping in October. You know, just before the leaves start to fall. When it's not quite cold enough for winter coats, but a jacket is too light, and the heat of the campfire keeps you toasty warm. The kind of night to cuddle up in a sleeping bag with someone special and…well, you get the picture. Do you remember nights like that, doc?"

Unfortunately he did. Vividly. And he couldn't help imagining himself snuggled up, sharing a sleeping bag with someone like her.

He tried to swallow, realizing suddenly that his mouth had gone bone-dry. She was messing with his head. And she was good at it.

"You know what else I was thinking? If you really don't care what people think of you, why would you bother putting on cologne in the first place? Hell, why bother shaving? I was also wondering, if you no longer care about your career, why you were reading a medical journal when I came in earlier? Then I was thinking, if you're so content sitting in that chair, why does it bug the hell out of you every time I get close and you have to look up at me?"

Because I'm not used to having breasts shoved in my face? He couldn't very well say that now, could he? "You seem to have all the answers. Why don't you tell me?"

"You're afraid. You're afraid to be anything less than perfect. I'll let you in on a little secret, doc. You weren't perfect."

"Is that so?"

"You only think you were."

Pete glared up at her with piercing blue eyes—eyes filled with a world of hurt and horrors she could only imagine. Which was why she was even more determined to see this through. He seemed so close to cracking, but she wasn't quite there yet. So many people would be disappointed if she failed. She'd been chosen for this job because she had a reputation for dealing well with difficult clients. The man just didn't realize how much everyone at the hospital cared about him. She cared, too, probably too much for her own good—and his.

But whatever he could dish out, she could take. God knows she'd been through much worse.

She sat casually on the sofa, as if she didn't have a care in the world. "So what do you say, doc?"

Pete wheeled himself to the window behind her so she could no longer see him, but she couldn't miss the exasperation in his voice.

"I never thought I was perfect," he said. "And while your insight on my life is truly fascinating, you couldn't be further off base."

"Okay. Prove it."

"If I do, will you go away?"

The hopeful ring to his voice made her laugh. "Yeah, prove to me without a doubt that I'm completely wrong about you, that you don't need me, and I'll go away."

There was a pause, then he said, "Maggie, turn around."

Something about the way he said her name sent chills across her skin. She shifted around to see him and found herself looking directly at…his crotch? Her eyes traveled up all six-feet-however-many inches of him as he walked—okay, limped—around the couch, until he was *standing* in front of her. He was *standing*. Then he leaned down and wedged his hands on the back of the loveseat on either side of her head, caging her in. Instinctively she pressed herself deeper into the cushions and her heart started to pound like crazy.

Oh. My. God.

He leaned in close, until they were nose to nose, flashed her a cocky smile and said, "How do *you* like it?"

If her jaw hadn't been fixed to her skull it would have been lying in her lap. "You sneaky son of a bitch. You can walk!"

"Are you convinced?"

She scrambled from under his arm and jumped to her feet. "How long have you been walking?"

He lowered himself onto the arm of the sofa, wincing slightly as he brought his foot to rest on the floor. "A while. I use the equipment at night, when I'm sure I'll have some privacy."

She circled him, examining his knee, wishing she could get a better look. Now didn't seem the time to ask him to drop his pants. "What's your range of motion?"

"It's stiff, and total extension is still tough. Impossible really."

"Your muscles are short from all the weight lifting you used to do. You're not working with enough resistance. We'll fix that."

His eyes widened. *"We?"*

"Yes, *we*. You've done a lot on your own, but with my help there's no telling what you could accomplish. I thought you'd been sitting around letting your muscles deteriorate. This will cut months off your therapy. We should start today. *Right now.*"

"I can't do that," he said, his voice rich with resignation. "Not today. Not ever."

"What do you mean you can't? You've come so far. I want to help you. Everyone will be so thrilled—"

"No!" He shot up so fast that he lost his balance and almost fell into her. She grabbed hold of his arm to steady him, but he pushed her hand away. "I don't need your help, and I don't want you telling anyone anything. I don't want anyone seeing me this way."

At that moment it became perfectly clear. He was embarrassed. He didn't want anyone, not even his closest friends and family, to see him struggling. Pride was getting in the way of his recovery, making him feel he had to do it alone, when now, more than ever, he needed help. He needed the support of the people who cared about him. Didn't he understand that he could only take this so far on his own?

Obviously, he didn't. She could tell him that it didn't matter that he wasn't perfect, that he was still the same man inside. That when he stood, even on a bad leg, he was still a powerful presence. She could even tell him that when he'd pinned her to the couch like that it had made her heart go berserk, and that his classically handsome features still left her a little breathless. That seeing him in the hospital had always lifted her spirits, and often she would make excuses to visit the ER just to get a glimpse of him.

She could tell him that she almost didn't take him on as a patient, for fear that she was too emotionally attached. But she knew she would never have the guts to say it. Not only would it be completely unprofessional, she would never humiliate herself that way. He was a million miles out of her league.

"I'd like you to leave now," he said, hobbling back over to his chair and lowering himself into it. "I can do this on my own. And though I can't force you, I'd appreciate it if you didn't tell anyone what you saw today."

"You need me, doc. Deep down, you know that."

He wheeled himself toward the door. "I'm sure you can find your way out."

She was losing ground fast. It was time to pull out the *really* heavy artillery. "Is this what your fiancée would have wanted?"

He turned to her, his eyes blank. "Goodbye, Maggie. Thanks for stopping by."

Just like that, she'd lost the battle.

For now, anyway.

Three

Pete woke to the squeak of his bedroom door opening, but he was too tired to pry his eyes open.

"Go away," he mumbled, pulling the blanket to his chin, silently cursing whoever it was for rousing him from one of the most erotic dreams he'd had in his life.

He'd dreamed Maggie had stolen into his room in the middle of the night. She'd stripped for him in the burnished moonlight in front of the open window, her slinky form hardly more than a shadow, leaving his imagination to roam. Then she'd climbed into his bed and the dream had become a blur of soft skin and slick heat and intense sexual sensation. He'd just been getting to the really good part when—

"Morning, doc. Time to get up."

He groaned, opening one eye to find the object of his dream hovering over him. "You again?"

"Get out of bed."

He closed his eye and sighed. *Why don't you slide in here with me?* The aftereffects of the dream weren't lost when she'd roused him—or, more to the point, *a*roused him.

She poked him through the covers. "Come on, wake up. We have work to do."

"Get lost," he said, pulling the blankets over his head. He'd been up half the night using the PT equipment and his body ached from the vigorous workout. He wondered if she was trained in massage therapy....

Before he could ask, she tugged the covers down to his shoulders. "I'm not leaving until you're up."

Up? I'm up, all right. He peered at her through half-open lids, in time to see her reach out and grasp the covers, knowing exactly what she was about to do.

"I sleep in the—"

The covers flew off him. "Rise and sh—"

"—nude."

The comforter fell and came to rest somewhere south of his thighs.

"Ooops!" She slapped a hand over her eyes and spun around so fast, for a second she was a blur of denim and white cotton. "Sorry about that."

"I tried to warn you." He sat up and reached for the covers, pulling them to his waist.

"I guess I just assumed you would be wearing pajamas."

"Yeah, well, I don't."

"I see that."

"Do you wake all your clients up this way?" he asked, yawning and raking his fingers through his hair. "In the wee hours of the—" he glanced at the digital clock beside his bed "—afternoon."

"Most of my clients are up before one o'clock."

"I told you yesterday that I like to work out at night." She was still turned away, and he stole the opportunity to check out her behind. She was wearing another pair of snug jeans that flaunted every curve, and the arousal that had begun to ease was threatening to rise up for a repeat performance. Time for a change of scenery. "You can turn around."

"I apologize if I've embarrassed you," she said, facing him.

"I have nothing to be to be embarrassed about." He wrinkled his brow and lifted the covers, looking down. "Or do I?"

Maggie bit the inside of her cheek, trying hard not to blush. Yes, she deserved his teasing. It had been presumptuous of her to barge in and rip the covers off him, and it was a mistake she would certainly not be making again. But to admit that the glimpse she'd gotten of his…well, it had been enough to assure her that he indeed had nothing whatsoever, at all— even the least little bit—to be embarrassed about. As a matter of fact, she was thinking that he ought to be pretty darned proud of himself.

And would she tell him that? Hell no. It was imperative they keep the line between caregiver and patient abundantly clear, now more than ever considering the proposition she was about to toss at him.

"Are you asking for my professional opinion?" she said. "Because sexual therapy really isn't my area of expertise. But if you're concerned that you're…*inadequate,* I could get you the name of a good therapist."

The corners of his mouth quirked up into an honest-to-goodness grin. It wasn't a big grin, but it was a start. She'd forgotten how gorgeous he looked when he smiled. Too gorgeous, in fact. He was also uncovered from the waist up and his chest was…well, he hadn't lost quite as much muscle as she'd suspected. He was still nowhere near as bulked up as he'd been before, but—she held back a sigh—he looked better this way, as far as she was concerned.

And, she realized, she was standing there staring at him. She backed toward the door. "Why don't I wait out here for you while you get dressed?"

"What's the matter?" He eased the covers down. "Afraid you'll see something you like?"

She shrugged, trying to look uninterested. "Sorry, doc. I sort of feel like if you've seen one, you've seen them all." Her back hit the door and she groped for the handle, hoping he didn't notice her sudden loss of coordination. "Take your time."

"Just give me a minute or two to get dressed and brush my teeth," she heard him say, and as the door snapped shut, she could swear she heard him laugh.

Ugh! What was wrong with her? It was understandable that she had been awestruck by the guy four months ago, but now he was a patient and that kind of behavior was inexcusable. Of course, she didn't usually see her patients naked. Not to mention that the majority of her male patients were wrinkly, shriveled-up old men.

She planted herself on the sofa. Okay, Mags, get a grip. It's not like you've never seen a naked man before—an *aroused* naked man. A really aroused and gorgeous naked man. Aroused and gorgeous and—

Sheesh! Get over it already. She'd fallen for a patient before and it had been a disaster. She was never making that mistake again.

By the time the door to the bedroom opened and Pete wheeled himself out several minutes later, she was back in professional mode, and intended to stay that way.

"Stop right there," she said. "I want to see you walk again."

His brow furrowed. "What for?"

"Humor me, okay?"

He glanced at the door.

"Don't worry," she said. "I locked it. The only way anyone is going to see is if they scale the side of the house and peek in the windows. It's just us."

Pete blew out a frustrated breath. She looked awfully determined, and a long, drawn-out debate didn't sound like a whole lot of fun right now. He had the sneaking suspicion that he would lose, anyway.

He'd humor her, just this once.

Pushing himself up on the arms of the chair, he rose to his feet, wincing at the familiar sting as he put weight on his bad leg. He'd taken only a few unsteady steps when she vaulted herself up off the couch.

"No, no, no! Not like that!"

"Jeez," he said, startled by her outburst. "What did I do?"

"You're favoring your good leg. You'll never get used to the prosthetic if you don't use it."

"I can't put that much weight on it. It hurts like a sonofagun."

She circled him, her brow crinkled. "Straighten it out."

He grabbed hold of a table for support. "I can't."

"When you work out, do you spend much time stretching it?"

"A little. Mainly I've been trying to build the muscle back up."

A pained look crossed her face, and he saw her take a very long, deep breath. "Don't take this the wrong way, but are you out of your friggin' mind?"

He mirrored her irritation. "What's wrong with trying to build up the muscle? The stronger my leg, the better I'll walk, right?"

"You doctors can be so dumb sometimes." She pointed to the couch. "Sit."

"Get up, sit down, get up, sit down—this is worse than Sunday mass," he grumbled, but he hobbled over and sat down anyway. She cringed with every step.

"Okay, give me your leg," she said, kneeling in front of him. When he hesitated, she sighed loudly. "I'll give it back."

He lifted his leg and she grasped his calf firmly. Then she pulled and he nearly went through the roof. "*Hey!* That hurts!"

She gave him a satisfied smile. "Do you know why it hurts, doc?"

"Gee, I don't know, it might have something to do with you *pulling on it!*"

She popped the bottom snap on his exercise pants, then paused, glancing up at him. "May I?"

"What, you didn't see enough in the bedroom?"

"Funny." She yanked the pant leg open to his thigh. He waited for her to gasp at the angry red scar tissue surrounding his knee, but she didn't even flinch.

"You must have been a lot of fun in the hospital," she said, fingering the muscle. "The nurses must have loved you."

He stifled a grin. "When I left the ICU, they threw a party. They said I was a lot more fun when I was in a coma."

She laid a hand on his thigh, just above the knee, and eased his calf up, watching his face. "You were that bad?"

"Yeah, I was pretty bad." He winced and she eased back. "I was still in the angry stage of my recovery."

"It's a wonder the nurses didn't murder you in your sleep."

He let a smile slip through. "You know what they say about doctors making lousy patients."

She pulled the leg of his pants together and fastened the snaps. "That's the second time you've smiled today."

The fact that she'd noticed, that she cared, made him smile again. It was an odd sensation. So many of those muscles in his face hadn't been exercised in a very long time. "You're counting?" he asked.

"I wouldn't normally, but I get the feeling you don't do it very often." She gave his leg a pat, then sat next to him on the couch. "But you should, it's nice."

Her comment made him feel better than it should have. It shouldn't have mattered at all that she liked his smile, but at that moment in time, it meant everything.

Moments pass, he thought ruefully. "So, Maggie, what's your diagnosis?"

She drew her knee up and used it as a chin rest. "You need to cool it on the weights, doc. Now is not the time to be trying to look like He-Man. Not only are you working the wrong muscles and completely defeating the purpose of the exercises, but the muscles you should be extending are actually getting shorter. You need to work on stretching the leg first, then add some resistance. We'll work out a routine together."

"I told you—"

She held out a hand. "Before you get all defensive and cranky, hear me out, okay? I know you don't want people to know what you've been up to, but I have an idea."

He scrubbed a hand over his face, realizing belatedly that he never should have gotten out of bed. He should have known she would be impossible to get rid of once she'd infiltrated his afternoon. "Okay, what's your idea?"

"Have you ever been to Gaylord?"

"I've passed through on my way to the Upper Peninsula a few times. Why?"

"Have you ever been to Turtle Lake?"

He didn't like the sound of this. "I don't think so."

"And you don't know anyone there, right?"

"Not to my knowledge. Is there a point to this?"

She smiled brightly. "Then it'll be perfect."

He really wasn't liking the sound of this. "Perfect for what?"

"For us. You don't want people you know to see you during your rehabilitation, so the obvious solution would be to go somewhere else, right? You don't know anyone at Turtle Lake, so that makes it the perfect place to go."

"What did you mean by *us?*"

"I mean pack your bags, doc. We're going to spend the rest of the summer together at Turtle Lake."

He was off the couch in a millisecond. *"No way."*

"Give me one good reason why it isn't a great idea," she said. "My grandparents have a small place up there. It'll be perfect. I've already arranged for the other PTs to cover my regular patients."

He limped right past his chair toward the bedroom. "You want me to stay with your grandparents? I don't think so."

"It's not like they'll be there. They live in Florida year-round, but they keep the cottage so my parents and my sister and I can use it. It's right on the lake and it's semi-secluded. It's perfect."

"Nothing about this sounds perfect to me." He tried to close the door on her but she pushed it open and followed him. "Will you stop following me!"

"Nope. I'm going to come to your house every morning and follow your stubborn rear end around until you agree to come with me. I'll follow you around for the rest of your life if I have to."

He spun around, towering over her with a menacing glare. "You really would, wouldn't you? You would make my life miserable just to get your way."

She didn't even flinch. "You bet I will. I'll be here every morning when you wake up. For two hours a day you'll be stuck with me. I'll be your shadow, pal." She poked him in the chest with her index finger. "You may be stubborn, doc, but I'm worse."

She was going to be harder to shake loose than he'd thought. "Even if I wanted to, my parents would never go for it. They want me close by so they can frown at me and give me disapproving looks."

"Already taken care of. I discussed it with your parents before I came up here. It took a little bit of persuading, but they finally listened to reason."

"*My father,* the king of I'm-right-and-you're-wrong, listened to reason? Why do I find that hard to swallow?"

"By the time I finished explaining it all to him I had him convinced it was his idea in the first place, and your mother seems to agree with just about anything he says, so she wasn't too hard to sway. So, whaddaya say, doc? A few months up north?"

He was running out of excuses—and energy. "What about

your boyfriend? What will he think about you picking up and spending the summer with a stranger?"

"Don't have one. And you, doc, have run out of excuses."

His knee was beginning to throb, so he sat on the edge of the bed. "Give me a minute. I'm sure I can come up with something else."

She sat down next to him, close enough that he could feel the warmth of her arm next to his, though she wasn't quite touching him. "Believe it or not, I know how difficult this is for you. And frightening, and confusing. I want to help you." She laid a hand on his forearm, her voice barely above a whisper. "Let me help you."

He looked down at the fingers curled around his arm, disconcerted by the contrast between his pale, almost translucent skin and her rich, sun-burnished complexion. He'd become a ghost. A shadow of a man.

Was that really what he wanted?

Maybe a few months in a completely different atmosphere would do him some good. If he was looking for a compelling reason to go, he didn't have to look any further than the woman next to him. What man in his right mind would pass up a few months alone with a woman like Maggie?

The kind of man who knew that she deserved better—that she would expect it. To her, he was just another damaged human being she could fix. One that she was probably being paid well to fix. She'd said it herself yesterday, she didn't really care if he rotted in the chair, it was just a job to her. A paycheck.

But this wasn't about her. It was about him, and damn it, as much as he would have liked to deny it, he wanted his life back. Besides, if he did go, and failed, he'd be no worse off than he'd been before. Right? With her help, he'd at least have a chance.

"If you say no, I'll have to reduce myself to kidnapping. You don't want me to commit a felony, do you?"

An honest-to-goodness chuckle rose in his chest and it felt…good. It had been a long time since anyone had made him feel this way. "You win. When do we leave?"

Four

"**A**ren't you driving a little fast?"

Maggie gripped the steering wheel with both hands. It was all she could do to stop herself from wrapping them around Pete's neck and strangling him. He'd done nothing but complain since they left. She was driving too fast, or the music was too loud, or he didn't like the station she was playing. It was too hot in the car, or it was too cold.

He was *never* happy.

At the rate they were going, this was going to be a really long summer. "I'm going the same speed as everyone else."

He glanced at the speedometer. "I'd like to get there in one piece if you don't mind—and alive."

Yep, a *really* long summer.

"I'll get you there alive," she said, and added silently, if I don't kill you first. Although it would be really tough to strangle a guy who smelled so darned good. Maybe duct tape over the mouth would be the more practical solution. She was sure she had a roll in the back somewhere....

"When was the last time you cleaned in here?" he asked, nudging two empty diet-soda bottles under the seat with his foot.

Her grip on the steering wheel tightened and her knuckles went white, but she kept her mouth firmly shut. She knew he was just saying these things to annoy her, as some sort of revenge for dragging him from the safety of his suite.

He was scared.

"So what is this place called that you're taking me to?" he asked.

"Turtle Lake. It's about ten miles outside of Gaylord."

"You went there a lot when you were a kid?"

Maggie felt a familiar, deep sting of resentment. She'd spent *her* summers on the fat farm while her parents and sister went to the cottage. Until she turned fourteen and flat-out refused to go to that horrible place again.

"Not as often as I would have liked to," she told Pete.

"You have brothers and sisters?"

"One sister. Molly." The perfect child. The thin, pretty daughter who could do no wrong. Straight A's in school, valedictorian of her class—a feat she repeated in college. Met the perfect man five minutes after graduation and married him in a fairy-tale wedding complete with horse-drawn carriages. When Molly got pregnant six months later, Maggie secretly hoped she would balloon up to two hundred pounds, get horrible stretch marks and have fat ankles. Of course she didn't gain an ounce over the acceptable twenty-five pounds, and she'd lost it all by the time Maggie's niece was a month old—

complete with pancake-flat stomach. No stretch marks either, thank you, cocoa butter. Molly had the perfect body, the perfect husband, the perfect child, the perfect house. The perfect *life*.

It was so unfair.

"How about you?" she asked Pete. "Any brothers or sisters?"

"Only child."

"Were you spoiled?"

He shrugged, and looked out the window. "I was away at boarding school most of the time."

As they approached the exit for Gaylord, she merged over into the right lane. "Now there's a concept I've never understood. Why bother having kids if you're just going to ship them off to live somewhere else?"

"Never made much sense to me either, but as you pointed out, my parents aren't exactly warm and fuzzy."

She detected a distinct note of bitterness there. "I suppose you went to an Ivy League college, too."

"University of Michigan. I'll be paying off student loans for the next ten years."

"You paid for your own college?"

He flashed her a look, one that said back off. "Long story."

Point taken.

She took the exit for 32 and headed into town, passing the IGA and Wal-Mart, remembering they would need supplies. Although she doubted Pete was in any condition, physically or mentally, for a trip to the grocery store. On the way up she'd suggested stopping at a greasy spoon for lunch, but had to settle for drive-through fast food when he refused to get out of the car. Not that she was surprised. His confidence had been shattered. It would take him a while to get that back.

They had all summer.

She would get him settled in the cottage first, then make a trip back into town.

"Before we get there we should probably hammer out the specifics of living together," she told Pete.

He just smirked and shook his head.

"What?"

"I've never lived with a woman, much less one I've known for only three days. This is going to take some getting used to."

"You didn't live with your fiancée?"

He looked out the window again. "She came from a very traditional family. She wouldn't move in with me until we were married."

And from what Maggie had gleaned from the rumor mill at the hospital, she'd hit the road not long after the shooting. Maybe the prospect of having a disabled spouse was more than she'd bargained for. God knows, Maggie had seen it before, though the majority of spouses and significant others stood by their partners. The strong ones did, anyway.

"Well," she told Pete. "I don't do anyone's laundry but my own, I'm a lousy cook, and don't expect me to clean up after you. I think it's only fair that we share the chores."

When he didn't respond, she glanced over at him. His brow was furrowed. She knew exactly what he was thinking. "Give me a little credit, doc. I'm not going to ask you to do anything you're not physically capable of. We'll take it one day at a time, okay?"

He nodded and absently rubbed his knee.

"Maybe someday you'll tell me about it," she said.

"About what?"

"The shooting."

Not likely, Pete thought. He'd never talked to anyone about that day. They'd tried to get him to go to a shrink a couple of times—his parents had even had a few come out to the house—but he didn't need to rehash what he'd been through. God knows he'd been over it a thousand times in his mind— what he could have done differently. If he'd only run away from the sound of the gunfire and not toward it, if he hadn't stayed to work that double shift because half the staff was out with the flu. If only.

What happened had happened, and talking about it wouldn't change anything. It wouldn't give him back his knee, or make his colleague Rachel any less dead.

It was over and he was putting it all behind him.

"Interesting architecture," he said, noting the Bavarian theme and chalet-style buildings as they passed through the main part of town.

Maggie nodded. "Butt out. Gotcha."

At least she could take a hint. Although he still wasn't quite sure what to make of her. He'd tried, without much success, to push all of her buttons on the drive up. He didn't even do it on purpose anymore. He was just so used to antagonizing people, to pushing them away, it was second nature. But it made sense, if he was to be stuck with this woman for the entire summer, that he should at least make an attempt to be civil.

They exited town and hit a long stretch of green, rolling

farmland. The road twisted and turned for several miles, then Maggie veered the SUV down a narrow dirt road. She hadn't been kidding about the remote location. They appeared to be in the middle of nowhere.

Beyond the dense treeline and thick underbrush he caught occasional glimpses of a house here and there and flashes of shimmering blue water beyond. The scent of clean lake air washed over him. He used to love the water. It should have been soothing, yet it only reminded him of waterskiing and windsurfing and all the other things he could no longer do.

She followed the road about a half mile around the lake, then pulled onto a long dirt driveway. Weeping willow branches brushed the top of the SUV and dappled sunlight dotted the windshield. The trees opened up to deep-blue water—miles of it—and an endless stretch of clean white sand. The cottage was small and quaint and meticulously kept. The entire setting was picturesque—like a scene from *On Golden Pond.*

So why did a hollow, relentless ache settle deep in his chest?

Maybe because he'd just realized what he'd agreed to— an entire summer of torture. A summer to contemplate all he would never do again. And he couldn't back out. Not now. He was stuck here.

Wonderful.

"Home sweet home." Maggie pulled up in front of the cottage and cut the engine.

Pete opened the door and eased himself down. She'd insisted on leaving his chair back at his parents' house, so negotiating the uneven ground to get to the door was going to be tricky. He was still having a hell of a time putting any real weight on his leg.

"Stay right there," Maggie said, "I have something for you."

She walked around back, opened the hatch and fished something out, then continued around to his side. When he saw what she was holding he shook his head.

"*No way.* I refuse to use a cane."

"It's temporary. You need something to get you through the first couple of weeks, until we get that leg stretched out."

"I told you before, I am not going to limp around on a cane."

Maggie shrugged. "Have it your way. When I'm in town I'll stop by the medical supply and get you a walker."

He narrowed his eyes at her. "That's a joke, right?"

She shrugged again. "It's this or a walker, take your pick."

Oh, she was evil.

He looked down at the cane she was grasping. To her credit, it wasn't the silver, geriatric variety he often saw his older patients using. It was crafted from deeply stained cherry, with a gold band and a flat, ornately carved handle that showed a fair amount of wear.

"It was my grandfather's," she said, gazing at it with affection. "He used it for a couple years, before he needed a wheelchair, so it has sentimental value."

She was even more evil and scheming than he'd imagined. If he said no now, it would be some slight against this grandparent who she obviously held dear to her heart.

"He was your height, so it should be just about the right size," she coaxed, waving it in front of him.

Pure evil.

"Two weeks," he told her. "Two weeks and this thing goes in the closet."

"Whatever you say, doc," she agreed, handing it to him.

Tentatively, he reached out and took it from her.

"Do you know how to use it?"

He gave her an exasperated look.

"Save the sarcasm. It actually takes a fair amount of coordination. Particularly since you'll be using your left hand. You have to keep your steps in sync with the cane. To your benefit you have exceptional upper-body strength. You try it out while I take the bags inside."

Maggie disappeared behind the SUV and Pete gripped the cane in his left hand. It was comfortable, but strange and unfamiliar at the same time. He looked over to be sure Maggie wasn't watching—the last thing he needed right now was an audience—then took a few tentative steps, stumbling on the rocky ground. Damned if she wasn't right, it was difficult to coordinate his movements. His left hand wanted to swing forward with his right leg, but that meant his left leg bore the brunt of his weight. That was bad.

He tried again, slower this time, resting his weight on the cane as he stepped with his right leg, then, centering his weight on his right leg, he stepped with his left. He managed two successful steps before he nearly fell flat on his face.

Rather than let himself get discouraged, he took a deep breath and tried again. The afternoon sun beat down hard on his back, and sweat beaded his brow, but he was determined to get this right. If he could cross-country ski, he could do this, damn it.

Maggie watched Pete through the car window as she unloaded the bags. She knew if she could only get the cane in his hand, get him to try it, he would learn to use it. He was too proud not to. She also knew he wouldn't want her standing and watching, telling him what to do. He would want to figure it out for himself—which was both good and bad. And though he'd had a rough start and a bit of stumbling, already his steps were more in sync. What the cane would do, even more than aid his walking, was build his confidence. He would be able to move faster and worry less about stumbling or falling.

She watched the muscle in his bare left arm flex and contract as he moved slowly forward. His brow was knitted deeply in concentration and sweat had begun to soak through his shirt. He stumbled again, this time nearly taking a nose dive into the dirt, and she cringed. She wanted to run to his aid, but knew he'd only brush off her help. He needed to do this on his own. Stubborn bastard.

And she admired the hell out of him for it.

He stopped for a moment, both hands braced on the cane, and she wondered if that was it, if he'd had enough. He took a couple of deep breaths, straightened up and started over again. Then she had no doubt that he wouldn't stop until he'd perfected his technique. She breathed a quiet sigh of relief, hefted the last of the bags from the back and carried them to the door.

The truth was, it made her ache to see this once larger than life man so beaten down—and by his own pride. She would use whatever means were necessary, no matter how unconventional, to rehabilitate Pete, and when she'd taken him as far physically as she could, she was determined to make him see that living with a disability wouldn't make him less of a man.

Failure wasn't even an option.

Pete stretched and opened his eyes, disoriented at first by his unfamiliar surroundings. The cottage.

Dark paneled walls came into focus, lined with row upon row of framed family portraits. Red-checked curtains hung in wood-paned windows and a rickety wooden storm door led out to a screened-in side porch that overlooked Turtle Lake. The air was musty with a vague hint of some kind of flowery potpourri. It was all so…*quaint*. A pleasant change from his parents' mausoleum of a house.

On the rare occasion his parents had taken him along for family holidays, they'd stayed in five-star resorts and hotels. He tried to imagine his mother in a place like this, with no one to wait on her hand and foot. With no silk sheets, fine china or gourmet cuisine.

It was enough to make him grin.

He pushed himself to a sitting position on the threadbare old couch—which was a lot more comfortable than it looked—and glanced at his watch. He'd wandered around outside for a good hour after Maggie had left to get groceries, investigating his surroundings, practicing his new walk, until his arm trembled from the physical exertion. He hadn't meant to doze off, only to relax for a few minutes. But he felt surprisingly well-rested for having slept only an hour and a half. He was a little sore, but he felt, well, *good*. As if he'd actually accomplished something today. Something important.

The storm door squeaked on its hinges as Maggie stepped inside from the back porch. When she saw him sitting there, she smiled a bright, happy-to-see-you smile that instantly lifted his spirits. The body-hugging, low-cut tank top and short-shorts didn't hurt either. Her figure was above average with modest clothing on. Like this, she was…*wow*. On a scale of one to ten, she ranked right up there in the low twenties. Her breasts were full and round, and he'd bet his medical license they would feel fantastic pressed against his chest—or other places.

And if he didn't alter the direction of his thoughts, her body was going to raise more than his spirits.

"Well, look who's up," she said. "Have a good nap?"

He yawned and stretched. "Yeah, I didn't mean to doze off."

She gestured to the small kitchen at back of the cottage. "I got a bunch of deli meat and cheese and some whole grain bread if you're hungry."

"Maybe later," he said, looking for his cane, finding it just where he'd left it, on the floor beside the couch.

"In that case, would you like to join me for a swim?"

She didn't tack on the "it would be good for your leg" line, even though he knew she was thinking it. And knowing she was thinking it dashed his enthusiasm. Maybe he just didn't like someone telling him what to do. Or maybe it was because lately everything seemed to revolve around his disability. For once he would like to do something for the sake of doing it, not because it would be good for him. But he was stuck here, so he might as well make the best of it. The sooner he got on with the rehabilitation, the sooner he got on with his life.

Besides, a swim sounded pretty good.

"Yeah, I'll come with you," he said, using the cane to hoist himself up off the couch. "I just need a minute to find my swim trunks."

"Great. I'll meet you outside."

She disappeared into her room, and he hobbled into the adjacent bedroom and closed the door. It was on the small side and had the same dark paneling as the rest of the cabin. The full-size bed was made up with flowered sheets and a colorful hand-stitched quilt, and in the middle of it sat his bags.

He unzipped the one with his clothes and fished around for his swim trunks. He was tempted to take a moment to unpack and organize—a practice that had been hammered into him in boarding school. Instead he changed and grabbed a beach towel from the closet Maggie had pointed out to him earlier, then slowly navigated his way out the door to meet her on the beach. He'd pretty much mastered regular walking, but the wood steps from the porch proved to be another new challenge, as did walking on the beach. When he put weight on it, his cane sank deep in the sand, throwing him off balance.

Pete was so focused on not tipping over, he didn't notice Maggie standing knee-deep in the water. And when he did look up and see her, he was so stunned, he nearly fell flat on his face. He wasn't sure what he'd expected when she suggested they go swimming, but it sure as hell wasn't this.

She was wearing a bikini. And to call it brief would be a gross understatement. It was practically nonexistent. She might as well have gone out naked considering how little the four small, neon-yellow triangles covered. On a scale of one to ten, she'd just been bumped up to a solid thirty-five. Her breasts were perfect, her stomach smooth and flat, her arms and legs toned to perfection. She packed one hell of a body into that frame, even though in his opinion she was bordering on too thin. And though he was her patient, he was still a man.

He glanced up and down the beach, wondering who else might be enjoying the view. The only people he saw were too far away to get a good look. With the exception of a few boats slicing across the water, and a couple of swimmers here and there, the lake was practically deserted. He was guessing the area activities wouldn't really pick up until after the fourth of July—which was a mere week away. For now, the solitude would be nice.

Maggie turned her back to him and bent over, dipping her hands in the water, her bikini bottoms creeping further up her perfectly rounded backside. He wasn't sure what she was trying to prove dressing that way, or if she was trying to prove anything. Maybe it was a tactic she used for motivating her difficult patients—a definition he most definitely fell under. It would explain her impressive success rate. He'd done his homework, calling the hospital and inquiring about her reputation, and was told that indeed she was the best money could buy. Not that he'd expected any less from his parents.

Oh, if his parents could see her now...

Maybe this was normal for her. Maybe she was a nudist, and for her this was modest.

Either way, at this rate, it was going to be a really *long* summer.

Five

"The water's a little chilly," Maggie called out.

Oh good, Pete thought, peeling his eyes from her rear end. That would save him the hassle of a cold shower.

Although now that he thought about it, he hadn't considered *how* he would get into the lake. He didn't want to use the cane in the water and without it his leg hurt like hell, thanks to the vigorous workout earlier that afternoon.

"Come on," she called, waving him toward her.

"I better not," he called back. "I don't want to ruin your grandfather's cane."

"Here, let me help." Maggie waded toward him, her breasts swaying with every exaggerated step. "You can lean on me."

Oh yeah, Maggie's near-naked body pressed up against him. Don't think so. He took a retreating step. "If it's that cold, I think I'll skip it."

"Oh, don't be a wuss. It's not *that* cold."

Considering the tightly peaked nipples clearly visible through her bikini top, he would beg to differ.

She stepped up beside him and took his arm, wrapping it around her shoulders. Her other arm went around his back and her hand came to rest on his waist. The sexual urges that had lain dormant inside him for so long roared to life with a vengeance.

He couldn't do this. He couldn't touch her this way if they planned to keep the relationship professional.

"I really think I'd rather not," Pete said, attempting to lift his arm from her shoulder, trying to put a little space between them. "I don't want to hurt you."

"You won't hurt me," she insisted, gripping his wrist and molding herself up against him. "I'm a lot stronger than I look."

Aw hell, he could feel himself getting aroused, and with only swim trunks on, it was going to be real obvious in about thirty seconds if he didn't either get back into the cottage, or waist-deep in the water. And since the water was right there in front of him, that seemed the way to go.

"We'll take it slow," she said, easing forward, her grip on his waist tightening as he leaned his weight into her.

His right foot hit the water and he sucked in a breath. He usually only trekked into water this cold wearing a wet suit. "You call that a *little* chilly? It's freezing!"

"If you take it slow, you'll adjust." She took another step, urging him forward, then another, until the water reached his calves. She smelled exotic, like pure sex, and her right breast was cozied up against his side, which made concentrating on his steps more than a little difficult. Kind of like impossible.

Which would explain why he stumbled, losing his balance, and though Maggie was strong, he outweighed her by at least half. Once they started to go down she was helpless to stop it. And because their arms were wrapped around each other, they plunged face first in the water.

Frantically untangling themselves from one another, they both sat up, gasping at the shock of the extreme cold. It was like being tossed headfirst into a tub of ice. On the bright side, any concern Pete had of a conspicuous erection was doused by the frigid water.

This was a hell of a lot more effective than a cold shower.

"Or, we could just dive right in," Maggie wheezed, shaking the water from her hair. Holy cow, that was cold.

Pete slicked his hair back from his face. "I guess you're not as strong as you thought, huh?"

"I am so sorry." She put her hand on his bad leg. "Are you hurt?"

"Nope. Just cold and wet."

"This is my fault," Maggie said. "I shouldn't have pushed you to do something you weren't ready for."

"It's okay. No harm done."

She still felt guilty. She didn't know what had happened exactly. She should have been able to hold Pete upright. But when he had started to lean forward, her equilibrium had been thrown completely out of whack and she'd lost her balance. He could have been hurt.

But boy, did he look good sitting there, chest glistening in the sunlight. Even if he did have the pallor of the undead. The guy could really benefit from a couple of hours in the sun. Despite that, when they'd stood so close a minute ago, arms around each other, she'd felt the patient/physician line growing fuzzy. It must have been residual feelings from her former crush, when Pete hadn't even known she was alive.

Considering the looks he kept sneaking in the direction of her breasts, he noticed her now. Now that it was too late. Now that an intimate relationship would be immoral. Besides, she was sure he was only staring at her breasts because they were convenient, and he probably hadn't seen any for a while, locked up in the house the way he'd been. So in other words, he'd have been happy looking at any old pair of boobs, not necessarily hers.

Which made her feel worse instead of better.

What on earth was wrong with her? Physical contact was an integral part of therapy and it had never bothered her before. Not that she was *bothered* per se, just a little more *aware* than usual.

"You know what's really going to be fun?" he asked, goose bumps forming on his arms. "Getting me out of here."

"Do you think you can get up?"

"Honestly, I don't know. But if I don't get up soon, I'm going to turn blue."

She was beginning to shiver herself. "I guess it was a little bit colder than I thought. It doesn't really warm up until mid-July."

"That would have been nice to know."

"I could get the cane."

He shook his head. "It's an heirloom. I don't want to ruin it. Why don't you try pulling me up to my feet?"

"Are you sure?"

"I don't exactly relish the idea of crawling up to the sand. In fact, I don't even know if I *can* crawl."

Maggie pushed herself to her feet, bracing herself against a wave of dizziness. What the devil was wrong with her? It wasn't like her to lose her balance this way. Maybe it was hormones or pheromones or something.

Pete grabbed her hand. "You okay?"

"Yeah," she gave her head a little shake. "Just stood up too fast. Must be the cold." The late-afternoon breeze kissed her icy skin and she shivered. When she was sure she had her bearings, she held out her hands. "Okay, I want you to take my hands—and get a good grip. On the count of three, push up with your good leg and I'll pull you to you feet. If you feel yourself falling, just grab a hold of me and I'll steady you."

He shook his head in obvious disgust. "Christ, I'm glad no one can see us."

She would tell him he had nothing to be ashamed about—that his surviving the shooting was nothing short of a miracle—but she knew that wasn't what he wanted to hear. She held out her hands and he grasped them. "On the count of three. You ready?"

He gripped her firmly and nodded.

"Okay. One…two…three!" She pulled hard on his arms and he pushed off with his good leg, propelling himself upward. When he was upright and starting to tip forward, Maggie countered the action by stepping into him, arms around his back so she could steady him. Which put her at eye level with his throat—man, was he tall, and he weighed a ton. Nowhere near the one hundred and seventy-five pounds they'd recorded on his chart. She was guessing he was closer to two hundred—and not an ounce of that was fat. With him pressed against her, she could feel nothing but lean muscle flexing and contracting under her palms as he struggled to steady himself. His arms had circled her. One hand curled around her shoulder while the other rested firmly on her hip. So much skin touching skin.

A sizzle of awareness zinged through her bloodstream. She used to fantasize about Pete holding her this way—about what it would feel like. Fantasy paled in comparison to the real thing.

A good reason to let go.

"Well, you're up," she said, trying to ease back, but Pete held her firmly against him. God, did he feel good. She wanted to run her hands up his back, down his arms. She wanted to touch him all over.

Back away, she warned herself. But when she tried, he held on tight. "Um, Pete?"

He rested his chin on the top of her head. "Yeah?"

"Since you're up now, maybe you should let go?"

The hand on her hip tightened and wandered an inch or two lower. "I probably should. But it's been a long time."

"Since what?"

"Since I've held a woman this way."

You're just convenient, she told herself. He doesn't really want you. That didn't stop her legs from going soft, her head from feeling dizzy.

"You have to try not to think of me that way," she said. "I'm not a woman, just a therapist. Non-sexual. There's no reason to think of me as anything else."

"There are two pretty good reasons, and they're pressing against my chest."

Oh. My. God. "You know we can't do this. You're my patient."

He sighed, slow and deep. "I know. It just feels nice. I guess I missed it more than I realized."

"That will pass," she assured him. She would know. It had been quite a while for her, too. But as time passed, she began to lose that craving for physical contact, that need to be close to someone. She instead sated her craving for intimacy with books and movies and casual friendships.

He finally loosened his grip and she slipped under his left arm, so he could keep the brunt of his weight off his bad leg. Very slowly they made their way to the beach. Though it was only a few feet, it took several minutes, and she could see that he was in a considerable amount of pain. This had been a really bad judgment call on her part. For about a hundred different reasons.

When they reached the sand, she grabbed his cane and handed it to him, then helped him up to the cottage. When they were inside, Pete seated on the couch, she breathed a quiet sigh of relief. Only then did she really look at him and see the stark frustration on his face.

"I know you probably won't believe this, but you're doing really well, doc." She sat beside him. "It's just going to take time. We pushed a little too hard today."

He leaned his head back and closed his eyes.

She had the distinct feeling she was losing him, that he was going to give up before they had even gotten started. "First thing tomorrow we'll start stretching that leg. You'll be amazed what a difference it'll make."

He nodded.

The sarcasm and the bad attitude she could handle. It meant he was still feisty, still prepared to fight. The silence scared her. If he turned in on himself, she might not have the skills to draw him back out.

They had taken a huge step backward today, and she couldn't help feeling that she'd failed him somehow.

"Sonofabitch." Pete peeled the blood-coated latex gloves from his hands and tossed them on the floor. "Time of death, 11:36 p.m."

The metallic stench of blood filled the room—from the body of a fifteen-year-old who'd come in moments ago, his body riddled with bullets.

"He was too far gone, Pete." Rachel Weathers, the doctor assisting him, shook her head sadly. "He was a gang member, this was bound to happen sooner or later."

While the rest of the team cleared the room, Pete grabbed the kid's chart off the rack by the door. His student ID was clipped on top: Simon Richards, ninth grade. Jesus. They seemed to get younger and younger every year.

"Did his buddy make it?" he asked Rachel.

"You mean the one he blew two holes into? They took him up to surgery a few minutes ago. One bullet nicked his left ventricle and another shattered his spine. If he lives he'll be a quadriplegic."

Pete pinched the bridge of his nose. At times like this he almost wished he'd become a pediatrician or a dermatologist, though he knew, if given a choice, he wouldn't trade this for anything. Here in the ER, he knew he was making a difference, he was saving lives. Well, usually he saved lives. On nights like tonight the multiple traumas, the senseless violence, made him wonder why they bothered.

Rachel took the chart from his hands. "When word gets out what happened, there will probably be retaliation, which means more bodies. Why don't you run down to the cafeteria and grab us a bite to eat," she said. "You look like you could use a break. I'll hold down the fort until you get back."

He nodded, trying to remember the last time he'd eaten and, because he couldn't recall, determined that it had probably been too long. "Fruit salad?" he asked.

"And an Evian. Take your time, okay?"

He peeled the shoe guards off his feet, tossing them in the hazardous waste barrel, and started down the hall toward the elevator.

"Hey," Rachel called after him. "I'm seeing that new intern up in OB. Why don't we double for drinks tomorrow night?"

"I promised Lizzy I'd teach her how to water ski," he called back.

"In February?"

"Her parents have a place in Florida. We're flying down for the day."

"Didn't you guys just go rock climbing?"

"That was last month," he said, walking backward toward the elevator.

Rachel laughed. "You're going to wear the poor girl out before you make it to the altar—or is that the idea?"

Pete shook his head and smiled, watching as she disappeared around the corner. She knew as well as everyone else that he couldn't wait to get married and settle down.

He raised his hand to press the elevator button when he heard a loud pop—

Pete's eyes flew open and he sat up in bed, the last remnants of the dream clinging like a malignancy in his mind, his breath coming sharp and fast. Fingers of light slipped past the curtains and birds chirped outside the bedroom window.

He was safe in the cottage. Nothing bad could happen to him here.

It had been weeks since he'd had the dream. At least this time he'd been able to stop it before it got to the bad part. Before he relived the shooting, when he saw Rachel's lifeless body sprawled across the hallway.

If only he hadn't taken a break, he might have gotten to her sooner. Or if he'd been there with her, it might have been him instead…

He shook the thought from his head. He wasn't even going to go there. He'd already run it through his mind a million times and the conclusion was always the same.

He'd let his best friend die.

Tossing back the covers, he sat up and swung his legs over the edge of the bed. Cool, fresh lake air rustled the curtains as he grabbed his cane and hoisted himself up. His arm was still a little sore and his knee ached from yesterday's escapade, but he was determined not to let it get him down. He threw on a T-shirt and a pair of shorts and straightened the covers on the bed.

He glanced across the hall into Maggie's room and found it empty. Clothes were strewn everywhere, the covers on her bed a disheveled mess, and two half-unpacked bags sat beside the bed, their contents spilling over onto the wood floor.

He brushed his teeth and cleaned up, then headed out to the kitchen. She wasn't there either, but he found evidence of her breakfast. An open, half-empty container of low-fat cottage cheese sat on the counter next to a bowl of fruit salad half-covered with plastic wrap. Beside that sat a dirty bowl and spoon that she obviously hadn't bothered to wash.

Either she'd been in an awfully big rush to leave—although he couldn't imagine what pressing business she could have at eight in the morning—or she was a slob. Judging from the condition of her room, and the junk littering the inside of her SUV, he was guessing it was the latter.

He looked out back but didn't see her anywhere. Where the hell had she gone? At least the SUV was still parked out front, meaning she hadn't taken off on him. Not that he thought she would. She seemed pretty determined to keep him motivated. She'd looked downright complacent after the lake fiasco yesterday. It was obvious she blamed herself for pushing him too hard.

He only blamed himself. And he'd be a liar if he tried to tell himself he hadn't been damned close to giving up. It seemed as if, lately, his life was one disappointment, one frustrating setback after another. But yesterday he'd made some real progress. Feeling the sun beating down on his shoulders, the wind in his hair, the length of a soft, warm female body pressed against him, had made him feel the tiniest hint of his old self, the Pete he thought had died on that cold hospital floor alongside Rachel.

As always when he remembered Rachel, a shaft of pain sliced through his heart. She'd barely finished her residency, and was by far one of the most promising medical students he'd had the pleasure of working with. Working with her had made the long, seemingly endless double shifts so much easier to tolerate. It had been fun.

But no matter how adamantly he'd denied any romantic feelings toward Rachel, his fiancée, Lizzy, had been jealous of their friendship. She had always been terribly insecure, always fishing for compliments, needing reassurances that she was the center of his universe.

Pete swore that after he was released from the hospital, Lizzy had been relieved that Rachel was no longer around. All she talked about for those first few weeks was everything they would do when his leg was better. When he was back to normal. The sight of his healing wounds had appalled her. She was much happier pretending it was all a bad dream that would soon end.

It hadn't taken her long to grow frustrated by his slow recovery. For the first time in their year-long relationship the focus was no longer centered on her. Every day he didn't make a miraculous recovery, her aggravation grew more keen. Her mounting resentment hung like a lead curtain between them until he finally recognized the truth—less than perfect would never be good enough for her. She would never be satisfied married to a man with a permanent disability.

When he'd asked her to leave and never come back, sparing her the guilt of being the one to end the relationship, behind the hurt and rejection, he saw relief in her eyes. And somewhere deep down, he'd been relieved, too.

That was all in the past, he reminded himself. There was no point in dwelling on something he couldn't or wouldn't want to change.

Figuring the food would spoil left out in the heat, he put the cottage cheese and fruit in the fridge, then propped his cane in the corner and washed the dirty dish and spoon. He was just finishing up when the porch door opened and Maggie came through. He turned to ask her where she'd been, but all the air backed up in his lungs, making it temporarily impossible to speak.

She was wearing a pair of running shorts that hugged her like a second skin and a matching sport bra that crushed her breasts together to form a deep cleft. Man, did she have the cleavage, and she didn't seem the least bit shy about showing it off. Both items of clothing were soaked with sweat and her hair hung in damp ringlets around her face. When she saw him, she smiled.

"Morning, doc. You just get up?"

"Yeah. Looks like you got an early start."

"Up at the crack of dawn. I do forty-five minutes with free weights and jog for an hour every morning."

He used to jog, too. That was one more thing he would never do again.

Maggie joined him in the kitchen, opening the fridge and taking out a bottle of water. She smelled of sweat and sun and fresh air—a tantalizing combination. She threw back her head and took a long swallow of water, exposing her long, slender neck. There was something about her that was just so…elegant, despite her tendency to be sarcastic and downright belligerent.

The truth was, that was what he found so attractive. Her spunk, her zest for life and her passion. And he *did* find her attractive. There was no denying that. A man would have to be blind not to find a woman like Maggie desirable.

She dragged a hand across her sweaty brow, pushing her hair back from her forehead. "Have you eaten?"

"Not yet."

"I'd have a hearty breakfast if I were you. I'm going to work your tail off today."

He leaned against the counter. "I can hardly wait."

"Give me fifteen minutes to shower and change." She set the bottle and cap on the counter and trotted off to the bathroom.

Pete capped the water and put it back in the fridge. He found eggs, cheese and a variety of vegetables, so he fixed himself an omelet. He was just starting to clean up when Maggie reappeared, hair damp, dressed in a snug, low-cut tank top and terrycloth short-shorts.

Did the woman own a *single* modest article of clothing?

"Let's get started," she said.

"Give me a minute to clean up this mess." He set his dirty dishes in the sink.

"Just leave them. You can do it later."

"Why wait until later when it'll take me about two minutes to do it now?" he said, running the hot water and squeezing a drop of dish detergent on the sponge—both of which he found deep in the cabinet under the sink.

Maggie let out a long, exasperated sigh. "They're not going to go anywhere, you know."

"All the more reason to do it now." He scrubbed egg off his plate. "Then it won't be hanging over my head all morning."

"You mean there are men who voluntarily clean?"

"I can only speak for myself."

She propped her hip against the cupboard beside him and folded her arms under her breasts. "Well, I think you're some weird freak of nature."

"Gee, thanks."

"My mom would have needed dynamite to get my dad out of his chair to wash dishes. They're very traditional. She was a stay-at-home mom, and he's the breadwinner. She cooks and cleans and does the shopping, he works nine to five then sits in his chair and watches TV. How about your parents?"

"Boarding school, remember?" He rinsed the dishes and set them on the draining board. "I wasn't around to see what my parents did."

"Did it bother you? Being away from home, I mean."

"I hated being home. At least at school I had friends. Being home meant being alone."

"That's really sad," Maggie said, looking genuinely distressed. "And it explains why you had such a lousy attitude living there again. So many bad memories."

He was about to snap back with a sarcastic comment when he realized she was right. He'd been miserable. She'd done him a huge favor dragging him out of there. And he'd practically molested her on the beach yesterday. Talk about disrespectful. He was sure that catering to his overactive sexual urges wasn't part of the therapy, yet she'd been nothing but kind and patient and respectful. And he owed her a huge apology.

"Maggie, about yesterday—"

"No sweat. These things happen."

"I just want you to know, I have a lot of respect for you as a medical professional."

"You should. I'm damned good at what I do."

And only a little modest. He dried his hands and hung the dish towel on the refrigerator door. "Okay, I'm ready."

"I hope so, doc. We have a lot of lost time to make up for.

When I'm finished with you, you're going to be begging for mercy."

After all he'd been through, whatever she could dish out, he could take. "We'll just see about that."

Six

"Christ, that hurts. Aren't we finished yet?"

"You know what they say, doc. No pain, no gain." Maggie knelt on a pillow in front of Pete, grasping his calf, extending his leg and stretching the muscle. Sweat rolled down the side of his face and he clutched the couch cushion with both hands. She bent his knee, giving him a few seconds to relax, then eased it straight, going as far as the short muscles would allow—then farther.

He gasped in a sharp breath. "Do you get off on torturing people?"

She eased back. "Oh, stop being a baby. For someone so macho, you sure have a low threshold for pain."

He scowled down at her. "I am *not* being a baby. You're stretching it too far."

They'd been at it for nearly two hours. First she did a full evaluation to gauge his condition and see exactly what he was capable of. The past hour they'd spent doing various stretching exercises to lengthen the muscles. Honestly, he was holding up pretty well considering how hard she was working him. The problem here was pride, and it wasn't uncommon. Even though he'd agreed to the therapy, he was still having a lot of trouble accepting her help. He didn't like anyone, even her, seeing him this way. Seeing him struggle.

It made him cranky.

"Has anyone ever told you that you have a lousy bedside manner?" Pete asked.

"Okay, is this better? Oh, you poor baby," she cooed and patted his leg. "Does that hurt?"

He fixed her with a look that could burn through concrete.

"Yeah, that's what I thought. Now stop whining and give me one more stretch. One more and I promise we'll stop."

"That's what you said five minutes ago."

"Yeah, well, this time I'm not lying." She grasped his calf firmly. "Come on, doc, one more."

"Like I have a choice," he grumbled, gripping the edge of the couch. Teeth gritted, he braced himself as she eased his leg up. She watched his eyes, noting the exact instant it started to hurt, holding his gaze. A bead of sweat rolled down the side of his face and dropped to his T-shirt. "Breathe through it, doc. Stay focused. Stay with me."

When she finally eased it back down, he collapsed against the cushions, breathing hard. "That's it, I'm done. My leg is toast."

"You did good." She rubbed her thumbs along his calf, massaging the muscle. She didn't want him cramping up. Now, *that* would hurt. "Now we get to do something fun."

"How about a nap? That sounds like fun."

"How about berry picking? There's a patch of wild raspberries about a mile up the road."

"Berry picking?"

"It'll be fun." She propped Pete's foot on her folded leg to lift it so she could reach the underside of his thigh. His skin was clammy from the intense workout, his leg hair crisp under her thumbs as she kneaded them into the muscle. The skin they had grafted onto his knee had healed well, but there would always be scars. She wondered how he felt about that— not that she didn't already have a good idea.

"You can stop now," Pete said from above her.

"We have to cool the muscle down," she said. "You don't want to cramp up."

"Maggie."

Something in the way he said her name gave her shivers. She looked up at him, at the intense, steel-blue eyes staring down at her, and her stomach did a flip-flop. He looked as though he might eat her alive.

"You really *need* to stop." Pete's eyes darkened a shade and Maggie's blood began to simmer.

"Massage is an important part of the therapy," she said, not removing her hands from his leg.

If he was uncomfortable with any part of the treatment, she should stop immediately. The problem was, he didn't look uncomfortable. He looked as if he was about two seconds from tearing her clothes off. Which was beyond inappropriate and completely unprofessional—so why was her heart beating a million miles an hour? Why did her head feel soft and fuzzy, her breasts tingly?

"I'm telling you this for your own good. It's been over four months since I've been with a woman, and I'm about fifteen seconds from doing something I shouldn't."

This was his fault really, forcing her into these casual circumstances. If they had been in a professional setting, in the therapy center at the hospital, she wouldn't be having all these inappropriate urges to touch him.

She wondered what he would do if she slid her hands farther up his thigh. Sitting nearly eye-level with his crotch, she could clearly see the effect this was having on him. She should have been embarrassed by her behavior, but all she felt was excited.

And naughty.

"Five seconds," Pete warned, sitting up, as if preparing to pounce. She could feel the muscles in his thigh tense under her fingers. She could see the fire in his eyes.

"Four…"

She really needed to pull her hands away, but felt frozen in place.

"Three…"

He was leaning forward, as if he were getting ready to kiss her.

"Two…"

Her lips tingled in anticipation, her head tipped to the right.

"One."

What was she *doing?*

She yanked her hands away from his leg and sat back on her heels. "Sorry. That was unprofessional of me. If you were…*uncomfortable,* I should have stopped right away. It won't happen again."

Uncomfortable. That was a mild way to describe what he was feeling right now. If she hadn't pulled away that exact second, he'd have her on the floor right now, bad knee or not, professionalism be damned. She would never know just how close he'd been to tearing that skimpy top off her with his teeth.

"This is your fault," she said, but her voice sounded whispery and soft and he could see the flutter of her heartbeat at the base of her throat. She was just as excited by this as he was.

Interesting.

He sat back and folded his arms across his chest, not even trying to hide the fact that he was turned on, amused to see her eyes stray to his crotch, widen slightly, then dart away. "And how is it *my* fault?"

"This wouldn't happen back at the rehab center. The atmosphere here is too...casual."

He shrugged. "Hey, it was your idea to come here."

"Only because you wouldn't come to the hospital, or use the room in your parents' house. You didn't give me a choice."

It took an awful lot to ruffle her, but once she got her panties in a bunch, Maggie was a lot of fun to tease. "So you got fresh with a patient, it's not the end of the world."

She bristled at the accusation. "I did *not* get fresh with you. Massage is a part of the therapy. It's not my fault you have sensitive thighs."

"That's not the only thing I've got that's sensitive right now," he said, his gaze straying downward.

Maggie let out a snort. "What is this, *junior high?*"

"You have the hots for me. Admit it."

"In your dreams, pal." She stood up, grabbed the pillow she'd been kneeling on, and threw it at him. "You are *so* not my type."

He caught the pillow and laughed. As the sound filled his ears, he realized it was the first time since the shooting that he'd really laughed.

And damn, did it feel good.

But not nearly as good as Maggie's lush lips would feel against his own. Not nearly as good as her body had felt pressed against him as they'd stood in the icy water yesterday.

He wanted to feel that again.

He really shouldn't. He'd promised himself he would keep their relationship professional, but that was before he knew she was attracted to him. Before he realized how attracted he was to her. There was something about her, something that appealed to him, and it wasn't just her body. He *liked* her. And he had to know what it would feel like. What *she* would feel like.

No, he shouldn't, but he was going to anyway.

"Help me up?" he asked, holding his hand out. She grasped it and helped pull him to his feet. As soon as he was upright and steady, he cupped one hand behind her head, slipped his fingers through her dark, silky hair, lowered his head, and kissed her.

For a second she seemed too stunned to move. He waited for her to push him away, or possibly slap him. Instead, she sighed against his mouth. Her head tilted and her lips softened and she leaned into the kiss. Her lips were as soft and sweet as he'd imagined.

Just to see her reaction, he nipped her lip with his teeth. She whimpered and pressed herself against him.

He knew he should end it right there, but now that he'd come this far, he had to taste her. He touched his tongue to her lower lip.

She planted her hands on his chest, and he knew he'd gone too far. He waited for that inevitable shove, for her to push him away. Instead she curled her fingers into the fabric of his shirt. Her lips parted, inviting him in, and he would never turn down an invitation like that. Not from her.

Though he would have guessed her to be the take-charge type, she was almost shy as his tongue slid over hers. She tasted sweet and tangy and his insides instantly caught fire. He lost himself in the heat of her mouth, the softness of her body pressed against him. It was just so…sweet. So not like the aggressive, outspoken Maggie he was used to.

But to hold this sort of power over her, to alter the dynamics of their relationship, felt wrong somehow. Frankly, it scared the hell out of him. But man, he wanted her. He had to do something to break the mood, before this got out of hand.

He shifted her head so he could kiss his way along the line of her jaw up to her ear. She shivered in his arms.

"I told you," he whispered.

Her eyes were closed and she had a dreamy look on her face. "Told me what?"

"That you have the hots for me."

Her eyes slowly opened and she looked up at him, confused for a second, then her eyes narrowed and she shoved him back. "You kissed me just to prove you're *right?*"

Oh, if she only knew. Instead of gathering her back up in his arms and showing her what he was really feeling, he flashed her a slow, cocky grin.

"Oh, you are *low.*" She whirled around and stomped off, mumbling to herself, and Pete felt like slime. Despite his bad leg, it would seem he hadn't lost his ability to seduce a woman.

And if her reaction was any indication, he'd done a pretty fair job of hurting her, too.

"This is dumb."

Maggie looked back at Pete, filled with smug satisfaction. They'd been out there thirty minutes and he'd been complaining for twenty-nine. She watched him try to hold his cane and the metal pail while plucking wild raspberries off the bushes. He'd dropped the bucket four times, spilling his berries all over the ground, before he'd figured to hang the bucket on the wrist of the hand clutching the cane so he could pick with the other. She might have helped him if she didn't still feel like punching him in the nose.

That's what he got for messing with her.

She still couldn't believe she'd let him kiss her. That she'd been so susceptible to his charms. And as humiliated as she'd felt afterward, she recognized his behavior as a natural step in his recovery. He was reestablishing his sexuality, asserting himself as a man. She just happened to be the only female around to take up the slack.

That didn't mean she couldn't get a little good old-fashioned revenge.

"Dumb or not, we aren't leaving until your bucket is at least half full," she said. "Unless you want to walk back."

"There aren't that many berries here to pick."

"It's still early in the season. You have to look under the leaves. They like to hide."

Which would necessitate him bending and crouching, which was nearly impossible for him to do at this point. At the rate he was going, they might be out there all night.

"I'm getting eaten alive by mosquitoes," he complained. "If I get West Nile it's going to be all your fault."

"We put bug spray on."

"I must need more. Why don't you give me the keys to the truck and I'll go get it."

She gave him a how-stupid-do-you-think-I-am? look and he mumbled something about her being evil.

"This is your revenge for that kiss, isn't it?"

She just smiled at him.

"If I kissed you again, I'll bet I could talk you into driving me back."

She didn't doubt that he could. When he'd kissed her earlier, her brain had completely shorted out. He could have asked her to parade around naked on the beach and she probably would have done it.

"Keep those lips to yourself, buddy. There will be no more hanky-panky."

"You can't tell me you didn't enjoy it."

She plucked a few berries and dropped them in her pail. "That's completely beside the point. I'm a therapist and you're my patient. There are certain rules I have to follow. You're the last person on the planet I should be kissing."

"So you admit that you enjoyed it."

Did he really need an ego-stroking? Did he not have the slightest clue how gorgeous he was? How crazy he made her? "Yeah, doc, it was freaking wonderful—better than chocolate-covered cherries. But suppose an attractive woman came into the ER for treatment. Would you kiss her?"

"Of course not!"

"Then I rest my case." She set her pail on the ground behind her and crouched down to reach a cluster of low-hanging branches covered with juicy berries. She interpreted his following silence as a concession.

"I'm ready to go," he said a minute later.

"You wish." She dropped a handful of berries in her pail, and they landed in the bottom with a gentle thunk. "What the—"

Her pail was empty! Pete stood next to her, a look of complete innocence on his face, his own pail nearly filled to the top.

"You stole my berries! You cheater."

Pete shrugged. "You only said my pail had to be half full. You never said anything about me picking them myself."

She shook her head. "You'll stoop to any level, won't you?"

"There's something you should know about me, Maggie."

"Oh yeah, what's that?"

"When I set my mind on something I usually get it." He flashed her the sexy smile that made her heart beat faster, and pinned her with his steel-blue eyes. "And I always play dirty."

Pete raised his hand to press the elevator button when he heard a loud pop from the direction of the ER, as if someone had set off a firecracker.

"What the—" He spun toward the noise. Who would be dumb enough to blow off fireworks in a hospital? Light one a little too close to an oxygen tank and they would all be blown to kingdom come. Three more quick pops split the silence, followed by the shatter of breaking glass and a bloodcurdling

scream. Then all hell broke loose. People were rushing down the hall toward him, away from the ER. It took his mind several seconds to register that a few people were sprayed with blood, though no one appeared to be injured.

Instinct kicked in and his legs were moving on their own. He fought his way back toward triage as another round of popping reverberated through the halls. When he rounded the corner, he saw Rachel lying face-down in the hallway, a bright-red stain seeping across the back of her shirt.

"No!"

Pete woke with a start, sitting up on the couch. He was soaked with sweat and nausea churned his stomach.

It was the dream. It always made him feel nauseous.

He tried to swallow but his mouth was dry.

"You okay, doc?"

He turned his head, saw Maggie standing in the kitchen looking concerned. He caught the scent of seared beef drifting in from the back porch. He must have dozed off while she was making dinner.

"Yeah," he said, his voice raspy. "Bad dream. Could I have a glass of water?"

"Of course." She grabbed a bottle of water from the fridge and brought it over to him, sitting on the arm of the couch beside him.

He twisted the cap off and took a swallow, felt the nausea begin to ease, the swimmy feeling in his head clearing.

Maggie reached up, touched his forehead. "You're all sweaty. Are you sure you're okay?"

"Fine," he lied. "I'm fine. I probably just got too much sun this afternoon."

Though she didn't look altogether convinced, she didn't press the issue. "I was just about to wake you. Your steak is ready. I hope you're hungry."

"Starving," he said, even though the thought of eating anything right now was enough to gag him.

He grabbed his cane and pushed himself up from the couch, his legs—even his good one—feeling wobbly from all the exercise, and joined Maggie at the kitchen table. She'd fixed him an ear of corn that was slightly scorched on one end, a side salad, and an enormous, juicy steak. Looking at it, he felt the slightest twinge of hunger. "I thought you said you can't cook."

"Ask me to follow a recipe and I always forget some essential ingredient and ruin the entire thing. Tossing a steak on the grill, I can do."

"Where is yours?" he asked, gesturing to her lone salad.

"I don't eat beef."

"You're going to eat something other than lettuce, aren't you?"

"I'm not very hungry."

"You had cottage cheese and fruit for breakfast, a diet shake for lunch. When do you eat *real* food?"

"For me, this *is* real food. I'm still on a diet."

He looked her up and down. "What for?"

She folded her arms under her breasts and glared down at him. "If you think that's going to get you back on my good side, it won't work. I have no illusions about the way I look."

"I'm serious, Maggie. You look fine the way you are. Why would you want to lose more?"

"Only a former fat person can understand. I have a goal weight and I won't be happy until I reach it."

"Even if that means being *too* thin?"

She slid into the seat across from him. "There's no such thing as too thin."

Boy, was she wrong about that. "Apparently you've never seen any pictures of me when I was a kid."

"You were skinny?"

"In tenth grade I was six feet tall and weighed about a hundred and thirty pounds fully dressed."

She raised a skeptical brow. "*You* were that skinny?"

"I was a bean pole."

She stabbed a forkful of salad and shoveled it in her mouth. "So, what happened?"

"I got tired of the other kids teasing me, and the pretty girls ignoring me, so I started drinking protein shakes and going to the weight room every morning for half an hour before class. After about a month, when I really started to see results, I upped it to an hour.

"I joined the lacrosse team, started playing soccer. Girls started to notice me. By my senior year I was in the weight room every day by 4:00 a.m and again after classes for another hour or two. When I started college, I was six-three and weighed two-twenty."

"Which explains why all that muscle you lost since the shooting didn't turn to flab. You're naturally thin." She said it like he was some freak of nature.

"We're not so different, you know. You have to work to keep weight off, and I have to work to keep it on."

She speared her lettuce, staring at it with distaste. "Frankly, I'd rather have your problem."

"Maggie, you look great just the way you are, and I'm not

saying that just to get on your good side. I think it's pretty obvious I find you attractive."

Instead of being flattered by the compliment—which, *silly him,* he would have expected—she bristled with indignation. "And I must have seen you a hundred times in the hospital when I was fat, and you didn't look twice at me."

"I was engaged. I didn't look twice at anyone."

How did the guy always manage to say exactly the right thing? And if he loved his fiancée that much, he must have been devastated when she had ended the relationship. He had to be hurting, and she probably wasn't helping. She had to remind herself, as cocky and frustratingly charming as the guy could be, he'd been through hell, and there was a fine line even she couldn't cross.

She couldn't let it drop either.

"You still can't deny that looks are important to you," she said. "I saw your fiancée. She was gorgeous. You guys were the perfect couple."

Something flashed in his eyes. Not hurt exactly. Something darker. And she had the sinking feeling she'd pushed too far, that her toes had edged over the line.

"You can't believe everything you see, Maggie. Things are not always what they seem."

Seven

"**O**kay, push against my hand again. This time try to hold it."

Pete sat on the deck floor at the top of the stairs, his foot braced against Maggie, who knelt on the sand four steps down. Gripping the wood plank, he pushed with his leg, wincing as pain shot up to his knee. They'd been stretching the leg extensively every morning, and again in the evening, for ten days now, gradually adding resistance. It still hurt like hell though.

Between the stretching and resistance, the long walks on the beach she was taking him on every day and the swimming in the evenings, he had to admit he was walking better. So much so that he was getting a little antsy for the real therapy to begin.

Though he couldn't deny he enjoyed the time they spent together. He'd never been the long, casual stroll type—if it didn't make him sweat, what was the point?—but with Maggie it was different. She was easy to talk to and she had a good sense of humor. He *liked* talking to her. Sometimes they didn't even talk, they were just together. He liked just *being* with her.

He thought of all the things he and Lizzy had done together—the skiing and parasailing and cycling and a dozen other activities—but he couldn't recall a single time when they'd just sat together on a warm evening drinking iced tea and talked. He couldn't recall her laughing much, or making him laugh. Their relationship had been one of mutual respect and common interests. And whenever they did talk, it was usually about her law practice, or fashion or her latest hairstyle.

They'd never talked about things that mattered. About feelings. Now that he considered it, she was a lot like his parents in that way.

The thought gave him a cold chill.

Maggie, on the other hand, seemed to hold nothing back.

"Make sure you extend the leg as much as you can while you push," she said, and he tried to comply. Sweat poured from his forehead and dripped into his eyes. It was the second day in a row that the temperature had hit ninety before noon and the humidity was so thick the air sat like wet cotton in his lungs. He didn't dare complain though, or she would only point out that he wouldn't be melting in the heat if they were at the hospital PT center. That if he weren't so stubborn that's exactly where they would be.

And she would be right.

If the heat wasn't distracting enough, Maggie was wearing another low-cut, form-fitting tank and from his higher vantage point he could see right down the front it. He was trying hard not to stare at her openly, but come on, even he had his limits. Her skin was golden from the sun and lightly freckled. Her breasts were so full and round and soft-looking…

"You're not pushing." she said.

He tore his eyes away from her cleavage. "Sorry."

She abruptly let go of his leg. "If you're not even going to try!"

"I am trying," he said. "I just got distracted. It's your fault."

"How is it my fault?"

"Are you kidding? Look at you."

She looked down at herself. "Yeah? Here I am. What about it?"

"Your clothes," he said.

"Yes, I'm wearing clothes."

Man, was she a sass. "*Barely.* Your shorts couldn't be any shorter, and look at that shirt. If it were cut any lower you'd be falling out of it."

"What do you want me to wear? Jeans and a turtleneck?"

"What do you wear at the hospital?"

"Scrubs."

"So why don't you wear that?"

"What are you, a prude? You haven't noticed that it's about a million degrees out?"

"I just don't think it's very professional," he said, already seeing this was a losing battle. Once she got on the defensive, it was all over.

"*Professional?* You're one to talk, Mr. It's-too-hot-for-a-shirt. Did it not occur to you that seeing you half-naked might be a distraction to me?"

If it was, she sure didn't let it show. He was so used to women staring at him, her total lack of interest lately had been disconcerting. If what she said was true, and he *was* a distraction, she did a fair job of hiding it.

But hearing it straight from those luscious lips was a much-needed confidence boost.

"That's different," he said, knowing he was really going to get her hackles up now. In fact, he was kind of hoping he would. Though he felt like a degenerate for it, getting her panties in a twist was a major turn-on. "I'm a guy. Guys are supposed to go shirtless in hot weather."

She closed her eyes and took a long deep breath, as if gathering all her patience. "Look, doc, I worked hard for this body and I'll be damned if I'm going to cover it because you're a male chauvinist pig."

Pete suppressed a smile. "So you think we should be equal, that what's considered socially acceptable for me, should be the same for you?"

"Exactly," she said.

He shrugged. "Okay. Take it off."

A little wrinkle formed in her brow. "Take what off?"

"Your shirt. I don't want to be accused of being sexist. If you want to make this fair, we'll both do my therapy topless. Problem solved."

She looked as if she couldn't tell whether he was serious or poking fun at her. "You know that isn't what I meant."

"Hell, if you're that proud of your body, show it off. Here, I'll help." He grabbed his cane and boosted himself up.

Maggie rose to her feet, swaying a bit before she righted herself. "Sit back down, we're not finished."

He lowered himself down one step, toward her. "Not until the shirt comes off."

She watched him, eyes wary, as if she thought he might actually be serious. But she held her ground. "Like you really think I'm going to do your therapy topless."

He nodded thoughtfully, taking another step. This time she took a step back. "You're right, that probably would be a bad idea. Someone might see. There is still the issue of you distracting me though. Unless..."

Her eyes narrowed. "Unless what?"

"I think I know what we can do to fix the problem."

She propped her hands on her shapely hips. "I'm afraid to ask what that would entail."

"It's simple. You show me your breasts, then I'll know what they look like, then they won't distract me anymore."

She glared up at him. "You're enjoying yourself, aren't you?"

He stepped down onto the sand, right in front of her. "Although you know, once I see them, I'm going to want to touch them."

She was trying hard to keep her composure, but he could tell he was ruffling her feathers. Her pulse fluttered at the base of her neck and color climbed high up her cheeks.

The truth was, all this talk of her breasts was getting him hot. He'd been working hard to think of her in professional terms only. But after that kiss, after she'd practically melted in his arms, he was having a hell of a time. Maybe he should just say what the heck...

"Oh no you don't," Maggie said, her heart hammering about a million beats per second. He had that look again, the one he'd had when he kissed her.

She took an involuntary step back.

"Oh no I don't what?" he asked taking another step toward

her, until they were nearly touching, and she had to look *way* up to see his face. Why did he have to be so darned big? And why did he have to smell so delicious? Soap and sweat and man. It was doing funky things to her head.

"You look like you're going to kiss me. And if you try it, I'll have to do something drastic."

"Like what? Kiss me back?"

"Yeah, you wish."

"Yeah, I do," he said, and the hungry look in his eyes…suffice it to say, her knees instantly went weak. But she refused to back down, to let him get the best of her. Though somewhere, deep down, she wanted him to kiss her—she ached for it even. She could be happy kissing Pete every day for the rest of her life.

Oh yeah, like that's gonna happen, the rational part of her brain taunted. The man is so far out of your league. Why would he settle for a woman like you? You're just convenient.

"This isn't professional," she tried, knowing how lame it sounded. It didn't help that her voice was shaky.

"I won't tell if you don't." He reached up and touched her hair, wrapping one curly lock around his index finger. It made her think of the last time he'd kissed her, the way he'd slipped his fingers through her hair and cupped her head, taking control. How much she'd enjoyed being allowed to relinquish control for a while. Sometimes she got so tired of this driving need to keep the upper hand in all situations.

And he knew as well as she did, if she really didn't want him to kiss her, all she had to do was tell him. If she insisted, he would back off. Unfortunately the message was getting scrambled somewhere between her brain and her mouth.

Pete lowered his head and her eyes drifted shut. She felt his fingers slipping along her jaw, through her hair.

He was going to kiss her again…

And then what? she wondered. Where would it go from there? A summer fling? Would she sleep with him, only to become desperately attached, then they'd have to go their separate ways when the summer was over, when his therapy was finished? She'd played that game before, and all it had gotten her was a broken heart. It wasn't her that Pete wanted, he was merely looking to assert himself as a man, to feel whole again. She just happened to be the only willing and available female. And she was very easily replaceable.

She felt the whisper of his breath on her lips, felt his fingers sliding through her hair, then his lips brushed against hers…

"No!" she said it so fiercely she startled them both.

Pete dropped his hand from her hair and took a step back.

"I can't do this, doc. It's not that I don't want to. Believe me, I do. I just don't feel it would be right. It's almost like I'd be taking advantage of you."

"Maggie—"

"If the way I dress really bothers you I can run into town this afternoon and pick up some scrubs."

"You don't have to do that."

"I don't want you to be uncomfortable."

He took hold of her arms. "Maggie, it's okay. I was teasing you and it got out of hand. I'm sorry."

So what was he saying? He'd never really wanted to kiss her in the first place? That it was all just a joke?

She tried not to let it sting. Isn't that the way it had always been? She was a lot of fun in the back seat of a car, convenient to fool around with, but when it came down to relationships, guys always went for the skinny girls. The eye candy. She'd thought that would change when she lost weight. Apparently she'd been wrong.

Maybe it hadn't been her body at all, but her personality that had driven people away. Maybe the only time guys could tolerate her was when her mouth was occupied doing something other than forming words.

The idea made her sick to her stomach.

"You want me to sit back down?" he asked.

"No, I think we've both had enough of that for today. I'll grab the pails and we'll go berry picking."

He rolled his eyes. *"Again?"*

Well, he was back to his old stubborn self. How refreshing.

"Aren't they out of season yet?"

"Nope."

"How about some real therapy for a change?"

She ignored the sarcasm. "After that we need to run into town for some groceries. You're eating us out of house and home."

She saw instant wariness in his eyes.

"I think I'll hang back."

"You need to get out around people, doc. You can't hide away forever."

He started up the steps to the porch. "When I'm walking better."

"But you *are* walking better. Look how easily you just walked up those stairs. Four days ago it would have taken you twice the time."

He turned to her. "Maggie, I'm just not ready. I'm going to go throw on a shirt. Grab the pails and I'll meet you at the truck."

Maggie sighed as she watched him limp away. If only he were even half as confident physically as he was sexually. She knew he was afraid he might stumble and embarrass himself, and truthfully, that could happen. It could also happen a month from now, or six months from now. He was going to have to learn to live with that. He couldn't stay cooped up inside forever.

"If you don't come out with me soon," she called after him. "I'm going to have to do something drastic."

"Do you have any fives?"

Pete mumbled a curse and handed over his five to Maggie. "I think you're cheating."

With a smug grin, she set the pair down in her ever-growing pile on the coffee table. "Anyone ever tell you you're a poor loser?"

What did she expect? After being creamed at Connect Four, slaughtered at Aggravation, and completely sunk at Battleship, he was beginning to get a complex. He was sure with Go Fish being a game of luck, he would have a shot of winning at least a few hands.

"Do you have any queens?"

He cursed again and handed it over. "What are you, telepathic?"

She dropped the queens on her pile.

Outside, thunder rumbled and rain tinged against the aluminum awning over the porch. It had rained all afternoon and into the evening. With no television to keep them amused, and his refusal to go into town, Maggie had raided the game closet.

"This isn't fair," Pete said. "You probably played these games a million times when you were a kid, you and your sister."

"Oh, don't be such a baby. Do you have any aces?"

"Go fish."

She chose a card from the center, smiled, then set another pair down. "Your turn."

"Why is it, when I ask you about your past, you change the subject?"

Her brow tucked into a neat little frown. "I don't do that."

"Yeah, you do. When I asked if you came here a lot as a kid, you said not as much as you would have liked to. What did you mean by that?"

The frown deepened. "It's a long story."

He tossed his cards down on the table and hoisted himself up off the floor onto the couch. "Anything to circumvent another humiliating loss." He patted the couch beside him. "Come on, let's talk."

Though she didn't look thrilled with the idea, she set her cards down and circled the table to sit on the couch beside him, close enough that their thighs were just barely touching. She seemed to do that a lot—walk just close enough so that her shoulder bumped lightly against his biceps, touch his arm when she talked to him, lean over him during the therapy so that her breast would very lightly rest against his leg. Though he might have thought so at first, he was sure she didn't do it on purpose. Maybe she was just a naturally physical person. Something he'd never been. But he liked the way it made him feel. The intimacy of being physically close to another person.

He liked being close to Maggie.

"I'll talk," she said. "But first you have to tell me why you had to pay for your own college."

"Simple. I didn't want to be stuck under my father's thumb anymore. As long as he paid for my school, he controlled what classes I took, where I lived. I refused to let him run my life any longer. After the shooting, he jumped at the chance to have me back under his roof, to manipulate me again."

"So why did you go? Surely someone else could have helped you."

"Oh, no," he said. "Now it's your turn. You have to tell me why you said that about coming up here."

"Until I was fourteen, my family spent their summer vacations up here," Maggie said, looking down at her clasped hands. "I spent mine at camp."

"Why would they come up here and send you to camp?"

Somewhere deep down he could see an old wound split open and ooze bitterness.

"It was fat camp, doc. For overweight kids."

He'd heard of places like that, but he had always been under the impression they were for kids so heavy their health was at risk. "I've seen pictures of you on the wall, you didn't look that heavy to me."

"I was chubby. Not huge or anything. Actually, I was pretty small compared to a lot of the other kids, so they always kind of resented me being there. But I come from a family full of naturally thin women. Being fat wasn't acceptable."

He slid his hand down over her clenched fingers, felt her relax the slightest bit. "And traumatizing you was acceptable?"

"I think my mother believed my weight reflected on her as a parent. She really resented me for not being perfect. I used to hear her talking to her friends when she thought I wasn't around. She would say, 'Molly is my special child. She plays the piano and paints beautiful pictures and gets honors in school. Maggie just likes to eat.'"

Pete felt a sting of resentment on her behalf. "That's cruel."

"Yeah, it did wonders for my self-esteem." She said it casually, but he didn't miss the bitter undertone. He gave her hand a squeeze. "It's probably what prompted me to let Joe Murphy get all the way to third base in the backseat of his car when I was fourteen."

"Fourteen?" He hadn't even been to *first* base by then. "How old was he?"

"Seventeen. Bear in mind, I was in a D-cup bra by thirteen, so I looked a lot older than I was. And most guys saw right past the fat and focused on the breasts. Unfortunately, that's *all* they saw."

Pete had to admit, they were kind of hard to ignore. To a hormonally challenged teenaged boy they would be a beacon.

"Joe told me how beautiful I was and how much he liked me. Imagine my surprise the next day when I saw him in the hall and he had his arm around Christine D'Angelo. Who, of course, was a toothpick."

"Guys can be jerks," Pete said, feeling the need to apologize on behalf of the entire male population. "I'm sure it wasn't personal."

"Joe's best friend Dave came up to me in the hall and said he was sorry for what Joe did, that he was a real jerk. I was beautiful and nice and any guy would be lucky to go out with me. Of course I swooned, and when Dave asked if I wanted to go out with him, I practically fainted at his feet."

Pete winced, afraid he wasn't going to like what was coming next. He turned Maggie's hand over, laced his fingers through hers and she didn't stop him. Touching her, showing her that he cared was the only way he knew how to console her. "I don't think I want to hear the rest of this."

"You'd think I would have learned my lesson the first time," she said. "But that night, there I was in the back of Dave's car, and the next morning at school, he avoided me like the plague."

Pete gripped her hand tighter, shook his head with disgust.

"You would think at that point I would have caught on. But remember, I was a low self-esteem girl. Reid was next, then Mike. Finally it got back to my sister Molly what was going on and she had the extreme pleasure of informing me that all these guys had some kind of bet going to see who could get me to go all the way."

Pete mumbled a foul word under his breath.

"At this point everyone at school had heard about it, so, of course, it got back to my mother, and I went from being Maggie the fat one to Maggie the slutty one. You can probably imagine how well that went over. She said I should have known better."

It had happened years ago, when he didn't even know her. Even so it made Pete feel like putting his fist through a wall. How could anyone be that cruel? How could they use an innocent, vulnerable girl that way?

He rubbed his thumb along the edge of her palm, wishing there was something he could do, something he could say to erase the hurt in her eyes. To show her that those boys didn't matter anymore.

"My mom told me that if I ever wanted to date a nice boy I'd better lose some weight. Like, a nice boy would never date a fat girl. Maybe she thought I deserved what I got."

"I don't think I ever want to meet your mother. I'd probably end up saying something I'd regret."

Maggie shrugged and pulled her hand free, leaned forward and began gathering the cards from their abandoned game. "She did the best she could. If nothing else it toughened me up."

"That's no excuse for the way you were treated."

"No, but it's just the way things are." Maggie yawned and looked at her watch. "I didn't realize how late it is. I'm beat."

It was barely nine-thirty, but Maggie usually went to bed around ten, if not earlier. Not unusual considering she was up at the crack of dawn exercising. It was no wonder she ate like a bird and worked out so much. Those boys had humiliated her, her mother had shattered her self-esteem. And he was guessing he probably hadn't heard everything. What other horrible things had Maggie dealt with growing up?

He wasn't sure he wanted to know.

"We have a long day ahead of us tomorrow, so make sure you get a good night's sleep," she told him, rising from the couch.

He grabbed her hand again. "I know you probably won't believe this, but it wouldn't have mattered to me."

"What wouldn't have mattered?"

"Your weight. It's what's on the inside that counts."

She gazed down at their hands linked together and only looked sadder. More lonely. "I'll bet you told yourself that very same thing while you were slaving away in the weight room." She gave him a look, one that said he was full of it, then she pulled her hand free and walked to her bedroom, shutting the door behind her.

He had no reason to feel guilty, to feel as if he'd wronged her somehow, but he did anyway.

Eight

Pete raised his hand to press the elevator button when he heard a loud pop from the direction of the ER.

It's happening again, he thought. I have to stop it this time.

People were running past him, knocking him from side to side, their faces masks of terror.

Rachel. He had to get to Rachel.

He fought his way back toward triage. More gunshots rang out, more screaming. He tried to run faster, but his legs felt as if they'd been encased in cement. If he could just get there sooner he might be able to save her this time.

He rounded the corner, saw Rachel lying facedown in the hallway.

"No!"

His world shifted into slow motion as he started down the hall toward her, barely aware of the gunfire. His only concern, as blood began to pool around her midsection, was getting her out of that hallway. He racked his brain to remember her blood type.

He heard another pop. Then another, closer this time, then a third and a fourth, and pain seared him like a red-hot brand through his chest, knocking him off balance. Another pop and he felt the sickening thud of bullet to bone, felt the flesh of his knee as it was torn away. His leg gave out and he crumpled like a rag doll, his cheek smashing hard against the cold floor. Pain such as he'd never imagined possible slammed the air from his lungs. He squeezed his eyes shut, forcing down the bile filling his throat. Rachel was only inches away, if he could just....

He lifted his arms, tried to pull himself across the floor, and saw that his left hand was soaked with blood. His blood. The pain was all-encompassing, making him dizzy and limp. He struggled for breath and realized his lung must have been pierced. He was going to die right there on the floor before he could help Rachel.

Feeling himself slipping into unconsciousness, he forced his eyes open. He was going to Florida tomorrow to teach his fiancée to water-ski. He was going to get married and have a family—he had plans, damn it. He couldn't die, not like this, not without a fight. Closing his eyes in concentration, he thrust his hand out, stretching until he felt the cotton of Rachel's scrubs. Clasping at the fabric, he pulled himself closer, fumbling to feel for a pulse at the base of her throat. Nothing. He tried to pull himself closer, to stop the bleeding, but he couldn't make his arms move. His eyes drifted closed again and his head dropped onto the floor.

Then he heard shouting. It was fuzzy, but close. He felt hands on his arms and legs, recognized the pressure being applied to his wounds, felt himself being lifted. He saw lights and movement through bleary eyes.

"She's gone," he heard someone say, and forced his eyes open, looking down at his colleague—his best friend—still sprawled on the floor. Eyes cold and hollow and lifeless.

"No," he moaned, closing his eyes. He hadn't been able to save her. He'd failed her again.

"Doc."

"Hang in there, Pete," someone was urging. "You're going to be okay. Keep fighting."

"Doc."

He didn't want to live. He just wanted to die, he wanted it to be over with. The pain was too intense, too deep. But someone was shaking him—

"Pete, wake up!"

Pete gasped in a breath and shot up in bed, heart slamming against his ribcage, bile rising in his throat, choking him. Blackness surrounded him and for a second he didn't know where he was, or if the hands rubbing his back, the calm voice soothing him, were part of the dream or just a figment of his imagination.

"It's okay. It was just a dream."

Then he realized, it was Maggie's voice, Maggie's hands. As his vision cleared and his eyes adjusted to the dark, he saw her silhouette crouched beside him on the bed. Her arms went around him, her sweet scent erasing the bitter metallic stench of blood still haunting him.

"I couldn't save her," he said, tears stinging his eyes. "I let her die."

"Shhh." Maggie rocked him gently. "It's okay. It's over."

But it wasn't over, not as long as he kept reliving it again and again in his sleep. It would never be over. "I didn't get to her fast enough. I had to lie there and watch her die."

She leaned back against the headboard, easing him down with her. "Lie down, try to go back to sleep."

Exhausted, he curled up beside her, head in her lap, shivering as the fan across the room blew cool air over his damp skin. Maggie reached down and untangled the sheet from his legs, covering him with it. He was too damned cold, too sick in his soul to care that she was seeing him this way—even to care that he was naked.

He only cared that he wasn't alone.

"Relax," Maggie said, gently stroking the hair back from his forehead. "Go back to sleep."

His lids began to feel heavy, so he let his eyes drift closed. He wrapped an arm around her waist, pulling himself closer, absorbing her heat.

With Maggie's hands soothing him, her gentle voice lulling him, he slipped into a deep, dreamless sleep.

Pete opened his eyes, but when he reached for Maggie, he found himself hugging a pillow instead. He would have thought it was all a dream if not for her scent still clinging to the pillowcase, the form of her body pressed into the sheets beside him. The air was thick with humidity from last night's rain and the sheet clung to his skin. It was going to be another unbearably hot day.

He glanced over at the clock and saw that it was after eight, meaning Maggie was probably out for her morning run. At

least he'd have a minute or two to pull himself together before he had to face her. He could only imagine what she would
think of him after the way he'd behaved last night. At least
he'd managed not to throw up this time, and he hadn't woken
wracked with sobs as he had so many times that first month
he was out of the hospital.

When the dreams had gradually tapered off, he'd thought
he'd seen the last of them. Working with Maggie, being forced
to deal with this on a daily basis, was dredging it all up again.
It seemed as though whenever he tried to get on with his life,
to put the shooting behind him, something kept dragging him
back down, forcing him to relive it.

From the other room he heard the squeak of the porch
door opening and footsteps on the creaky wood floor. Maggie was back. He heard the fridge open as she got herself a
bottle of water, then a loud thump, as if maybe she'd closed
a cupboard door.

Could it be possible that she was actually cleaning up after
herself? Wouldn't that be a novelty? he thought with a wry
smile. Cleanliness wasn't exactly one of her strong suits.
Every morning he came out to find the remains of her breakfast waiting for him on the kitchen counter, and she never
picked up her wet towel from the bathroom floor after she
took a shower. Not to mention she usually left her clothes discarded there, too, and her shoes all over the house for him to
trip on. He was constantly stuffing her clothes in the hamper
and dropping her shoes by the back door. She never cleaned
up when she made a meal either, and since dirty dishes in the
sink grated on his nerves, he usually cleaned that up, too.

It all seemed trivial when he thought about everything

she'd been through, and all she'd done for him. The way she'd been there for him last night.

He swung his legs over the edge of the bed and sat up. No point in trying to put off the inevitable. He was going to have to apologize for last night, and try to figure out some way to explain what had happened—without her thinking he was a big wuss.

He got dressed and brushed his teeth, then headed out to the kitchen, confused at first to find the refrigerator door hanging open, until he looked down and saw Maggie lying on the kitchen floor, out cold. She looked peaceful, as if she'd just decided to plop down and take a nap. It took a full ten seconds for the reality of what he was seeing to kick in—pretty pathetic for an ER doctor. The thump he'd heard hadn't been a cabinet door closing, it had been Maggie hitting the floor.

As fast as his legs would carry him, he was at her side. Ignoring the ache in his knee, he lowered himself to the floor and knelt beside her. "Maggie, wake up."

When she didn't open her eyes a slug of fear lodged itself in his gut. Sweat soaked her clothes, her skin was clammy and deathly pale, and she had dark smudges under her eyes. He pressed two fingers to the inside of her wrist, wishing he'd brought a stethoscope and blood pressure cuff with him. "Maggie, can you hear me?"

He grabbed the bottle of water from the floor beside her and poured some into his hand then patted her cheeks. "Come on, Maggie, wake up."

Her eyes fluttered open, she gazed blearily up, and for a second he didn't think she was really seeing him. Then she blinked a few times, and recognition seemed to set in—then confusion.

"Hey, doc. Why am I lying on the floor?"

"My guess is that you're dehydrated and you've pushed yourself too hard on too little food. But I'm going to want a second opinion on that. Can you sit up?"

"I think so."

"Take it slow," he said, taking her hand and helping her. She swayed halfway up, clutching his arm to steady herself. "Easy."

When she was upright and steady, he handed her the water. "Drink this slowly."

She took small sips of the water. Already the color was returning to her cheeks, but she still looked like hell.

"Have you ever passed out before?"

She shook her head. "Nope, this is new for me."

"But you've been dizzy lately?"

"Sometimes, but it's probably just from the heat."

"Nausea?"

"Also from the heat."

"Missed periods?"

She shot him a scathing look. "You have to have sex to get pregnant, doc."

"You can miss periods for a lot of reasons other than pregnancy."

"No, I haven't missed any periods. Not completely."

"But you've been irregular?"

"A little."

"How little?"

She frowned. "I don't know that I'm comfortable having this conversation with you."

"I'm a doctor, Maggie. How irregular?"

"Last month I just spotted."

Pete slowly rose, gripping the edge of the counter to pull himself to his feet. "Where are your car keys?"

"Why?"

"You said you would do something drastic if I didn't go to town with you. I guess you weren't kidding."

"You think I did this on *purpose?*"

"Your keys?"

"In the bedroom. Where are we going?"

"I'm taking you to the hospital."

She shook her head. "No way. I'm okay, doc."

"No, you're not. You're dehydrated, malnourished and I'm guessing you're probably anemic."

"I feel fine." To illustrate her point, she pulled herself to her feet…and lost her balance on the way up. If Pete hadn't been there to grab hold of her she would have wound up right back on her butt on the kitchen floor.

"No arguments," he said when she opened her mouth to plead her case. "You're going."

"Your blood pressure is low, you're dehydrated and though I won't know for sure until we get the results of your blood tests back, you're most likely anemic."

Pete shot Maggie an I-told-you-so look.

She stuck her tongue out at him.

Dr. Cartwright, who looked to be about the same age as Pete—and was almost as cute in a preppy sort of way—gave them an odd look. He had run down a laundry list of about a million questions, and spent the last fifteen minutes poking and prodding her.

"I'll get you started on an iron supplement, but the best way to keep your iron levels up is through a balanced diet."

"That could be a problem considering she never eats," Pete said, and Maggie glared at him.

"I do so. I eat three meals a day."

"What's your typical daily intake?" the doctor asked.

Maggie faltered, knowing it was going to sound like a lot less than it really was. To lose those last five pounds, she needed to keep her calorie intake low and her activity level high.

"She eats cottage cheese and fruit for breakfast," Pete said for her. "A diet shake for lunch and usually a salad for dinner."

The doctor regarded her with a lifted brow. "Does that sound about right?"

"And she works out vigorously for about two hours a day," Pete added.

Maggie shot him another scathing look. He was making it sound a lot worse than it was. "I'm trying to lose the last five pounds and I hit a plateau so I cut my calorie intake," she explained to the doctor. "As soon as I lose the weight, I'll eat more."

"What do you weigh now?" he asked.

Maggie chewed the inside of her cheek. "I'm not sure exactly. The cottage doesn't have a scale. But my clothes haven't gotten too much looser."

"How can you tell?" Pete asked. "Everything you own is a size too small."

Oh, he was really asking for it now. So she liked her clothes snug, big deal. Was that a crime? He didn't seem to mind so much when he was ogling her breasts.

"Why don't we take a trip to the scale?" Dr. Cartwright suggested, sliding back the curtain. Maggie hopped down from the bed and followed him, holding her gown closed so her rear end didn't hang out. Pete trailed behind them.

Maggie climbed onto the scale and Pete watched over her shoulder as the doctor slid the weights over. She expected him to stop at one-thirty, where she'd been stuck for the past month, but that didn't balance the scale. She watched, stunned as he tapped the weight all the way down to one-fifteen.

One hundred and fifteen? How was that possible?

She shook her head. "That can't be right."

"These scales are calibrated monthly. It's right."

Why didn't she feel thin? How could she be ten pounds *under* her goal weight and still feel fat?

"This can't be right," she insisted. "It has to be wrong."

"It's not wrong," Pete said from behind her.

"A woman your age, with your frame, should weigh between one-twenty-five and one-thirty-five," the doctor said. "You're about ten pounds underweight."

Maggie stepped down from the scale. "So why don't I feel thin?"

Pete and the doctor exchanged a look, and Maggie knew exactly what they were thinking, but they were wrong.

"Don't even look at me like that. I do not have an eating disorder."

"Let's go back in the exam room," Dr. Cartwright said. When they were there he pulled the curtain closed. "I know you don't want to hear this, Mrs.—"

"Ms.," Maggie corrected. "I'm not married."

He looked questioningly at Pete.

"He's my patient," she said. "I'm a physical therapist."

The doctor nodded, but still looked as though he didn't get

it. "I know you won't want to hear this, but you're making yourself sick. You need to start eating a healthy diet or you run the risk of severe health problems. The worst being heart failure."

"No more of this diet crap," Pete said, and the ferocity with which he spoke startled her. He sounded…worried. *Really* worried. "You're going to start eating balanced meals until we get your weight back up." He turned to Dr Cartwright. "Any possibility you might have a spare blood pressure cuff lying around I could borrow for a while?"

"I could probably scrounge one up. You know how to use it?"

"I'm a doctor—emergency medicine," Pete said, and held up the cane. "Medical leave. I'm recovering from an…accident."

"Where do you work?"

"Henry Ford Hospital in Detroit. We both do," he said, nodding to Maggie.

"I know of it. They had that terrible shooting earlier this year. One doctor killed, another one…" He trailed off when he saw the tight look on Pete's face. "You weren't…?"

Pete shifted uncomfortably, leaning on his cane. "Yeah, that would be me."

An awkward silence followed. What did you say to something like that? *Sorry* just didn't cut it. This was exactly the kind of thing Pete didn't want to deal with, and the very thing he would have to learn to.

"Jeremy Cartwright," the doctor finally said, shaking Pete's hand.

"Pete Morgan."

"How long are you two planning on being in town?"

"Through the summer," Pete said.

"If you're up to it physically, and you can spare a few hours a week, there's a free clinic in Alma, about thirty miles from here. We're desperate for volunteers. It's not going to be as fast-paced as an urban ER—mostly ear infections, poison ivy, allergic reactions, things like that. But it's for a good cause."

For a second Pete looked interested, then something dark passed over his eyes. "I'm not sure if I would have time with my therapy."

He wanted to do it, Maggie was sure of it. In his heart, he would always be a doctor, whether he was practicing or not. The desire to help people wasn't one that went away.

This might be just the thing he needed to bring him around.

"We can adjust your therapy schedule," she said. She didn't want to push, but this was too good an opportunity to pass up. He *needed* to do this—even if he didn't realize it.

And now she had leverage.

"We have openings in pretty much every shift, so you would be free to make your own hours. And we're never short on patients." Jeremy jotted a few numbers down on a piece of paper and handed it to Pete. "Here's my beeper and home number. If you change your mind, call me."

"Could you excuse us for a minute, doc?" Maggie asked Pete. "I need a couple of minutes alone with the doctor."

Pete regarded her suspiciously.

"Female stuff," she said.

He nodded, but she could tell he didn't believe her. "I'll wait for you outside."

He left, and Maggie peeked out the curtain, to be sure that he wasn't lurking outside eavesdropping. When she turned back around, Jeremy was grinning.

"I'm guessing there's no female issue."

She shook her head.

"How bad was it? His injuries, I mean."

"Bad. He was shot twice in the chest and once in the knee. He's lucky to be alive."

"And the other doctor?"

"Killed instantly. Witnesses said that when Pete saw her lying there, he just started running toward her. He didn't even notice there was a kid with a gun standing at the end of the hall. All he cared about was trying to save her."

"It's normal to see gunshot wounds in the ER, maybe not so much here. But when it's one of your own…" He shook his head. "He seems to be getting around pretty well though."

"Most of his problem now is accepting his disability. He thinks he can't have a career in medicine because he can't keep up with the fast pace of the ER. I think working in the clinic will help him realize that he's capable of a lot more than he thinks. He needs to take this volunteer position. I want to incorporate it into his therapy."

"I'll be happy to help out any way I can, but I can't force him."

"You won't have to." A devious smile curled her mouth. "If I've learned one thing as a therapist, it's how to be persuasive."

Nine

Maggie walked out to the emergency center parking lot and found Pete leaning against the back of her SUV, arms folded over his chest, a grim look on his face.

Despite that, he looked good. Better than he had living in that tomb in his parents' house. He looked…healthy. His hair was still on the long side, but he'd lost that pasty white pallor. His skin was deeply tanned from all the long walks they'd been taking and he spent a lot of time in the afternoons on the beach doing sit-ups and push-ups, trying to maintain his upper-body strength.

He was nowhere close to having the muscle mass he'd had before the shooting, but he looked healthy and happy, and in her book, that was all that mattered.

Pete jingled her keys from his finger. "You okay to drive?"

"Actually, I'm still feeling a little woozy," she lied. "You can drive."

He opened her door for her, then walked around and got in on the driver's side. He set his cane on the floor. "Things are going to change around the cottage," he said.

She fastened her seatbelt. "Oh, yeah? What things?"

He started the engine and put the SUV into gear, backing out from the space and driving toward the exit. "Until your blood pressure is up and your iron levels are higher, you can forget about exercising."

Dr. Cartwright had said as much, but hearing it from Pete was entirely different. He wasn't her doctor. It made her feel rebellious. "Says who?"

"Says me."

"I have two words for you," she said. *"Bite me."*

"I'm serious, Maggie. You're going to start taking care of yourself." He pulled out into traffic, but in the opposite direction from the lake.

"You're going the wrong way, Einstein. Home is in the other direction."

"We're not going home. We're going shopping."

"We are? Mr. I'm-just-not-ready-to-go-out?"

"We need supplies," he said. "And I can't trust you to make the trip alone."

"Oh, that reminds me." She pulled the blood pressure cuff from her bag and tossed it at him. "Jeremy asked me to give that to you."

He set it on the seat between them. "We also need a scale. And more food."

Well, she'd wanted to get him out of the house and around people. And here they were. And she knew for a fact he hadn't driven since the shooting, so that was a step forward, too.

So why did she have a sinking feeling in her stomach?

"What kind of food?"

"Chicken, fish, beef. Foods rich in iron. We're going to weigh you daily until you're back up to where you should be."

The thought of eating meat was only slightly more offensive than the reality of hopping on a scale every day. "And if I refuse?"

"Not an option. I'll force-feed you if I have to." He pulled into the Carter's parking lot and swung into a spot. "Don't think I won't do it."

Oh, she would never make that mistake. Pete was a man of his word.

And then some.

He grabbed his cane, opened his door and lowered himself down. She hopped out and met him around back. Concern she understood, but he was being downright bossy.

"Why do you even care, doc? I'm not your patient." He started to walk around her and she stepped in his way. "What difference does it make how much I weigh?"

"Don't push me, Maggie," he said tightly. "I'm not in the mood."

He wasn't concerned, he was *angry* with her.

Her own anger sparked. "Do you really think getting mad at me is going to make this any easier?"

He grabbed her upper arm and backed her against the tail of the SUV. "What makes me mad," he said through gritted teeth, "is those jerks, for the way they treated you back in high school, and your mother, for making you feel inadequate for what was obviously her own damned neurosis."

Something dark and dangerous flared in his eyes. His gaze drifted lower, to her mouth, lingering there.

He was going to kiss her again. And the crazy thing was, she *wanted* him to, even though she knew it was wrong.

His head dipped lower, his eyes still on her mouth, and her lips felt warm and full. So ready to take whatever he offered. He held himself there for a second, as if he couldn't decide whether he really wanted to do it. Then he cursed under his breath, lowered his head, and crushed his lips against hers. This was no sweet, seductive kiss. This was a bruising, punishing kiss. She couldn't help wondering who it was exactly he was trying to punish—her or himself. She only knew there was more passion, more emotion in that simple gesture than in the last fifty times she'd been kissed. Her heart dropped to the pit of her stomach, her knees went rubbery and flames ignited in her soul.

He ended the kiss as abruptly as he'd begun it, and backed away just far enough to look her in the eyes. "Now, we're going in that store, and we're buying food, then we're going to find a medical supply store and we're going to get a scale. And you'll eat what I tell you to, and you'll get on the scale every damned morning until I say you can stop. Understand?"

Something told her now was not the time to argue, so she gave him a wobbly nod.

He let go of her arm. "That's more like it. Now let's get this over with."

He backed away and her knees were so weak and her head so swimmy she nearly slid down the back hatch and hit the pavement.

What was that?

She knew he found her attractive, and probably even liked

her a little, misguided as he was. But this concern for her health, for the way she'd been treated…she was stunned. If she didn't know any better she might think—

No, she wouldn't even let herself think that, because it would never happen. She wouldn't *let* it happen. It wasn't uncommon for patients to develop close relationships with their therapists. With her and Pete living together, being so close in every respect, and being two healthy—well, relatively healthy—adults, emotions were bound to be blown way out of proportion.

She'd seen it before, and she'd made some really lousy judgment calls.

She wouldn't be doing that again.

Maggie sat at the table, twisting her napkin in her lap, staring at her plate. Pete had made grilled salmon fillets topped with a butter-dill sauce and served them with steamed broccoli and seasoned brown rice. She mentally calculated how many zillions of calories were sitting on her plate and her stomach heaved.

"Dig in," he said. "You're not leaving this table until your plate is clean."

"Whatever you say, *Dad.*"

The insult rolled off his back. "Don't think you're going to sass your way out of this one, Maggie. I'm serious."

Which fit right in with her plan. It was time for the bargaining to begin. She took a deep breath and blew it out. "I'll eat this, but only on one condition."

His fork stopped halfway to his mouth. "What condition?"

"You have to agree to volunteer at the clinic."

He frowned and put down his fork. "You know how I feel about that."

"And you know how I feel about eating, but you're forcing me to do it anyway."

"Because not eating is unhealthy."

"Hiding yourself away from the world isn't healthy either, doc. You went out today, and did you have a problem? Did anyone point and laugh? Did you fall, or even stumble?"

He only stared at her.

"All I'm asking for is a couple of hours a day, twice a week. It'll be part of your therapy. Give it two weeks and if you really hate it, you can stop."

"And if I say no?"

She pushed her plate away. "You're eating alone."

"It's only been eleven days."

"And you're doing great, doc. You're ready for this." She pulled Jeremy's number from her back pocket. She gave him that and her cell phone. "Make the call."

For a full minute he only looked at her outstretched hand. Finally he took the phone and the number and dialed. "Jeremy, this is Pete Morgan. I'd like to take you up on that volunteer position." Pete nodded toward her plate.

Maggie pulled it back in front of her and picked up her fork.

"I was thinking two days a week to start."

She broke off a small bite of fish and lifted it to her mouth. She glanced up at Pete and he nodded.

"Tuesday and Thursday afternoons would be great."

Before she could talk herself out of it, or stop to think about the calories she would be ingesting and the rolls of fat she'd worked so hard to shed, Maggie closed her eyes and shoved the fork in her mouth. Her taste buds went into overdrive as the tangy sauce hit her tongue. The flavor was so intense she nearly gagged.

Instead, she forced herself to chew very slowly, then swallow.

"Eleven to four would be fine," Pete was saying, his eyes not leaving her face. He gave her another nod, as if to say, take another bite.

She loaded her fork with rice and her mouth actually watered in anticipation. The rice was spicy and cooked just right. It had been so long since she'd had real food, she'd forgotten how much she used to love to eat. It scared the heck out of her because it would be so easy to fall back into her old habits. So easy to become fat Maggie again.

"I don't know, let me ask," Pete said, then asked Maggie, "Do I need directions to the clinic?"

"I know where it is."

"Nope," he told Jeremy, "I'm good."

Maggie tried her broccoli next. It was seasoned with lemon juice and what tasted like garlic salt, so it couldn't have too many calories. And it was delicious.

"She's good," Pete said with another pointed look her way. "She's eating dinner right now." He laughed, then said, "Yeah, she is."

Maggie narrowed her eyes at him.

"Sounds good. I'll see you Tuesday." He snapped her phone closed and set it on the table.

"Yeah, I am what?" she asked.

"He asked if you were giving me any trouble about the eating. How is it, by the way?"

"Wonderful," she said, taking another bite of her fish. "Where did you learn to cook?"

He shrugged. "Here and there. When you're a bachelor, especially one with a crazy schedule, you either learn to cook, or you eat a lot of fast food."

"I never learned to cook, and I ate nothing but fast food for a long time. Which explains why I looked the way I did, I guess."

"I think genetics has a lot to do with it, too. I know for me it does. But it's always better for you in the long run to eat healthily." He looked up at her and grinned. "That's the doctor in me talking."

"Maybe you should do most of the cooking from now on," she said, "since you're so much better at it than I am."

"I'll cook if you do the dishes. And I mean *after* dinner, not the next morning."

"Dirty dishes really drive you nuts, don't they?"

"So do dirty clothes and wet towels strewn all over the bathroom floor. And shoes left in the middle of the room where I inevitably trip on them."

"I don't leave my shoes in the middle of the room. I take them off by the back door."

Pete nodded in the direction of the couch, and she turned to see her flip-flops lying there, in the middle of the floor, right where she'd kicked them off. "Oops."

"I'm the one who puts your shoes by the back door," he said. "You leave them all over the place."

"I'll try not to do that," she said.

"I would appreciate it."

"I'll try to remember to put my dirty clothes and towels in

the hamper, too." She pushed her rice around with her fork, working up the will to take another bite. "Despite all the little stuff, I think this is working out pretty well. I mean, we seem to get along okay."

"Yeah, we do," he agreed.

"When you're not being bossy and overbearing," she added.

He gave her a wry smile. "Yeah, because we both know you don't have a bossy bone in your body."

She smiled. The truth was, she liked that he kept her on her toes. It made life interesting. She'd never had a roommate like Pete before. And while she'd had lots of male friends over the years, there was something more than that with him.

Something…*special.*

He took a bite of fish, chewing slowly, eyes fixed on his plate. "By the way, I wanted to um, talk to you about last night."

She forced herself to take another bite. "What about it?"

"I wanted to apologize."

Chew…chew…swallow. "What for?"

"For waking you. For making you feel like you had to stay with me."

She'd kind of expected him to be embarrassed about the nightmare. It probably made him feel weak, and, like most men she knew, Pete hated feeling weak.

She took another bite. "Do you have nightmares a lot?"

"At first I did. Almost every night. They stopped after a couple of months. Now they're back."

Bite. Chew…chew…swallow. "Did it help having me there?"

"Yeah, it did, but—"

"Then don't worry about it. I didn't mind." Bite. Chew... chew...swallow. If she thought of eating as a process, and forgot about the ramifications, it was a little easier to do. "Out of curiosity, have you ever talked to anyone about it?"

"About my dreams?"

"No, about the shooting."

He shrugged. "What's to talk about? It happened, now it's over. I've dealt with it."

"Have you really?"

"Don't psychoanalyze me, Maggie."

"It was only a suggestion. Just know that I'm here to talk if you need to."

They ate in silence for several minutes, until Maggie's plate was nearly empty. And she felt full. She couldn't remember the last time she'd eaten until she was satisfied. But instead of satisfied, she began to feel edgy and panicked, like she'd just done something reprehensible. Like she needed to get the food out of her body, before it broke down and turned into fat. She could practically feel the fat cells forming and sticking to her insides. The waist of her shorts felt too tight and her top stretched snugly over her stomach.

Pete had piled twice the amount of food she'd had on his plate and had eaten every bite, down to the last grain of rice, but he wouldn't be gaining any weight.

It was so unfair.

What was wrong with being a little underweight, anyway? Maybe if she promised not to lose any more weight they would let her stay the way she was. How bad could it be really? There were lots of skinny people in the world.

The panic multiplied. Her stomach clutched, feeling

bloated and overfull. Sweat popped out on her brow and she felt nauseated. She glanced in the direction of the bathroom. Would it really hurt, just this once…?

"Don't even think about it," Pete said sharply and Maggie jumped at the sound of his voice.

"Th-think about what?"

"Losing your dinner. It's not going to happen, so just forget it."

She made an indignant noise. "Now you think I'm bulimic?"

"All I know is that you look like you're about to crawl out of your skin, and you keep glancing in the direction of the bathroom. But I won't let you do it. If I have to duct-tape your mouth shut, I will."

She resented the implication, but what bothered her even more, what had fear gripping her, was that he was right. She *was* actually considering making herself throw up. Suppose she did do it this one time. What would stop her from doing it a second time and a third?

"I've seen first-hand what happens to women who binge and purge, Maggie. Trust me when I say, it's not a pretty sight. It's a control issue. And once you start, it's nearly impossible to stop, not without intensive therapy. Is that what you want?"

She sucked in an unsteady breath and clasped her hands together to keep them from shaking. He was right, she wasn't used to this feeling of helplessness. She might have made her share of mistakes, but she'd always been in control of her life. She felt as if that had suddenly been snatched away.

"You'll get through this," Pete said. There was so much compassion in his eyes it made her go all mushy inside. He leaned across the table and put a hand over both of hers. "We both will."

The fact that she wasn't in this alone, that in a small way he understood what she was going through, made it a little less scary. She wondered what might have happened if Pete hadn't been there to boss her around. Would she have had the ability to see what she was doing to herself, or would she have just kept losing weight until there was nothing left of her?

Ten

Maggie flopped on her stomach, driving her fists into the pillow in a fit of pure frustration. This was the fourth night since Pete had taken her to the hospital that she couldn't sleep. The fourth night she'd tossed and turned until she felt like screaming and banging her head against the wall. She wasn't sure if it was the sudden lack of activity or the abnormally high calorie intake or the fact that she felt as though her life was spinning out of control. Whatever it was, it was driving her crazy.

She heard a noise from the other room and pushed herself up on her elbows to listen. Pete hadn't had a nightmare in days. He'd begun work at the clinic on Tuesday, as promised. After his shift, when he got home, she'd asked him how it went and he gave her a noncommittal shrug. She hadn't pushed. She knew when he was ready to talk about it he would.

Sure enough, during dinner, as she forced herself to choke down a grilled chicken breast and a baked potato, he mentioned how swamped he'd been with patients.

"You wouldn't believe how many people can't afford decent health care," he'd said. "Without the clinic these people would have no place else to go. I had a little boy in today suffering from recurring ear infections. He's had so many he has significant hearing loss."

"Can you help him?"

"He needs a myringotomy. It's a simple out-patient procedure, but his parents don't have health insurance. Without insurance it could cost thousands. His mother said her husband was laid off and they're barely making ends meet as it is. They just can't afford it."

"What about public assistance?" she'd asked.

"She makes enough money that they don't qualify. In the ER we treat everyone, whether they have insurance or not, so I never really considered the effect a lack of insurance would have for non-emergency health care."

"So, what you're doing there is good?"

He nodded. "Yeah, I guess it is."

That afternoon after work he'd told her about the other doctors who worked there and a few of his more interesting cases. "It's kind of a challenge," he said. "Trying to figure out the best and cheapest way to treat people. And the gratitude in their eyes...I feel like I'm really making a difference."

"You are, doc," she had told him, and he'd smiled. For the first time since they'd come here she could finally see the light at the end of the tunnel. She had real hope that Pete was beginning to accept his disability and his limitations.

Herself, now, that was another story altogether.

Maggie lowered her head back down on the pillow and closed her eyes, then she heard the noise again.

"Rachel, no!"

Oh, damn, Pete was having another nightmare.

She scrambled out of bed and darted across the hall. She didn't turn on the light this time, knowing she would get an eyeful if she did. And sure enough, as she stepped closer to the bed she could see that Pete was sprawled out, only half-covered by the sheet. She couldn't see a lot in the dark, but she could see enough to know that he was naked. Even with Pete in this distressed state, she wasn't immune to all that lean muscle and tanned skin.

His head thrashed across the pillow and he moaned in his sleep. She slipped into bed beside him, grabbed his shoulder, and gave it a shake. His skin was hot and slippery with perspiration. "Doc, wake up. You're having a bad dream."

He moaned and grimaced in his sleep.

"Pete, wake up!"

As he had the first time, Pete shot up in bed, his breath coming hard and fast.

"It's okay," she said softly, smoothing her hands down his back. "It was just a dream."

He looked dazedly around, as if he wasn't sure where he was. Then he blinked a few times and asked in a raspy voice, "What time is it?"

She combed her fingers through his damp hair. "Two o'clock."

"I woke you again," he said, dragging a hand over his face.

"It's okay. I was already awake." She eased him back against the pillows. "Lie down, relax."

"Are you leaving?" There was a note of panic in his voice that made her smile. He wouldn't ask her to stay, he was too proud for that. Too macho. But he wanted her to.

"I'm not going anywhere." She scooted down beside him and he shifted closer, wrapping his arm around her waist and resting his head on her shoulder. She enjoyed this far too much for her own good. The sheet was tangled around his legs and she did her best to keep her eyes from wandering south. If this became a habit, the man was going to have to think about wearing pajamas to bed. A girl could only take so much of that body before her thoughts turned wicked.

She was already ninety percent there.

"You don't have to stay," he said, though he had an awfully tight grip on her. His breath was warm against her neck, the hand wrapped around her waist so large and sure.

Things had been so uncertain for her lately, but here, lying with Pete, she felt…safe. Maybe she needed this as much as he did.

"I'm staying," she said.

"I'm naked, you know."

"I know."

"That doesn't bother you?"

"I have my eyes closed."

He paused then asked, "Do you really?"

"No, not really."

He chuckled lightly, and she knew he was feeling better. "Like you said, if you've seen one you've seen them all, huh?"

"Don't forget, I've seen *yours*."

He was quiet for a second, then said, "That's a little unfair, don't you think?"

"What is?"

"That you've seen mine. To make it fair, you should show me yours."

Oh yeah, like that would ever happen. "Who ever said life is fair, doc?"

He gripped her nightshirt, gathering the fabric in his hand, easing it up over her thighs. "Just one little peek…"

She didn't make a move to stop him, positive he was bluffing, or at the very least just trying to annoy her. And maybe a small part of her was intrigued by the idea of a little show and tell—until her shirt was up to her waist and he hooked his fingers in the top of her panties, lifting his head like he was really going to take a peek. Then she smacked his hand. Hard.

"Ow!" he said, yanking his hand back, but she could hear a smile in his voice. "Jeez, you're mean."

She tugged her nightshirt back down. "Try that again and you're liable to lose that hand."

"Yeah, but it would be worth it," he said, and the comment warmed her all over. If he was only saying it to be nice, to make her feel good, it had worked. That charm could play dangerous games with her head.

He was quiet for a minute then asked, "Do you think this is weird? Us sleeping together? I'm assuming you don't do this with your other patients."

She laughed softly. "No, this isn't usually part of the therapy. Of course, I don't move in with my other patients either. So, yes, I guess you could say the entire arrangement is a little weird."

"We've definitely transcended the typical therapist-patient relationship."

"Definitely."

"I think what we have is a lot more than a friendship, too."

"I do, too."

"You do know how much I care about you?"

Not as much as I care about you, she wanted to say. Too much to be anything but friends. "I care about you, too," she said.

He settled his head back against her shoulder. "Maggie, why don't you have a boyfriend?"

"Why do you want to know?"

"Just curious."

"I had a...bad experience."

"With a boyfriend?"

"He was sort of my fiancé."

He rose up on one elbow and gazed at her through the dark. "This isn't one of those stories that's going to make me feel like punching something, is it?"

"He was a patient."

"I thought you don't get involved with patients."

"Normally no, and it wasn't the first time one had a thing for me, but I really thought it was different with this guy. He really seemed to care about me."

"And..."

"And I was wrong." Yet another failure in the ever-growing list her mother had been keeping since Maggie had left the womb.

When she'd started dating her ex, her mother had been ecstatic. He was attractive, successful—the perfect man in her mother's eyes. When he'd asked Maggie to marry him, her parents had been over the moon with joy, and Maggie finally felt as if she had done something right, she'd pleased them—until her mother threw in a little disclaimer.

"You finally have a chance at real happiness," she told Maggie. "*Don't* blow this."

As if the relationship had been destined to fail otherwise. And maybe it had been. Maybe she was really that unlovable, that undesirable.

Telling her parents the wedding was off, that she'd been unceremoniously dumped, had been the most humiliating thing she'd ever had to do. And of course her mother saw it as another failure. Instead of drawing Maggie into her arms and soothing her, she'd berated her.

"I should have known," her mother had said, shaking her head. "I swear, Maggie, you do this on purpose just to hurt me."

Once again, she'd made it all about herself, how *she* felt. That had been the final straw for Maggie. It was the moment she realized that her mother didn't care about her feelings and probably never would.

"What happened?" Pete asked.

"He met someone else," she said. Someone thin and delicate and submissive.

You're so bossy, he used to tell her. *Do you always have to be right?* And he would nag her constantly about her weight. It was her mother all over again.

But she'd stayed with him. It was that or disappoint her parents. However, she'd discovered, there were worse things than making her mother unhappy. Being stuck in a relationship with a man who would have made her miserable, who would have constantly fed her low self-esteem—that would have been the ultimate mistake.

When she got over the hurt and realized how much better off she was, she was grateful he'd dumped her. She never would have had the courage to end it herself. And it had taught her an important lesson. Good things, happy relationships, didn't happen to people like her.

There was a long stretch of silence, then Pete said, "You know I would never hurt you, Maggie."

"People don't usually go into a relationship intending to hurt someone," she said. "But they still do."

"I like being with you. You're so different from anyone I've been attracted to before."

"You're in limbo, doc. Right now a lot of your world revolves around me. It's normal to form attachments. When you've finished your therapy, the feeling will fade. Trust me."

"You don't know that."

"Yes," she said, with a finality that shot a dagger of pain through his heart. "I do."

Pete woke with his hand cupped around something soft and warm. He didn't have to open his eyes to know it was still dark or that the warm body curled up beside him was Maggie. She lay in the crook of his body, pressed tightly against him, her head resting on his other arm, her cute little behind tucked intimately against his crotch with only a very thin pair of panties in between. He could feel her nightshirt bunched around her waist and the backs of her bare legs against his upper thighs. The soft thing in his hand was her breast, and he was more than a little aroused.

Well, this was awkward. And wonderful.

Her breathing was slow and deep, so he was guessing she was still asleep, giving him plenty of opportunity to rearrange them out of this compromising position. The problem was, he didn't want to move. It just felt too damned good. She felt so warm and sweet in his arms. He liked this softer, vulnerable side. She was usually so capable and independent. Meaning, the instant she woke, he ran the very possible risk of getting an elbow jab to the ribs.

Despite the inevitable consequences, the hand cupping her breast seemed to take on a will of its own. His thumb grazed slowly back and forth, until he felt the peak of her breast tighten into a rigid point. Maggie made a soft mewing sound and tucked her behind more firmly against him.

He felt like a degenerate, taking advantage of her in her sleep. Of course, she'd wanted to stay, and he'd warned her their second day here that it had been a long time for him. Sleeping in the same bed, something like this had been bound to happen eventually. She'd had every opportunity to go back to her own room, so this couldn't really be construed as his fault. And he hadn't even opened his eyes, so technically he wasn't awake yet. She couldn't expect him to be responsible for his actions while he was asleep. Right?

Any other excuses you can dredge up, Pete?

He gave her breast a little squeeze. She sighed, wiggling her backside against him, and he struggled not to moan. He felt like a ticking bomb. A little more of her squirming just might be enough to set off an explosion.

He felt like a hormonally challenged kid. It was taking every ounce of willpower he possessed not to rub himself up

against her. Even he had limits on how blatantly inappropri-
ately he would behave.

Maggie let out a sigh and rolled in his arms until she faced
him. She tucked her face against the crook of his neck and her
hand landed on his bare backside. Her breath was hot on his
throat, her breasts soft against his chest.

As if their position wasn't intimate enough before. This
was downright torture. He had no choice but to wrap his arm
around her.

Well, that wasn't exactly true. He had all kinds of choices,
like rolling over to the other side of the bed. Or, since falling
back to sleep at this point would be impossible, he could
climb out of bed altogether and take a cold shower.

Instead he found his hands sliding down her back, until he
cupped the swell of her behind. He was wide awake now.
Without the guise of sleep to hide behind he felt even more
guilty, more lecherous. That didn't stop him from stroking her
behind, dipping his thumb under the edge of her panties. Then
Maggie laid her hand over his and he froze.

Was she awake? And if so, why hadn't she slugged him?
It seemed clear he deserved it.

Instead, she took his hand and guided it to the front of her
panties. He was so astonished that for a minute he wasn't sure
what to do. Well, he knew *what* to do—he could think of a
couple of dozen things right off the top of his head—he just
didn't know if he *should*. If she was asleep, then touching her
would be wrong.

She'd been so adamant about keeping their relationship
professional, there was no way she was anything but sound
asleep.

There was one very simple solution. Give her a shake and wake her up. It was that or touch her, and risk having her wake right in the middle of…well, whatever they might be doing, and have her blast him for taking advantage of her.

So why wasn't he waking her?

Because deep down he wanted to believe she was awake and knew exactly what she was doing. He wanted to believe that not touching was just as damned hard for her as it was for him.

He held very still, waiting to see what she did. He would give her thirty seconds. If she didn't move by then, he would pull his hand away.

But she did move. She let out a little groan of protest and arched against his hand, as if to say come on, touch me. With an invitation like that, how could he *not* touch her?

Very lightly he rubbed her through her panties and she pushed herself against his fingers, muffling a moan against the crook of his neck. Her hand was back on his rear end, clutching and pulling him closer, her nails digging into his skin.

Okay, there was no way she could sleep through this. She had to be awake now, which meant he could stop rationalizing this and let nature take its course.

He slipped his hand under the edge of her panties, between her thighs, found her hot and slippery. She gasped and spread her legs.

She reached between them and wrapped her hand around his erection, and he nearly swallowed his tongue. As much as he would have liked to rip those skimpy panties off her and bury himself deep inside that wet heat, sexual petting was a far cry from making love. He'd abandoned the idea of casual sex back in med school.

But what they were doing now, this was...*exciting*. It made him feel sixteen again, when he'd touched a girl intimately for the first time. Only this time he wasn't fumbling his way through, hoping he was getting it right. He knew exactly what to do, where to touch, to give her pleasure. He cupped his free hand over her breast, pinching lightly through the fabric of her shirt, and her grip on him tightened, her pace quickened.

Aw, man, he was close. He didn't want to come first, but he could feel his control slipping.

Maggie's hips rocked back and forth, keeping time with his stroking fingers, then she moaned and arched against him, her body shaking with release. That was all it took to push him over the edge. Honestly, it was a miracle he lasted longer than thirty seconds. It was hot and fast and draining, as if all the tension, all the stress of the past five months had suddenly been lifted. He felt a little more like his old self.

And boy, did he need that.

Apparently, Maggie had, too. She burrowed against him and let a out a contented little sigh. Pete wrapped her in his arms and instantly felt himself slipping back to sleep.

Hours later, he finally pried his eyes open, squinting against the morning sun shining through the open window. He reached for Maggie, only to find himself alone, and had the bizarre feeling that it had all been a dream.

Maggie stood on the back porch, staring out at the water, sipping her coffee and trying to work up the will to feel guilty about what had happened last night.

How could something so wrong feel so *good?*

When she'd woken in the middle of the night with Pete curled around her, his hand on her breast, her body had screamed, oh baby! Her brain had done that short-circuit thing and instead of thinking oh, no, it had shouted a very clear oh, yes!

It had taken a good ten minutes of wiggling and shifting before he began to stir, but even then he hadn't gotten the hint. She would have thought turning in his arms and grabbing his butt would have done the trick, but still he'd faltered. Though she'd never considered herself the aggressive type when it came to sex, the guy just couldn't take a hint. She'd had no choice but to take matters into her own hands.

Literally.

When she thought about the way she'd taken his hand and put it between her legs, her cheeks burned with embarrassment. She burned with something else, too—sexual awareness. She felt it in her fingers and her toes and in the tips of her hair. She felt *alive,* in a way she never had before.

She also felt scared. She was setting herself up to be hurt again. Even if Pete didn't mean to or want to hurt her, it was inevitable. Though sometimes he seemed to genuinely care for her, when he got back home, back to his regular life, back to his old friends, he would feel differently.

"Good morning."

At the sound of Pete's voice Maggie's heart took a dive for her toes. She sucked in a deep breath and turned to him. He stood in the doorway, dressed in a pair of low-slung cut-off shorts and nothing else, his hair still rumpled from sleep. She would never be able to look at him again without remembering the way his body had felt pressed up against her, the way his fingers had teased her into ecstasy.

And while one part of her wanted to throw herself into his

arms, she knew that what had happened last night could never be repeated. No matter how badly she wanted it. Because it wouldn't last. One more good blow to her battered pride and she might never eat again.

"Morning, doc," she said, and turned back toward the water. She heard Pete sigh.

"Is that the way it's going to be?"

"What do you mean?" she asked, even though she knew *exactly* what he meant.

"We're just going to pretend that last night never happened?"

She closed her eyes. "I don't know about you, but I'd rather skip the we-shouldn't-have-let-that-happen speech."

He walked over and leaned on the rail beside her, gazing out at the water. Even at this early hour boats dotted the lake and gulls swooped down to scavenge off the beach. "Yeah, I guess I could live without that, too."

She only wished she could pretend it hadn't happened. She wished she could forget the way his skin had smelled musky from sleep, or how hot and hard he'd felt in her hand. His fingers had worked so skillfully and he knew exactly how to touch her until she completely lost herself. The memory was so fresh in her mind, so vivid, it was making her dizzy.

She glanced over at him and saw that his brow had tucked into a frown. He looked almost…hurt.

Maybe he thought she hadn't enjoyed herself. Maybe he thought he'd done something wrong. She didn't want him to feel bad or, even worse, feel as if he'd disappointed her. That couldn't be farther from the truth.

"Don't get me wrong," she said. "I had a good time."

He nodded. "So did I."

"It's just that things could get…awkward." She turned to look at him. "Things aren't going to be awkward now, are they?"

He shook his head.

"It was just an impulse thing, you know? A fleeting…" she waved her hands, searching for the right word. *"Whatever."*

A smile quirked up the corner of his mouth. "For someone who doesn't want to have the morning-after talk, you're having a hard time dropping it."

"You're right, I'm sorry. I just…" She sighed. "I guess I don't want you to feel guilty, as if you did something wrong. I mean, I started it, so it's completely my own fault."

He only stared at her, one brow lifted, as though maybe he wasn't certain of the exact chain of events, and she felt compelled to explain.

"If I hadn't been, you know, wiggling around, then you wouldn't have gotten, you know—"

He flattened one large hand very gently over her mouth. "I was there, I don't need a play-by-play of the action. All that will do is land us back in bed together, where you insist we shouldn't be. You don't need to beat yourself up over this, okay?"

She nodded, wondering what he would do if she bit him—or licked his palm—then decided that wouldn't be wise.

"Look," he said. "I was raised not to talk about my feelings, so this isn't exactly easy for me to say, but I really care about you, Maggie. You know that, don't you?"

She nodded. Though he didn't often say it, his actions spoke of his feelings for her. That didn't change the fact that his judgment was impaired. What he was feeling now would be very different from what he felt a month from now.

"We're both going through some heavy emotional stuff right now. As much as I would like to explore exactly where this relationship might go, I respect the fact that you're not ready for that. And as for last night, don't feel guilty. What happened was one-hundred-percent mutual. It was obviously something we both needed. It happened, and it's over, and we won't let it happen again. That *is* what you want, right?" He moved his hand so she could answer.

"Right," she said, her lips tingling from his touch. Which of course made her think about last night, and the other things he'd made tingle.

But he was right. And the way he'd explained it made sense. It probably *was* something they had both needed. Stress relief, or something like that. And now that they had gotten it out of their systems, not touching each other wouldn't be a problem.

She hoped.

Eleven

"Well, how is it?"

"One-oh-seven over seventy-five," Pete said and jotted the reading down on the chart he'd been keeping.

"So that's better, right?"

He pulled the blood pressure cuff from her arm and set it on the kitchen counter. "Yeah, it's better. Hop on the scale."

She looked with disdain at the scale sitting on the kitchen floor. In the past two weeks she'd grown to really hate that thing. What a god-awful way to start her day. "Can't we just skip it this one time?"

He crossed his arms and gave her his yeah-right look.

"Fine," she grumbled. She stepped over and lifted her foot—

"Shoes *off*," he said sternly, and she shot him the evil eye. "Don't look at me like that. You know the rules."

Mumbling under her breath, she kicked her tennis shoes

off, shut her eyes and stepped on the scale. She always kept her eyes closed. It was bad enough knowing she was gaining weight, she didn't want to see it, too.

On the bright side—and thank heavens there *was* a bright side to this—some of the clothes that had begun to feel a little loose were fitting again. She didn't get dizzy every time she stood up either, and she had more energy. She'd also had her first normal period in months.

"You've gained another pound." He marked that down on the chart as well. "Only three more to go."

"Does that mean I can start exercising again?" she asked.

"Don't push your luck. Besides, we've been walking. That's exercise."

Though it was nowhere close to the vigorous exercise she was used to, she had to admit the nightly walks they'd gotten into the habit of taking together—on the beach or through the woods or sometimes just down the dirt road—had become her favorite part of the day. It was a chance to relax and unwind and talk about everything or nothing in particular. Sometimes they didn't talk at all, they just walked side by side, quietly enjoying the evening.

One evening a few days ago, Pete had taken her hand to help her over a log that had fallen across the path, and he hadn't let go. He just kept walking, his fingers twined through hers, as if it were nothing out of the ordinary. She'd spent the next half hour debating; should she pull away, or just go with it and see what he did? Something about walking with Pete like that just felt so…natural. And every night since then, he'd automatically taken her hand when they left the cottage.

Besides, to worry about something as trivial as holding

hands seemed silly considering Pete had woken with bad dreams six times in the last two weeks—the last three nights in a row—and she'd wound up sleeping with him. And while nothing overtly sexual had occurred, Pete was a cuddler. He didn't seem content to sleep in the same bed unless he was lying all over her. And despite this becoming a regular thing for them, he still didn't wear pajamas. It hadn't escaped her attention that a certain part of his anatomy usually woke up well before he did.

She couldn't deny that she'd had the inclination to peek under the covers once or twice. Not that he would have known. Once he was out, the man slept like the dead. And it wasn't like she hadn't seen him naked before. The only problem was, she knew that once she looked, she would want to touch. She thought of how he'd shuddered when she'd wrapped her hand around him that night, how he'd felt long and hot and silky-smooth. The memory alone made her feel restless and needy.

So yeah, she definitely would want to do that again. And doing that could get her into a lot of trouble. So when she got the urge to peek, that was usually the point when she untangled herself from his arms and climbed out of bed.

"Three more pounds," Pete was saying, but she'd completely forgotten what they'd been talking about. She must have given him a totally blank look, because he waved a hand in front of her face and said, "Earth to Maggie."

She gave her head a little shake to clear it. "Sorry, what were you saying?"

"You asked if you could exercise and I said you have to gain three more pounds. Are you okay?"

"Fine." Just a mild case of sex on the brain.

"You sure? You really zoned out."

"I'm sure." And since she was feeling more than a little overheated, she opened the fridge, grabbed a bottle of water, and offered Pete one.

He took it and twisted the top off. "By the way, Jeremy called while you were in the shower."

"And…?"

"He wondered if I could fill in for another doctor and take on a couple of extra days at the clinic next week."

"How many?"

"It would be a full week."

She didn't doubt he was ready. She glanced over at the cane leaning in the corner by the door. The only time he used it now was when he was in an unfamiliar situation, or on uneven ground. And even then she didn't think he really needed it. He just wasn't yet ready to let go completely. He was still walking with a limp, but the truth was, that would probably never go away. She wasn't sure if he was ready to hear that, though. He still needed time to adjust—to heal. If not physically, then emotionally.

Working more was definitely a step in the right direction.

"So, what did you tell him?" she asked Pete.

He flashed her a grin. "I said I would have to check with my therapist first."

"Do you *want* to work extra days?"

He shrugged and took a swallow of his water. "If there's no one else to do it, I guess it couldn't hurt. I figured if you need the car you could drop me off and pick me up."

That was a big yes, if she'd ever heard one. "Well, even

though you won't admit it, you seem to really like volunteering, and God knows you've been a lot less cranky."

He raised an eyebrow at her. "I'm *cranky?*"

"And I can easily readjust your therapy schedule. I say go for it."

"You won't get bored here all by yourself?"

"Are you kidding? I can't wait to be rid of you."

He grinned, and his eyes locked on hers. He gave her that penetrating, soul-deep look that made her go all wishy-washy. She hated when he did that. It made her ache that much more for the things she knew she would never have. Though he didn't often come right out and say how he was feeling about her, he showed her in a million little ways.

She lowered her eyes. "I wish you wouldn't look at me like that."

"I just realized, I haven't thanked you for all you've done for me."

She lifted her shoulders in a casual shrug, eyes lowered to the floor. "No need to thank me. It's a job."

He tucked a finger under her chin and lifted, so she had to look at him. "You and I both know this has been more than a job."

She knew right then, by the look in his eyes, by the way his gaze wandered to her mouth, he was going to kiss her. She wanted to pull away, and she didn't want to. His head dipped lower and her lids slipped down. She felt his breath on her lips, his hand cupping her cheek, and her knees felt as if they might buckle out from under her. His lips brushed over hers and everything inside her went liquid. She found herself leaning into the kiss, into him, sliding her arms around his neck.

She felt his tongue teasing her lip, his teeth nipping lightly, and she went dizzy with desire.

"I want you, Maggie," he whispered against her lips.

But for how long? Though she was trying like hell to fight it, she couldn't deny she was falling in love with him. It was a lazy, easy kind of love that felt like a natural extension of herself—the logical next step in their relationship. But there was nothing logical about it. What would happen when summer was over and it was time to go home? How would he feel when he got back to his own life?

The ache in her heart became a persistent dull throb. She dropped her hands from around his neck and lowered her head. "I can't."

He sighed and rested his chin on the top of her head. "You want this as much as I do. Why do you keep fighting it?"

"You know why."

"We get along, we have fun together. We're sleeping together, for goodness' sake!"

"Not in the biblical sense."

"Why not? What can I do to prove to you that I have genuine feelings for you, Maggie? I'm probably one of the most emotionally stunted men you're ever going to meet, but if you tell me what it is I should say, what I should do, I swear I'll do it."

"If this about sex—"

He cupped her face in his hands. "You know damn well, this is not about sex. Why can't you trust this? Trust *me?*"

"This isn't a trust issue. I don't doubt that your feelings are genuine. For now, anyway. But you're going to feel differently when we go home."

"What if I don't?"

"What if you do?"

"But what if I *don't?*"

She closed her eyes and leaned her head against his chest. And Pete held her, because he didn't know what else to do. He felt like banging his head against the wall. He hated those bastards from her high school for making her feel unlovable, and her mother for making her feel inadequate. And she was wrong about one thing. This *was* a trust issue. And it wasn't him she didn't trust, it was her own convoluted feelings that were messing with her head.

Short of getting down on his knees and begging, he didn't know what to do or what to say to make her understand how deeply he cared for her. He might even love her. In fact, what he felt for Maggie went far beyond any form of love he'd felt before. It was complex and peaceful and exciting and *frustrating*. And the best thing that had ever happened to him. But he knew she wasn't ready to hear that. To tell her now would only drive her farther away. But eventually he would tell her. He would make her see what was so completely obvious to him— they were a perfect match. He would find the right time.

The only question was, when?

Pete reached up, watching his hand as it neared the elevator button, feeling an overwhelming sense of déjà vu. He'd done this before, he was sure of it. He heard the loud pops and spun around.

Then he knew, it was the shooting. It was happening all over again. Maybe this time it could be different. Maybe this time he could save her.

He ran past the screaming people, down the hall that seemed to stretch for miles, so far there seemed to be no end to it. He ran faster, feeling lighter than air, as if he were flying, still it stretched on. There was more gunfire, more screaming, but it sounded fuzzy and far away. Then he saw it, the junction of the hallway, where he would turn and find Rachel, and he already knew it was too late. Still, he couldn't stop, even though it meant facing the bullets that were sure to rip through him. He couldn't make himself turn around.

He finally rounded the corner, and there she was, lying in the hallway, soaked in her own blood.

No!

He knew what was next and he tried to stop it, tried to hit Rewind, but it was no use. His legs refused to stop moving. Then he felt it, the searing pain as the first slug hit his chest and stopped him dead in his tracks.

"Pete!"

The second slug threw him backward, then his knee exploded, sending him crashing to the floor.

"Pete, wake up!"

Pete gasped and surged up in bed, his breath coming in hard rasps, bile rising in his throat. "Damn it!"

Maggie knelt on the bed beside him, rubbing his shoulder. "It's okay."

No, it wasn't okay. Not at all. Instead of getting better, this was only getting worse.

He scrubbed both hands across his face, but he couldn't erase the vision of Rachel lying there. He could still feel the sting of the bullets. The pain. That would *never* go away.

"I am so damned sick of this," he said. "Is one night of uninterrupted sleep too much to ask for?"

As she had been every other night, Maggie was his voice of reason. "You're still healing. Give it time."

She was right. Though physically his wounds had healed, emotionally he was a still a wreck, and he didn't know how to fix that.

"I didn't save her," he said. "I failed Rachel."

"She died instantly, doc. There's no way you *could* have saved her."

Her words tore through him with the same ferocity as the bullets that had ripped through his chest. "If I hadn't taken my break, if I had been there with her—"

"You would *both* be dead."

He shook his head. "No. I could have gotten in front of her, I could have blocked it."

"And the second you went down, they would have shot her, too. It doesn't even matter, because it happened, and it's over, and all the guilt and remorse and what-ifs are not going to change the fact that she died and you lived."

The rational part of his brain knew that. He'd replayed that night a thousand different ways, and every time, as irrational as it was, he'd drawn the same conclusion; he should have been able to save her.

"It wasn't your fault, Pete."

"I know that."

"Then forgive yourself."

He shook his head. "I can't."

Maggie lay back on the pillow. "Come on, let's go to sleep."

He lay down and curled up beside her, his arm around her waist, his head resting on her shoulder. And as on every other night they'd spent together, she wrapped her arms around him and held him. He breathed in the scent of her skin, her hair, felt her stomach rise and fall as she breathed, needing her so badly he ached. She was in his arms, yet so damned far away.

"You're not sick of having to get up and come in here every night?" he asked.

She stroked the hair at the nape of his neck. "I know it's wrong, but I like sleeping with you."

It wasn't wrong. In fact, nothing had ever felt so right. All she had to do was say the word and he would have her out of that nightshirt. But unless she threw herself at him and said "take me," or gave him at least a vague sign that she wanted anything other than a platonic relationship, he would respect her wishes. Sleeping together—in the platonic sense—would have to be enough to sate this ever-growing need to be close to her. He was a patient man, so he would give her time. Time to see that what he felt for her had nothing to do with gratitude.

She was downright bossy at times, stubborn as a mule and annoyingly independent. She was also funny and sweet and understanding. And vulnerable. She was the first woman he'd felt he could really talk to. He *liked* talking to her. She knew more about him than Lizzy had ever known, or had ever *wanted* to know.

He and Lizzy had never been much for socializing with each other. They had always been busy doing other things— physically challenging activities that required little conversation. Now that he thought about it, he'd been engaged to a woman he barely knew. Not the way he knew Maggie. All those things he used to do, the activities he thought he would so miss after the shooting, had barely crossed his mind. Despite all the crap he was going through with the nightmares and the therapy, he couldn't remember a time when he'd been happier.

Beside him, Maggie's breathing had become slow and deep. She always fell asleep first. And as he had every night, he pressed a kiss to her temple, laid his head on her shoulder, and fell into a deep, dreamless sleep.

Twelve

"**H**ave you got a minute, Pete?" Jeremy stood in the door of the small, shabby little office the doctors at the clinic shared. It had been a long, busy five days, and now that Pete's Friday shift had ended, he was taking some time to catch up on his charts.

"Sure," he told Jeremy, setting his pen down. "What's up?"

Jeremy took a seat on the edge of the desk. "Just wondering how it went this week. It wasn't too much too soon?"

The truth was, it felt damned good to be practising medicine again. The hours he worked here were nowhere close to the long, grueling shifts in the ER. This was a cakewalk. In fact, the end of his shift seemed to come too soon, and he found himself stalling, taking one or two more patients before he quit for the day. "It's been good," he said.

"I noticed you're not using the cane anymore. The therapy is going well?"

"The truth is, I haven't had much time for therapy this week, but I've been trying to keep active. I swim in the mornings and Maggie and I go for walks every evening. She's talking about getting bikes this weekend, now that her weight is up."

"She's eating better?"

"Not as much as I'd like, but we're getting there."

"That's good. She's quite a girl."

Pete grinned. "She definitely has her moments."

"I'm having a barbecue a week from Saturday and I'd really like to have you and Maggie there. It'll mainly be staff from the hospital and their families. We're a pretty tight-knit group."

"I don't want to intrude…"

"No, it wouldn't be an intrusion. A lot of people are interested in meeting you."

"Why is that?"

"How do you like it up here, Pete?"

Pete sat back in his chair and folded his hands in his lap, wondering where exactly Jeremy was going with this. "I like it. Why do you ask?"

"Would you ever consider relocating here permanently?"

"I guess that all depends."

"The doctor you're filling in for this week has just been offered a private practice in Arizona. We're looking for a replacement."

"For the clinic?"

"The clinic and the ER. With your experience, you'd be a hell of an asset to the team. It wouldn't be the hectic pace you're used to in the city. The only gunshot wounds we get here are from hunting accidents, and stabbings are pretty rare. But Gaylord is a good place to live, a nice place to raise a family."

Pete's mind whirled with the possibility. Him and Maggie moving up to Gaylord permanently, starting a life together here.

He liked it.

The truth was, he didn't have much to go back to in Detroit, and he hadn't missed it since he'd been gone. But was he ready for that kind of commitment? Did he know for sure that Maggie was the woman he wanted to spend the rest of his life with? It stunned him how quickly the answer came. He didn't even have to give it a second thought.

Yes.

Without question, Maggie was the one. But how did she feel about him? What if she didn't want to live here? What if she didn't want the same things he did? They'd never really talked about it, not even casually.

"Think about it," Jeremy said, rising from the desk. "Come to the barbecue Saturday and meet everyone."

"Yeah," Pete said. He and Maggie were going to have to have a talk. And soon. "I'll definitely do that."

"That's four of a kind," Maggie said, adding up the dice. "Twenty-six points."

As she always did on nights that it rained, Maggie had raided the game closet. This time she'd chosen Yahtzee, and as usual she was creaming him.

He offered her the bowl of low-fat microwave popcorn. She hesitated, then took a handful without his insistence, popping a few kernels in her mouth, chewing slowly. Two weeks ago, she would never have considered an evening snack without a fair amount of persuasion from him. Though it was a slow, frustrating process, he was convinced she was well on her way to a new, healthy attitude.

"Your turn," she said, popping a few more kernels in her mouth.

"I don't know why I bother," Pete grumbled, but he scooped up the dice and rolled—two ones, two threes and a six. "What the hell am I supposed to do with this?"

Maggie peeked over at his score sheet. "You could try for a full house."

"I already crossed that off. All I need are fives and a long straight." He picked up the entire mess and rolled it over, and again got nothing he could use. "This is stupid."

"You keep saying that, yet here we are still playing."

She was right. Because despite the fact that he consistently lost, and Maggie had done her fair share of gloating, he was having fun. He wasn't scaling a mountain, or zipping over the snow on skis. He wasn't challenging himself physically, yet somehow, he was still having a good time.

Because he was with Maggie, and no matter what it was they did together, even if he was just sitting and watching her, how her eyes lit up when she smiled, or the way she bit her lip when she was concentrating, he couldn't escape this feeling of utter contentment.

But did she feel it, too?

"You have one more roll," she said.

He grabbed all the dice, rolled again, and got a big fat nothing.

"Wow, this really isn't your night," she said, gathering up the dice and rolling a long straight her first try.

When the game was over, Maggie had once again slaughtered him. She yawned, stretching like a feline, and looked at the clock above the sink in the kitchen. "No wonder I'm so tired. It's after eleven."

"I guess we should call it a night," he agreed, covering a yawn with the back of his hand. Although to him, going to bed just meant waking in an hour or two, drenched in sweat and gasping for breath. It meant images of blood and death. And the more he worked in the clinic, the worse the dreams escalated.

Sometimes he wondered if it would never end. But he wouldn't give in, wouldn't let it interfere with his life any longer. He was going to beat this thing.

"You want the bathroom first?" Maggie asked.

"You can have it," he said. "I'll clean up our mess."

"Okee-dokee."

Maggie headed for the bathroom and Pete put the game away, then gathered the dishes they had used for their soda and popcorn. By the time he'd washed and dried them, Maggie was ready for bed.

Pete used the bathroom next, brushing his teeth and, of course, picking up Maggie's discarded clothes from the floor and tossing them in the hamper. It had become a regular part of his routine—one he didn't mind so much anymore. It seemed a small price to pay considering all she'd done for him—forcing him to come here and face his demons. He was a better man because of her. A better person.

He finished up in the bathroom and walked to his room, thinking for a second as he got there that he'd made a wrong turn. Maggie sat in his bed, dressed in her nightshirt, reading a book.

"Hey," he said, not quite sure what to make of this. Either she'd had a serious change of heart, or he was hallucinating. Either way, she looked damned sexy sitting there, her legs curled under her, her face freshly scrubbed. She looked almost...wholesome.

She looked up and smiled, setting her book in her lap. "Hey. I guess you're wondering what I'm doing in your bed."

"I guess I am."

"I have a theory."

He leaned in the doorway and folded his arms over his chest. "Oh, yeah? A theory about what?"

"You never have nightmares when I'm with you, right?"

He thought about it and realized she was right. Once she climbed in his bed, he slept like a baby. "Not so far, no."

"Then I was thinking that if I sleep with you all night, maybe you won't have a nightmare. And let's face it, I'm probably going to wind up here eventually anyway."

"There is a definite logic to that."

"Unless you don't want me to."

Oh, no, he wanted her to. He just didn't know how much more of this he could take, how much longer they could sleep in the same bed, wrapped in each other's arms, before he went off the deep end. But she was right. Maybe sleeping together all night would keep the nightmares away. It was worth a shot at least. He would sell his soul for a night of uninterrupted sleep. "I think it's a good idea."

She set her book on the night stand and patted the bed beside her. "Hop in."

Outside, rain beat relentlessly against the side of the cottage, and cool, damp air lifted the curtains. Good sleeping weather.

He walked toward the bed, unfastening his shorts, and Maggie's eyes widened a fraction. "You might want to either turn out the light or close your eyes."

Her gaze strayed down to his crotch and lingered there. "I, um, don't suppose I could talk you into wearing pajamas to bed?"

"I don't own any."

"Oh. Boxers then?"

"I've been sleeping in the buff since college. I don't think I *could* sleep with boxers on."

"And you're not shy, are you?"

He grinned. "Nope. I see naked people in the ER every day. I kind of feel like a body is just a body."

Maggie reached over and turned out the light, plunging them into darkness, and he dropped his shorts and boxers to the floor.

"So," she asked. "If I was sitting here naked, I would just be a body to you?"

"No. If you were sitting here naked, we wouldn't be talking." He climbed in bed next to her, covering himself with the sheet. "You want to know what we *would* be doing?"

"No, I think I have a pretty good idea." She slipped under the sheet beside him, and they both lay down.

Maggie turned on her side to face him, and he did the same. As his eyes adjusted, he could barely make out the contour of her body beside him, the shadowy features of her face. Normally, after one of his dreams, he didn't hesitate to cuddle up next to her. Tonight he wasn't sure if he should. If that would be too...suggestive. Too forward.

As if she'd been reading his mind, she said, "This is weird."

"Yeah, it is."

"But nice, too. I like sleeping with you. Even though you're a *close* sleeper."

"Close sleeper?"

"You hog the bed, doc."

He smiled. She was right. The way he looked at it, if you were going to share a bed with someone, you might as well enjoy it. He liked to be close to Maggie. In bed was the only time she really let him get that close. Even then it wasn't nearly close enough.

"In my own defense," he said, "it's not a very big bed."

"No, it's not." She was quiet for a minute then asked, "You said that Lizzy was old-fashioned. How old-fashioned?"

"Where did that come from?"

"Just curious."

It kind of surprised him that it had taken her this long to ask about his ex. Not that it was one of his favorite subjects, but he didn't mind talking about it either. "If you're asking if we were sleeping together, yeah, we were. She just didn't spend the night. She still lived with her parents, and out of respect for them, I always drove her home. The odd thing is, I didn't mind. I didn't really think about it. Things just were the way they were."

"You don't miss her?"

"Honestly, no. At first I missed the idea of her, of the future. But we wouldn't have been happy together."

"Why not?"

"We weren't friends. We never talked. But that was as much my fault as hers. If I had it to do all over, things would be different."

If he had it to do all over, knowing what he knew now about love and friendship, they wouldn't last a week.

"Tell me about your parents."

Definitely *not* his favorite subject. He'd resigned himself a long time ago to the fact that they were never going to change, and he could live with that. If nothing else, he'd learned from them how *not* to raise a family. "They're very…rich."

She gave him a playful poke. "Tell me something I didn't already know. What are they like?"

"Cold," he said after a moment. "I suppose they loved me, but they never said it. Or *showed* it. I spent an awful lot of time trying not to be like them, but I guess some things you're just born with."

"You're not cold."

"No, but don't ask me to talk about my feelings."

"But you show your feelings in so many other ways. You can say you care for someone, but if you don't show it, the words don't mean much."

He reached up, stroked her cheek. "I care about you."

Maggie closed her eyes and sighed as Pete's fingers slipped through her hair. "I know you do, doc."

"You never use my name," he said, and he sounded sad.

"I like calling you *doc*. It's a term of endearment."

"I don't think so. I think it's just your way of distancing yourself from me."

She was about to argue until she realized that he was right. That was exactly why she didn't use his name. Calling him Pete felt so personal. So…*intimate.*

And lying here in the dark, touching and talking, wasn't intimate? Waking wrapped in each other's arms wasn't intimate? Not to mention that he was naked. You just didn't get much more intimate than that.

In every way possible this had passed friendship and drifted into relationship territory.

In every way except for sex.

"Maybe I'm still trying to look at this as a job. Trying to see you as my patient," she said. "But I guess it's not like that anymore, is it?"

"No, it isn't. Not for me."

"You know, when your parents called the hospital, and the director asked me to take your case, I almost didn't. I thought it might be a conflict of interest."

"How could it be a conflict of interest? We hardly knew each other."

"Yeah, but I kinda had these…*feelings.*"

"What kinds of feelings?"

"Before the shooting, I sort of…well…" She bit her lip, felt her cheeks burning. Why had she started this? "This is embarrassing."

"Don't be embarrassed. You sort of what?"

"I sort of had a crush on you."

Through the dark she could see him smile. "You did?"

At least he didn't laugh and point and call her a fool—even though that was exactly how she felt. And when she would have been better off keeping her mouth shut, she couldn't keep the entire, humiliating truth from spilling out all over the place.

"Sometimes I would find reasons to go down to the ER just to see you," she said.

"Really?"

Oh, great, Mags, now you sound like a stalker.

"Not all the time," she amended. "I just…you were always so upbeat and friendly and, you know…*gorgeous.* If I was having a bad day, seeing you would lift my spirits. Pretty pathetic, huh?"

"Not at all. You should have talked to me."

"You were engaged, I was engaged. And even if we hadn't been, I was fat. I wouldn't have approached someone like you in a million years."

"You should have," Pete said, slipping his fingers through her hair, twisting a curl around his finger. "We could have been friends."

"Maybe."

"Maybe?" he said, and he sounded hurt. "Maggie, do you have any idea what you mean to me? I don't even want to think about where I would be right now if you hadn't dragged me out here. You *saved* me."

A lump formed in her throat, and for some stupid reason tears stung the corners of her eyes. She felt…hollow. How could she be so close to someone and still feel so empty?

So *lonely?*

"It was my job to save you."

"Damn it, it's more than that and you know it," he said, his voice tight with frustration. "Why can't you tell me how you feel?"

Simple. Because she loved him. She loved him more than she'd ever loved another person, and she couldn't tell him. She was *afraid* to tell him. Because he might say he loved her, too, then she would have hope, when she already knew it was destined to end.

If anyone was emotionally repressed around here, it was her.

"Talk to me, Maggie."

"Doc—"

"No," he said. "Don't do that. Don't hide from me."

Tears welled in the corners of her eyes and slipped down her cheeks.

"I want to hear you say it," Pete said softly. He was close, his lips a whisper away. "Say my name."

Somehow she knew that if she did, everything would change. They would be treading on territory previously forbidden. She would be admitting her feelings.

The God's-honest truth was, she was tired of fighting it. Didn't she deserve a little happiness, even if it was short-lived? Maybe all these weeks they had been building up to this. Maybe it had been inevitable.

She trembled from the inside out, with fear and longing and anticipation. She wanted this so badly, but she was terrified of being hurt again. Sometimes she felt as if her entire life was just one long, painful experience she was destined to live over and over again.

Pete's fingers tangled in her hair, his breath tickled her lips. "Say it, Maggie. Say my name."

She knew if she did, he would kiss her. And this time it wouldn't end there.

She didn't *want* it to end.

"Pete," she whispered, and heard him sigh. His hands slipped through her hair, caressed her face, and she could swear he was trembling. She hadn't realized how badly he wanted this, too. He wanted *her.* Plain old, nothing-special Maggie.

But when she was with him, when he touched her this way, she *did* feel special.

"I want to hear you say it again," he said. His lips brushed tenderly over hers, as if he thought he might break her.

"Pete."

"Again," he whispered.

"Pete."

He captured her mouth, kissing her slow and deep and long, putting his heart and soul into it. Tears rolled in earnest down her cheeks. She wasn't sure why. Maybe she was happy, maybe sad—she just couldn't seem to pinpoint the exact emotion.

Pete cupped her face, felt that it was damp. He lifted himself up on one elbow. "Why are you crying?"

There was no way she could answer him, not without crying even harder. Instead she slipped her arms around his neck, pulled him to her and kissed him with all she was worth. She didn't want to talk anymore. She didn't even want to think. She just wanted to lose herself in his kiss.

And she wanted to feel him, the way she had that night, and more. There was so much of him to touch, she didn't want to miss an inch of it. She let her hands wander across his shoulders, down his back. His skin was smooth and warm, the muscles taut underneath. Her hands drifted lower, over his muscular backside.

Pete pulled away long enough to drag her nightshirt up over her head, then he stopped and just looked, as if the sight of her body amazed him.

"You're so beautiful," he breathed. Then he was touching her. Just like she'd always wanted him to—stroking her face, her throat, the valley between her breasts. She felt herself falling, tumbling deeper into ecstasy, dissolving in his arms.

He kissed her, deep and searching but unbelievably tender.

They were so close. In body and mind and spirit. She didn't know it was possible to be so close to someone. Not like this.

With his mouth still locked on her own, he slid her panties down and she kicked them off. Their legs twined, breath mingled. It was as if they just couldn't get close enough. Then he slipped a hand between her thighs, parting her, and she gasped at the intense sensation.

"You're so wet," he said, and if her skin hadn't already been on fire, she would have blushed. She felt wanton and heavy with desire. She wanted him to make love to her, *needed* him to.

He tormented her with long, torturously slow strokes and she arched against his hand. She felt feverishly restless, out of control. Her thighs parted, her legs came up to wrap around his waist. She'd never acted this way, never so aggressively, but if he wasn't inside her soon, she felt as if she would go out of her mind.

Pete hissed out a breath and looked down at her through the dark. "Tell me what you want," he said, his voice a hoarse whisper. "Say the words."

She caught his face between her hands. "Make love to me, Pete."

"Oh, Maggie." He entered her in one long, slow thrust, and her entire world shifted. In that second, everything she ever knew about making love was irreparably changed. She would never feel this again—this soul-deep connection. Not with anyone but Pete.

It was frightening and wonderful at the same time.

He withdrew, thrust again and her hips rocked upward, driving him even deeper inside her. She cried out as white-hot pleasure pulsed through her, all the way to the tips of her fingers and toes and the ends of her hair. She felt her mind going fuzzy, spiraling into oblivion. The air was thick with the scent of rain and the tantalizing perfume of sex. Their skin was slick with perspiration. She clung to Pete, to her senses, not wanting it to end. She wanted to feel just like this, be this close to him, but she was slipping, floating away…

Pete shuddered and groaned her name and her grip on reality slipped. The world exploded before her eyes, she splintered into a million pieces and she soared.

Thirteen

His heart jumping wildly in his chest, their bodies still linked, Pete watched Maggie as she went still and quiet beneath him.

Holy cow.

He didn't know what had just happened, but he felt as if everything he knew about his life, about himself as a man, had been knocked upside-down, turned inside-out and twisted all around. If he wasn't certain he loved Maggie before, he sure as hell knew now. Because the only thing he could think about as she lay peacefully in his arms, the only thing he wanted to do, was find a way to keep her there.

He knew if he told her he loved her, especially now, she wouldn't believe him. But, damn, he felt as though he would burst if he didn't say something soon.

Maggie's legs fell away from his hips, and she breathed a long, blissful sigh.

"Hey," he said, nudging her nose with his own. "I'm the guy. I'm the one who's supposed to roll over and go to sleep."

Her lips curled into a lazy smile and she gazed up at him, her eyes half-closed and glassy. She wrapped her arm around his neck and pulled him to her for a kiss. She tasted salty and sweet and delicious. The ringlets of hair around her face were moist with sweat, the skin between their bodies warm and slippery.

"We need a shower," he said.

Maggie groaned and tightened her grip on his neck. "I don't want to move. You feel too good."

"You don't mind being all sweaty?"

"Uh-uh." She slid her hands down his back and up again. "I like you sweaty."

This was a nice change from what he was used to. As physically active as he and Lizzy had been, when it came to sex, she didn't like to sweat. Now that he thought about it, there wasn't a whole hell of a lot about sex she did like. Just your basic missionary style. No frills, no excitement—no *fun*. He'd initiated oral sex a time or two only to be cut off at the pass and she wasn't really into trying new positions. In all the months they had been together, they'd never been as close, never as connected as he was with Maggie.

He wondered what exactly she might be willing to try…

He kissed her chin, her throat, the curve where her neck met her shoulder, and she made a soft mewling sound, rubbing herself against him.

Oh, man, did she feel good.

He cupped the weight of her breast in his hand, kissed and nipped at her slick skin, working his way lower, down the ladder of her ribs over her flat, toned stomach. Maggie moaned softly and stretched her body longer, didn't resist him when he pressed her thighs apart, when he lowered his head and tasted her. She gasped and dug her fingers into his hair, holding him in place, as if she thought he might stop.

Fat chance. He wouldn't stop until she was writhing in ecstasy, until he'd done things to her that in the past he'd only fantasized about.

And when they were both limp and sated and drained of energy, he was going to start all over again.

Pinkish light peeked through the curtains, and outside the window birds chirped. Maggie woke to find herself alone. She yawned and stretched and when she noticed the condition of the bed, a little shiver of satisfaction rippled through her. The top sheet lay sideways over her and tangled around her legs, and the fitted sheet had been pulled loose and lay rumpled beneath her, exposing three corners of the mattress.

Last night had been sensual and sweet and...*adventurous*. She hadn't known making love could be so much fun. Or so enthusiastic. Her tired, achy muscles protested as she rolled out of bed and stumbled into the bathroom. She brushed her teeth and tried to fix her hair, realizing that she would need a shower to tame the unruly curls. Giving up, she wrapped herself in the top sheet and ventured out of the bathroom in search of Pete.

She found him sitting on the deck steps, wearing only a faded pair of cut-off denim shorts, gazing at the water, sipping a cup of coffee. Dragonflies darted across the surface of the lake and spiderwebs glistened with dew. The air was thick with humidity and scented with moss and pine.

"Morning."

He turned to her and smiled. "Morning."

"You're up early."

"Couldn't sleep." He turned back toward the water and a tiny jolt of alarm passed through her. Something was wrong.

She sat behind him, sliding her hands over his chest, resting her chin on his shoulder. He set his coffee down and slipped his hands over her own, rested his head against her cheek. She loved touching him, being close to him.

"Bad dreams?" she asked.

"As a matter of fact no, I didn't have bad dreams at all last night. I guess your theory worked."

Though he didn't sound upset exactly, something in his voice set her on edge. And she knew, if she wanted to find out what was up, she would have to drag it out of him.

"What are you doing out here?" she asked.

"Thinking."

"About...?"

"My therapy. How in the past few weeks it's just sort of tapered off. I kept waiting for the real therapy to start, but what we've been doing, the walks and the swimming and the berry picking, getting me used to the disability, *that* was the therapy, wasn't it?" He looked back at her. "This is it. This is as good as it's going to get."

Her heart sank. She'd wondered how long it would take him to figure it out. "Pete—"

"It's okay." He gave her hands a squeeze. "It's not so bad, really. All the things I thought I would miss, I don't really miss them. I think...I think I've accepted it."

It was what she wanted—all she'd *ever* wanted for him— so why did she feel as if he'd just ripped out her heart?

Because now that he'd accepted it, the therapy was done, her job finished. It would be time for them to go home soon. Then everything would change. Even if they didn't want it to.

She laid her head on his shoulder and squeezed her eyes shut. It was over before it had really begun. But she didn't want it to end, *she* wasn't ready.

"I have to say something to you, Maggie, but I'm not quite sure how. I've been sitting here for half an hour going over it in my head, trying to find the words to explain it in a way you'll understand, that you'll believe, but I'm no good at this kind of thing. So I'm just going to say it, okay?"

Her heart sank low in her belly and her fingers felt numb and tingly. She was too afraid even to consider what he could possibly mean. But whatever it was, it didn't sound good.

Swallowing her fear, she nodded. "Okay."

"I love you, Maggie."

If he'd whacked her upside the head with a dead fish she wouldn't have been more surprised. And as much as she wanted to scream with happiness and thank God or Cupid or whoever for their divine intervention, it didn't change the fact that this was temporary.

His loving her was both horrible and wonderful and she just couldn't figure out which emotion she should let herself feel.

"I know you probably don't believe me," he said.

"No, I believe you." She believed that he thought he loved her, but that had no bearing on what he would be feeling six months from now.

"So why do you sound so miserable? Is it because you don't love me?"

She closed her eyes and pressed her forehead to his shoulder. "It's not that."

"Do you?" he asked, turning to face her. "Do you love me?"

"There are different kinds of love, doc." She cringed when she realized she'd called him doc again. It was her internal defense mechanism kicking in.

"We're back to that again?" He sighed and looked away. "So, what kind of love is it that I'm feeling? The pretend kind?"

"Pete—"

"It's a simple question, Maggie, do you love me or not?"

Tears burned her eyes. Why was he doing this to her? Couldn't he see that he was making her miserable? Did he enjoy torturing her? "We're going to go home, and you're going to get back to your regular life and this thing with me isn't going to seem so important anymore. It won't last, so it doesn't really matter what I feel."

Pete turned and lifted her into his lap, so her legs were wrapped around his waist. The sheet pulled to the side, leaving her completely exposed. Her breasts pressed against his chest and his denim shorts chafed her between her thighs.

"Yes or no, Maggie. I *need* to know." Pete took her face in his hands and forced her to look him in the eye. "If the answer is no, don't be afraid to say it."

He was tearing her apart. If she lied and told him no, she would hurt him. If she told him the truth, she would be hurting herself.

But she couldn't do it, she couldn't hurt Pete, even if that meant hanging her own heart out to be filleted and chopped to pieces.

"Maggie—"

"Yes! I do love you."

A slow smile curled the corners of his mouth and he pressed a very gentle kiss to her lips. She kissed him back—it was that or burst into tears. She didn't want to talk anymore. Didn't want to think.

His hands slid over her bare back, across her shoulders. When he kissed her so sweetly, touched her so tenderly, she could pretend they had a chance. She could make herself believe this would last. She could pretend this would all work out.

She felt herself melting, dissolving in his arms as the hands caressing her became more bold and the kiss went from sweet and sensual to hot and urgent.

Only when the sheet dropped away altogether, landing in a pile on the stairs below them, did it occur to her that they were outside and she was naked.

"Pete," she said breathlessly. "Someone might see."

He cupped her backside, fitting her more snugly against him. "No one will see."

He kissed her mouth, her throat, the tips of her breasts, and she was so dizzy with desire she didn't care if someone *did* see. All she wanted was for Pete to be inside her again. She needed him to be.

She rose up on her knees and unfastened his shorts.

Pete shoved them down. "Make love to me, Maggie."

Very slowly, so she could savor every sensation, every nuance, she lowered herself onto him until he was deep, deep inside her. They fit so perfectly together she wanted to cry.

"I love you," Pete whispered. He gathered her face in his hands, kissed her softly. "Tell me you love me, Maggie."

"I love you, Pete." It didn't hurt so much to say it anymore.

When they were like this, she could pretend everything was perfect.

Pete's hands wandered over her skin, touching her intimately, and she couldn't hold herself still any longer. Her body began moving—slowly at first, then faster, thrusting against him. Already she had that light, floaty, dizzy sensation in her head. Her body hummed and crackled with energy. She didn't want this to end, but at the same time she wanted to feel that completeness, that absolute connection she'd felt with no one but him.

"Oh, Maggie," Pete whispered, and at the sound of his voice, as his muscles coiled tight with release, she came undone.

Maggie sat in the shade on the deck in Jeremy's backyard, watching as the party buzzed around her, letting herself pretend, if only for a few hours, that she might someday have a life like this. Wives stood in clusters chatting about hospital gossip and children splashed in the enormous in-ground pool.

There was food everywhere. Chips and dip, vegetables and fruit, and everyone seemed to be snacking. She wondered if it would ever be that easy for her. If she would ever be able to look at food and not feel disdain. Not view it as the enemy. It was getting easier, but she didn't think she would ever lose the fear of being fat again. But it was getting easier to live with. Pete no longer had to force her to eat.

He'd been so patient with her—so understanding, yet firm. She didn't even want to think where she would be without him.

Across the yard—a rolling carpet of pristine emerald-green grass—Pete stood by the barbecue with Jeremy and several other doctors from the hospital. He looked tan and healthy and happy. He still walked with a pronounced limp—and always would—but to see him standing there, no one would guess the hell he'd been through.

Before her eyes, he'd become the confident, sociable man he was before the shooting. And despite their new intimate relationship and the countless times they'd made love in the past week, she couldn't shake the feeling they'd reached the beginning of the end.

He didn't need her anymore.

"Maggie, can I get you anything?"

Maggie looked up to find Mel, Jeremy's wife, standing beside her. Her long auburn hair was pulled back in a ponytail, her tank top pulled tight over the subtle bulge of her belly. Her face was free of makeup, giving her a fresh, natural look the other wives lacked. There was something about her, a sincerity that had made Maggie like her the instant they were introduced. She had also noticed that while Mel was friendly with the other women, she kept her distance. She was more of an observer than a participant. She reminded Maggie a lot of herself in that way. There was a look in her eyes, an insecurity Maggie could identify with. Given the chance, she could see her and Mel becoming friends.

Too bad they would never have the chance.

Maggie smiled up at her. "I'm good, thanks."

"Why don't you come inside and keep me company while I fix the potato salad?" Mel said.

"I'd love to." Maggie pushed herself out of the deck chair and followed Mel through the sliding-glass door into an enormous kitchen with every modern convenience known to man. Every room that she'd seen in the sprawling, Colonial-style home had been impeccably decorated down to the finest detail. Professionally decorated, Maggie was guessing, and everything looked brand-new. "You have a beautiful home."

Mel opened the fridge and pulled out a bowl of boiled potatoes, setting it on the island in the center of the room. "I told Jeremy I didn't need anything this big, but he insisted."

"I'll help you peel those," Maggie said.

Mel took two paring knives out and handed Maggie one. They each took a potato and started peeling. "Don't get me wrong, I really like the house. It's just not what I'm used to. When I met Jeremy I lived an apartment the size of my bedroom closet."

"How long have you been married?"

"Four months," she said, and laid a hand over her belly. "And since you're probably too polite to ask, I'm five months pregnant. Not planned, obviously. The consensus among the other wives is that I trapped Jeremy."

"Well, if you two love each other, I guess it doesn't matter what people think."

"That's what I keep telling Jeremy. It upsets him, though, that I haven't been accepted into the inner circle."

Maggie finished one potato and grabbed another. "Does it bother you?"

She shrugged. "For Jeremy's sake, I guess it would be okay. And it's not that they're bad people. They're just not *my* kind of people, you know?"

Maggie nodded. "I know exactly what you mean."

She wondered, would Pete expect a wife who would blend into the social scene? Not one who would always be on the fringes of the conversation—on the outside, looking in. He definitely deserved better. She didn't like to use the term *generic,* but someone who better fit the mold of a proper doctor's wife. Like Lizzy would have been.

He'd said that if he had it to do over, he would have done things differently. Maybe that had been his subtle way of telling her, or subconsciously admitting to himself, that he wanted another chance with Lizzy.

"How long have you and Pete been together?" Mel asked.

"We're, um, not exactly together. He's my patient."

Mel grinned. "I've seen the way that man looks at you. Whether you think so or not, you guys are definitely together."

"It's complicated."

Mel laughed. "It usually is. That doesn't mean it won't all work out in the end."

Maggie didn't even want to think about everything she and Pete would have to work out if they were to make a relationship last. She wouldn't have a clue where to begin. They were just too different. And too much alike.

Yet she couldn't help imagining herself and Pete married, living in Gaylord, her belly round with his child someday. She imagined long walks holding hands and long nights making love. On the surface it sounded doable—conceivable even—until she reminded herself that his feelings for her were temporary.

"I know Jeremy thinks the world of Pete. He's really hoping he'll accept the offer."

"Offer?"

"The ER position at the hospital." When Mel saw the look on Maggie's face, her hand stilled on the potato she'd been peeling. "Uh-oh, why do I get the feeling I just let the prover-bial cat out of the bag?"

"It's okay," Maggie said, swallowing back a world of hurt and rejection. "I'm sure he was waiting until he made a deci-sion to tell me."

Pete was getting on with his life, making plans for the fu-ture. It was a good thing. She was happy for him—even though on the inside, she was shattering.

"I'm sorry, Maggie, I just assumed you knew."

"It's okay." Maggie forced a smile. "I hope he takes it."

"Maybe he'll ask you to stay here with him."

Maggie gave a vague nod. If Pete had any intention of ask-ing her to stay, he would surely have brought it up by now. But that was okay.

If he didn't ask her, it would save her the torture of having to tell him no.

Fourteen

"**D**o you miss your job, Maggie?"

Maggie lay in Pete's arms in the dark, legs looped, bodies slick with perspiration. They'd barely returned from Jeremy and Mel's party before Pete had begun kissing and undressing her, leading her toward the bedroom they now shared. And she'd let him, even though she was aching inside, knowing their time was almost up. She knew what she'd been getting herself into, and here she was, right where she thought she'd be—preparing for the end.

"Yeah, I miss it."

"You really love your job." He voiced it as a statement, not a question, as if he were trying to rationalize its validity. She loved her job, therefore she should go home and get on with her life.

"Yeah, I love it."

"So did I. I didn't realize how much until I started volunteering. I didn't realize how much I'd missed it." He held her tightly against him. "I'm ready to move on now. I'm finally ready to get back to my life."

Why didn't he just say it was over? Why did he have to hint around like this?

Guilt. He was too nice a guy just to blurt it out. To hurt her. He would try to let her down easily.

He stroked his fingers up and down the length of her spine, giving her shivers. "I think...I think it's what Rachel would have wanted."

Maggie squeezed her eyes shut. "She would have wanted you to be happy."

"I just wish I could close my eyes and see her how she used to be. But every time I try, I still see her lying in that hallway. I still see the blood."

"It won't be that way forever," she said.

"I'll always feel that her dying was unfair. I see people die all the time. But never someone I was close to. I guess I didn't know how to deal with it, and that was hard to admit. Kind of like your feelings toward food."

She gave a rueful laugh. "It's definitely a love-hate relationship. I thought when I lost weight my life would be perfect, but it doesn't get any easier, does it? I thought I was in control, but it was an illusion. I'd never been more out of control in my life."

"And now?"

"I know that life is work. There's no easy answer to anything. The important thing is that I'm healthy. And it's okay if I'm not always in control."

"How does your mom feel now that you've lost weight?"

"She doesn't know about it. I haven't seen her since I started losing."

"Why not?"

"Because I don't want her to think that I did this for her—for her approval. I don't need that anymore and I don't want it. I did this for me."

"So, what? You're never going to see her again?"

"I will eventually. When I can deal with the fact that she's never going to change. When I'm ready to forgive her. I haven't reached that point yet. But like you said about your parents, at least they taught you how not to raise a family."

"You want that?" he asked.

"What?"

"A family."

I'd like one with you, she wanted to say. "Someday," she said instead.

He was quiet for a minute, then asked, "Are you okay, Maggie? You seem…sad."

No, she wasn't okay, she was miserable. She couldn't lie here like this with him and pretend everything was all right when it wasn't. And at the same time she wanted to hold on to their last bit of time together.

"I'm fine," she told Pete.

"Didn't you have fun today?"

"I had a lot of fun. I really liked Mel." So much that she was sorry they would never have the chance to know each other better, to be friends. "I'm just tired."

Sick and tired of being the one who was stiffed in the end,

the one who walked away with the booby prize—her own battered pride.

If he couldn't come right out and say it, if he couldn't make the first move and just end this, maybe she would just do it for him.

Tomorrow, she thought as she snuggled against the long, lean warmth of Pete's body. As he sighed and held her closer.

She would definitely say something tomorrow.

Pete pulled the SUV up to the cottage, cut the engine and hopped out, an uncharacteristic spring in his step. Everything was in place. Today was the day he and Maggie were going to have a talk.

She'd been acting a little weird this past week, ever since Jeremy's party. Much quieter than usual. He was hoping his news would be enough to pull her out of whatever funk she'd slipped into. He hoped it would be enough to make her see that he really did love her. He'd told her at least twenty times each day, still, he didn't think she believed him. She said actions spoke louder than words, so he hoped his actions today would do the trick.

He walked to the door and stepped inside, nearly tripping over the suitcases stacked there. Maggie's suitcases.

"What the hell?"

"I'm going home."

Pete looked up to see her standing in the bedroom doorway. Her eyes were red, as if she'd been crying. He had the sinking feeling something terrible had happened. A death in the family, maybe? "What's going on?"

"I can't do this anymore."

"You can't do what?"

"I can't stay here and pretend everything is okay. It's tearing me apart. I have to go."

She was leaving because of *him?* For a second he was speechless. "I thought everything *was* okay."

She gave him that look, the one that said he was full of it.

"Okay," he admitted, "you have seemed a little quiet this week. I should have asked what was wrong…"

"But you don't like to talk about feelings."

Boy, did she have him pegged. "So tell me what's wrong."

"Did you take the job?"

"The job? How did you know—"

"Did you take it?"

"Not yet."

"You should take it. You'll be happy here."

He knew, from the way she said *he* would be happy here, she wasn't including herself in the equation. "*We,* Maggie. I wouldn't be happy here without you."

She lowered her head, looked at the floor. "You say that now, doc."

Oh for cryin' out loud, was she going to start with the doc thing again?

"You should call Lizzy," she said.

Lizzy? Where the hell had that come from? "Maggie, what are you talking about?"

"You said if you had a chance to do it all over, you would do things differently. This is your chance."

He smacked himself in the forehead. "Oh my God, Maggie, I was speaking *hypothetically.* I didn't mean I wanted to get back together with her."

"But she'd be the perfect woman for you."

"Lizzy is cold and spoiled and self-centered. How would *that* be perfect for me?"

She didn't seem to know how to answer that one.

"Do you love me, Maggie?"

She lowered her head again. "Yes."

"And I love you. So wouldn't that make *you* the perfect woman for me?"

She looked so hopelessly confused, so genuinely conflicted, he had to smile. Why she continued to fight this, why she wouldn't believe he loved her, was a mystery to him.

He walked across the room to her, tucked his finger under her chin and lifted her face. "Why can't you let yourself believe that this is real?"

"Because good things like this don't happen to me."

The hopelessness in her eyes made his chest hurt. He pulled her into his arms and held her and she pressed her cheek to his shirt. "*Ever?* I mean, aren't you about due?"

She was quiet for several seconds, then said, "I guess I never thought about it like that."

"I know it's tough, Maggie, but you've got to have a little faith. You have to trust your feelings, and you have to trust me."

"I thought, because you didn't tell me about the job, you weren't going to ask me to stay."

"Is that why you've been so quiet this week? Because you thought I was going to tell you I was staying here and say *so long*? You actually thought I would do that to you?"

She looked up at him and nodded, her eyes filled with guilt.

"Next time, instead of making yourself miserable, why don't you just *ask* me? As my therapist you've never had a problem getting in my face and giving me what-for. It's one of the things I like most about you. Don't turn into a doormat now."

Anger sparked in her eyes, and he could see he'd gotten her hackles up. Well, good. He didn't like it when she got quiet and withdrawn. It just wasn't her. He liked her feisty.

"Okay, fine," she snapped. "So why *didn't* you tell me? Didn't you think I might have wanted to know?"

"You're right," he agreed, "I should have told you, and I'm sorry I didn't. I just wanted to make sure all the pieces were in place before I brought it up. I had certain criteria they had to meet before I would even consider taking the position."

"What kinds of criteria?"

"Well, you said you love what you do, so I thought you might be more likely to stay here with me if you had a job offer."

The feisty look drained from her face. "A job offer?"

"I told them if they wanted to hire me, they would have to hire you, too."

"You actually *said* that?"

"Yep."

She couldn't believe he would do that for her. That he would hinge his career on her. These were not the actions of a man who didn't have a pretty darned good idea of what he wanted. She couldn't stop the hope from welling up inside her and spilling out all over the place. She didn't want to stop it this time.

And since he didn't seem in any hurry to tell her what had happened, she couldn't help demanding, "So what did they say? Did they have an opening?"

"They said first they would have to check your references.

So I gave them the name of your boss at the hospital. I hope that was all right."

"And…"

"And they called her."

She gave him the evil eye. Now he was just dragging this out to torture her. Not that she didn't deserve it just a teensy bit. She'd done her share of torturing him, by not trusting him.

What had she been thinking?

"And?" she asked.

He grinned. "And if you want the job it's yours."

"Well, jeez," she said, giving him a playful shove. "Why didn't you tell me?"

"I was going to, then I came home to find your bags packed."

She folded her arms stubbornly over her chest. "And what about you? Did you take the job?"

"I start September first…but only on one condition. That you stay here with me."

"And if I don't?" Like that would ever happen. He would need a crowbar to get rid of her now.

"Then I'll have to follow your stubborn behind home and try to get my old job back. I'll follow you around for the rest of your life if I have to. If that's what it takes to show you this is *not* my imagination." He reached up, touched her cheek. "Whatever it takes."

He really truly loved her, and she was kicking herself soundly for not realizing it before. For not trusting him.

For not trusting herself. It was time she started.

"Can I ask you a question, Maggie?"

She nodded.

"Your patient, the one you were engaged to, did you love him?"

"I tried to make myself love him. I think…I think I was in love with the idea of pleasing my parents, and I knew how much they approved of him. But when it ended, when I got over feeling bad, and feeling guilty for disappointing them, I was relieved."

"He didn't make you happy?"

"I tried to pretend I was. But deep down I was just fooling myself."

"Do *I* make you happy?"

Tears gathered in her eyes. "Always."

"Even this past week, when you were so *un*happy?"

The tears threatened to spill down her cheeks. "That was me making myself miserable. You never did anything wrong."

"Do you believe that I love you? Real, honest-to-goodness-until-the-day-I-die love?"

She grinned. "Yeah, I do."

Pete sighed and pressed his forehead to hers. "Thank God."

"No kidding."

He cupped her face in his hands, kissed her. "If we're going to make this work, Maggie, we have to be able to talk to each other. If you have any concerns or any doubts you need to tell me."

"And if you're planning on making any life-altering decisions, you have to tell me."

"Well, I'm thinking about asking you to marry me. That would be pretty life-altering."

There was so much love, so much sincerity in his eyes, she

knew this couldn't be anything but one-hundred-percent genuine. "Ask me."

He grinned. "Will you marry me, Maggie?"

She got on her tippy toes and gave him a big, toe-curling
kiss. "Absolutely."

That night, Pete had a dream.

*He was back in the hospital in Detroit, standing by the el-
evator, but this time there was no gunfire, no screaming people. No fear.*

*He turned, and from around the corner there was a light.
A light so radiant, so bright it should have hurt his eyes, but
for some reason, it didn't. He walked toward it, more curious than he was apprehensive. It was as if it was pulling
him, beckoning him closer. And as he rounded the corner he
saw her.*

Rachel.

*She stood in the hallway, waiting for him. All around her
the light glowed. It seemed to be coming from inside her, and
at the same time it didn't. It was coming from everywhere and
nowhere.*

*"Pete." She held out her hand. There was no blood, no hor-
ror, just her sweet, friendly smile.*

*He walked toward her, reached for her hand, and when
they connected, her touch filled him with a deep sense of
calm. That's when he knew: the nightmares, the bad memories—they were over. It was as if they had been erased from
his mind. Every time he thought of Rachel now, he would see
her like this. Full of radiance and life.*

"Be happy," she said, and he felt her squeeze his hand.

He had so much he wanted to tell her, so much to say, but already she was fading.

"Be happy," she said again, but she sounded far away. He grasped her hand tighter and realized he was holding air. But that was all right, because he knew now that everything would be okay.

Then the last of the light faded and she was gone.

Pete opened his eyes.

The room was dark. Maggie slept soundly beside him, her breathing slow and deep. They were alone, yet he had the eerie, almost surreal feeling they weren't.

It had been a dream. Right?

Then he realized, it didn't really matter. The message had been clear. It was time to get on with his life.

He loved Maggie, and she loved him. Being happy and happy with her, that was the thing he definitely planned to do.

* * * * *

FREE!

2 Books
and a surprise gift!

We would like to take this opportunity to thank you for reading this Mills & Boon® book by offering you the chance to take TWO more specially selected titles from the Desire™ series absolutely FREE! We're also making this offer to introduce you to the benefits of the Mills & Boon® Book Club™—

- ★ **FREE home delivery**
- ★ **FREE gifts and competitions**
- ★ **FREE monthly Newsletter**
- ★ **Exclusive Mills & Boon Book Club offers**
- ★ **Books available before they're in the shops**

Accepting these FREE books and gift places you under no obligation to buy, you may cancel at any time, even after receiving your free shipment. Simply complete your details below and return the entire page to the address below. You don't even need a stamp!

YES! Please send me 2 free Desire books and a surprise gift. I understand that unless you hear from me, I will receive 3 superb new titles every month for just £5.25 each, postage and packing free. I am under no obligation to purchase any books and may cancel my subscription at any time. The free books and gift will be mine to keep in any case.

D8ZEF

Ms/Mrs/Miss/Mr ....Initials ....

BLOCK CAPITALS PLEASE

Surname ....

Address ....

....

....Postcode ....

Send this whole page to:
UK: FREEPOST CN81, Croydon, CR9 3WZ